DEATH BY GREEK FIRE
DECIMUS JULIUS VIRILIS
BOOK ONE

B. R. STATEHAM

Copyright (C) 2022 B.R. Stateham

Layout design and Copyright (C) 2022 by Next Chapter

Published 2022 by Next Chapter

Edited by Charity Rabbiosi

Cover art by Lordan June Pinote

This book is a work of fiction. Names, characters, places, and incidents are the product of the author's imagination or are used fictitiously. Any resemblance to actual events, locales, or persons, living or dead, is purely coincidental.

All rights reserved. No part of this book may be reproduced or transmitted in any form or by any means, electronic or mechanical, including photocopying, recording, or by any information storage and retrieval system, without the author's permission.

I

7 AD
Dalmatia
On a hilltop overlooking a mountain valley road

D eath comes in the deepest portion of the night. Suddenly and without warning. Especially here. Deep in enemy territory surrounded by sullen mountains shrouded in dark forests underneath low-lying carpets of icy fog. Unseen death stalks the careless. An arrow from out of the darkness. The sudden *thud* of a hurled javelin cracking into one's *lorica segmentata*. The unexpected surge of a black figure rising out of the darkness followed by the swift stroke of cold steel across yielding flesh. In the night death comes sudden, swift and sure.

Especially here, on this strangely quiet, foreboding night in Dalmatia. The promise of death so near in the darkness, it was making the entire legion nervous and fidgety. He knew from his long experience soldiering what fear could do to a legion. A legion spooked and restless on the night before a possible battle contained all the ingredients for disaster. Fear could make a legion, led ineptly, to bend. To *yield* ground. And eventually to *shatter* like cheap pottery thrown onto a cold stone floor.

Not that the commander was inept. Inept was a harsh descriptor. *Inept* connoted incompetence and a casual disregard of assigned duties. Young would be a better description. Inexperienced. Thrust into the command of a legion long before he was ready for it. The young Gaius Cornelius Sulla was just old enough to be elected into the Roman Senate. Old enough, but contrary to tradition and Roman law, the young Senator had never served in the army. Never held one of the minor political offices which were normally prerequisites before running for a Senator's seat. Money, and his father's reputation, allowed the boy to bypass mere formalities. He was suitably impressed with the duties of being a legion commander. He wanted to prove to his father he was the man and son his father wanted. It was just that ... well ... the lad was but a boy. A boy given the command of a Roman legion which was sorely below nominal strength in manpower and finding itself hurled into the depth of enemy territory without proper training and equipment.

Youth untrained, and a legion improperly handled, were the ugly ingredients needed for a recipe of unparalleled disaster.

Twenty plus years serving in one legion or another had painted for him, on several occasions, what the end results of a legion shattering like a piece of thin glass would be. A horror beyond description. The killing would be endless. Roman soldiers throwing down their shields and swords as they ran from the battlefield in a mass panic only to be ridden down by the enemy's cavalry or assaulted by roving bands of sword and axmen. Hacked to pieces or ran through by fast riding cavalry, the memories of his past burned brightly in his mind. He knew if such a debacle happened on the morrow there would be few, if any, survivors. Especially here in this mountainous country overran with ravaging madmen filled with bloodlust and hate for anything Roman. That's why, throwing a heavy campaign cloak over his shoulders as he stood near the warmth of a burning brazier, he preferred inspecting the army's perimeter in person.

Stepping out of his tent, pulling the heavy wool cloak tighter around his shoulders, he took his time setting his bronze helm over his brow before reaching for his officer's baton firmly clamped under his right armpit. On either side of his tent's entrance, the two legionnaires snapped to attention and saluted in perfect unison. Acknowledging their salutes with a wave of his baton, he eyed the camp to his right and left in silence, then turned his attention to the nine legionnaires standing directly in front of him.

The young *decanus,* or a *contriburnium* commander of eight men, saluted smartly as the eight legionnaires behind him snapped to attention. One glance from his old eyes told him he and his men had spent some time getting their armor cleaned and smartly arrayed. The *decanus* was, at best, eighteen or nineteen years old. He, like his men, were not much more than raw recruits swept up off the streets of Brundisium and Rome and sent packing off to Dalmatia. Dalmatian tribesmen were in revolt. Again. And Roman authority, again, being challenged. The *decanus* was so young his beard was nonexistent. So frail of bone he wondered how in Hades the lad stood upright in the thirty or more pounds of standard legionnaire armor assigned to each man. Nevertheless, the lad was standing tall and proud. His men looked smartly attired and diligent. It didn't matter if the *contriburnium* was of the 7th cohort. The 7th being the cohort of the youngest, most untrained soldiers.

Lads beginning their long, arduous, and sometimes quite deadly learning phase of becoming a professional soldier. In the young eyes of these nine men, he could see they were looking for some sign of hope. Some gesture that they might survive in what was, obviously, a desperate situation. And without a doubt it was a desperate situation. Surrounded on three sides by determined foes who vastly outnumbered them. Intent on throwing off the yoke of Roman rule, the six or so main Dalmatian tribes united and waged war on anything which hinted of imperial power. This newly formed legion, *Legio IX Brundisi*, was within their grasp. A new legion, vastly undermanned, yet swept up into the fight because of the threat of a foe so close to the shores of Rome itself.

It was a hodgepodge collection of veterans and raw recruits. And he, Decimus Julius Virilis, being third in command, was the legion's *Praefectus Castoreum*. His main duty, of the many assigned to him, was to throw this collection of madmen together and hone it into a fighting machine as quickly as possible. A vastly important job given only to a professional soldier who had come up through the ranks and had proven himself to be both tough and enduring, as well as loyal and intelligent. A job that never ended. He had ordered a *contriburnium* from the 7th to be his personal escort tonight as he inspected the legion's perimeter. Yes, a move fraught with danger, perhaps. Especially so if the rebels decided to assault the legion's defensive lines hidden behind the veil of darkness.

In all the world there was no fighting force as well trained, well organized, and more victorious, than that of the seasoned professional legions of Rome. For almost four hundred years Roman legions fought the armies of just about every foe in what would become, eventually, modern Europe. Greeks, Etruscans, Carthaginian, Egyptian, Spaniards, Parthians, Germans, Gauls. The list was endless. For four hundred years Rome's steel had, by in large, remained victorious. Yet four hundred years of military dominance guaranteed one certainty.

There would be no peace, no tranquility in an empire forged from steel and strife. There would always be someone, somewhere, ready to rise up and defy the Roman yoke.

Eyeing the darkness and low hanging clouds of fog surrounding the hilltop the legion now commanded, Decimus could feel the weight of the coming battle resting on his tired shoulders. It would be a desperate fight. An unwanted fight. The legion was seriously undermanned. It was alone, deep in enemy territory, miles away from the main Roman army under the command of Tiberius Caesar.

Caesar, the adopted son of Caesar *Augustus*, had been summoned by his father to return to Rome and take command of the ten or so legions being assembled to fight the Dalmatian rebellion. The general had been in the north, beyond the Alps, fighting Gaul and Germanic tribes and trying to stabilize the northern borders. But the Dalmatian uprising, so dangerously close to the Latin homelands, took priority. The rebelling tribes were directly east of Rome—just across the watery finger of the narrow Adriatic Sea. A failure of her legions now would directly threaten Rome itself. Therefore, her best general was summoned to take command of the legions assembled to put the rebellion down.

Legio IXth Brundisi had been hastily recruited, marginally equipped, and shipped off to Dalmatia before being properly trained. The legion was almost two thousand men short of a legion's nominal six thousand men strength. Without its cavalry contingent of four hundred or more horsemen, with each of the legion's eight cohorts drastically undermanned, their disastrous arrival in the Illyricum port of Asa was like a prophet's decree of looming defeat to come.

A mysterious fire erupted among the ships in the harbor and spread its ravenous hunger across the small fleet which escorted the legion's troopships to Asa. Dalmatian spies infiltrated the Roman-held port and somehow set fire to all of the legion's troopships only moments after the last man of the legion had disembarked. The hungry flames spread from ship to ship, lighting up the harbor's night with a terrifying display of light and smoke, and continued to ravenously devour ships far into the next three days.

Bad luck continued to haunt the *IXth Brundisi* as they left Asa and marched into the depths of the rebel held territory. Leaving the port, rebels began to attack the rear and flanks of the columns of the marching legion with sudden, deadly attacks by small units of bowmen who hit hard, and just as swiftly faded back into the forests before any counterattack could be organized. The continuous loss of one or two men with each swift attack was telling. Untrained recruits not used to the hardships of war sulked and stewed in their thoughts when the legion finally made camp at night.

He saw it in the men's eyes. The lack of sleep. The lack of trust in the legion's legate. All of it was combining to create that deep-set feeling of fear which, if allowed to grip the hearts of all, was unquestionably a recipe for a disaster waiting to happen. It rested on his shoulders as the legion's *Praefectous Castorum*, the legion's most experienced veteran, to train these men into a fighting unit.

Nodding to the young *decanus,* Decimus set off with a firm step to inspect the legion's perimeter, not knowing that within moments, an unimaginable disaster was soon to turn the dark Dalmatian night into the raging fires and billowing roar of a Grecian Hades nightmare.

II

7 AD
Dalmatia
The Fires of Hades

Whatever it was which made him pause and turn his head to look, he would never be able to say. But he did. And it possibly saved his life. He came to a halt on a slight rise of dirt, surrounded by his escorts, his mind intent on keeping his men ever alert. The night was a thick envelope of dark and oddly silent to the ear. Not even a breath of cool mountain air stirred in the thick blackness. In the darkness, just below the hill, the ground opened into a wide space of flat valley floor. Meandering down the middle of the valley was a road which ran from Asa on the coastline deep into the Dalmatian interior. On both sides of the valley were high, forest covered mountains. Rugged forested mountains pockmarked with the burning pinpricks of hundreds of campfires of the enemy.

Clearly visible. A constellation of man-made fireflies flickering brightly in the cloying darkness of the moonless night. Dalmatian rebels who, each one, had in their chests a burning hatred for anything Roman.

To his right—the outer defenses of the legion's camp, rows upon rows of wooden stakes driven into the soft dirt of the small hill. Beyond the stakes, a deep ditch with sloping sides encased the camp. Work was completed by every last member of the legion in a matter of a few hours. Like all Roman camps, this one was an almost perfect square precisely mapped out and plotted by the legion's attached engineers hours before the first of the legion's cohorts came marching up the road. All legionnaire camps were the same. It didn't matter if you soldiered in Mauritania in far off Africa or slogged away in a unit a thousand leagues away in the cold and ice of distant Celtic Britain. A Roman army camp was the same. A legion would march for a little over half of the daylight hours in a precisely ordered marching formation, a concisely ordered marching order *all* legions of the army adhered to since the days of the legendary Scipio Africanus, the Roman general who defeated Hannibal and ultimately destroyed Carthage almost four hundred years earlier.

But, usually four hours before sunset, the legion would come out of its marching formation and build a fortified camp atop some piece of elevated terrain which gave the legion an unhindered 360 degree of visibility of its immediate environs. It was the Roman way. It was inviolate Roman tradition. It was one of the many little pieces of the puzzle which made the Roman Army invincible.

Each marching soldier not only carried his weapons with him, but a wooden stake, or a shovel, or a pick, as well. Each man pitched in to build the camp. It took about four hours to complete. But by the time it was done, every soldier in the camp knew exactly where his cohort resided and where his tent would be found. And it was Decimus' job to make sure the legion performed to exact standards without exception.

But on this night, he paused atop a small mound of freshly discarded dirt and turned to his left to look up the hill toward the legate's tent. The darkness in the direction toward the legate's tent was not quite as dense thanks to the burning torches and campfires which littered the camp's interior. It was not a high hill the legion resided on. Its slopes were relatively gentle to traverse. Decimus noticed the large tent on the summit of the hill, surrounded by soldiers from the general's personal praetorian guards. Rising above the general's tent was the masthead which, atop it, displayed the legion's cherished eagle, along with the many pennants of the legion itself and its eight cohorts underneath. In the semi-darkness of the camp's burning campfires, he saw the main flap of the general's tent open and a group of men exit the tent's interior in mass. In the twilight it looked like five army officers surrounding a large figure wearing a dark cape which covered his entire frame. Light reflected off the polished armor of the Romans as they gathered around the dark figure for a moment or two before disappearing behind the legate's large tent.

Decimus frowned. From this distance, and with so little light illuminating the night, it was hard to see the faces of the Roman officers. But he was sure he had never seen any of the men before. As for the heavy looking man in his black hooded cloak, his face was never revealed. But he moved like a soldier. A hand lifted up to pull the hood of his cape around his face as he turned to walk away. An act of deception, the *Prefect* thought to himself. An act of intrigue. But there was a confidence, almost an arrogance, in the way he straightened himself up and moved out of view surrounded by the five Roman officers.

An unexpected chill ran down the *Prefect's* spine. Half turning, his brown eyes fell onto the balding, white-haired little man who was his servant, a sour faced old man who had served for years with him in one legion or another. He leaned closer to the older man to speak quietly into his ear.

"Find out who those men were and when they arrived in camp."

The small man with the balding head and darkly tanned face nodded in silence and turned to leave. He moved through the small entourage of armor-clad legionnaires who surrounded the *Prefect*, and then started up the incline of the hill toward the legate's tent.

He took no more than ten steps before the explosion ripped through the night. A roaring crescendo shook the ground violently underneath his sandaled feet and lit up the night with the hellish light of a nightmare. A blast of hot, foul-smelling air threw Decimus, and everyone else standing at their posts, through the air as if he was nothing more than a child's rag doll. The roar of the explosion droned on and on even as large chunks of soil and rock began raining out of the semi-lit skies. Gigantic chunks of soil and rock hit the ground with a thudding jolt, guaranteeing death and severe pain if some hapless legionnaire stood or laid splayed out underneath the raining fury.

The hot, multi-colored flames shooting up from the top of the hill roared and exploded like the hissing fury of a metal smith's forge. A forge only conceivable by the gods themselves. Decimus, stunned and in pain, lifted himself up from the ground and staggered to one side as he faced the billowing inferno above him and stared at it in awe. As he watched he saw the flames weakening, the roar of its fury lessening perceptibly, and then, with the blinking of an eye, suddenly ceasing altogether. One moment Hades' fires burned and screamed in its fury. The next, gone altogether, the night's darkness suddenly enveloping one and all, the sudden silence slapping everyone across the cheek with a startling clarity almost as overwhelming as the explosion itself.

Reality flooded into Decimus' mind as he turned and began bellowing out names with the hammer-like staccato force that only someone with twenty years of soldiering could possibly do.

"Menelaus! Romulus! Crassus! Brutus! All tribunes and centurions... to me! To me! The rest of you bastards, off your asses. NOW! Up! Up! Get on your feet, or by the sweet graces of all that is holy, I'll personally peel the hides off each and every one of you with a cat o'nine tails in the morning!"

Decimus roared. He strode from one point to the next on the outer perimeter cajoling, barking, kicking men up and off their ground and throwing them physically back to their assigned positions. He organized small gathering of legionnaires to fight and subdue the innumerable fires which sprung up in the camp. As he roared and terrified one and all, burly men dressed in the armor of tribunes or centurions staggered or ran to join him. In the eyes of each, Decimus saw disbelief and terror filling their souls. But he knew. Knew this was no time for either emotion.

A catastrophe of Olympian proportions struck the *IXth Brundisi*. But an even larger, deadlier, catastrophe was about to happen when dawn arrived if the legion was not prepared for it.

"Gnaeus!" the *Prefect* yelled over the shouting of his centurions taking over at last and rousing the men out of their stunned silence. "Survey the camp. Assess the damages and loss of men and report back to me as soon as possible."

Decimus turned and stared up at where once the top of the

hill had been. Where the legate's massive tent, the holy shrines of the legion's namesakes, where the several tents of the officers would be found, all gone. Not just destroyed. But *gone!* Nothing remained. Not a shred of cloth, or a piece of armor, or even a body part of one of the dead remained. Now there was only a gaping hole twenty meters deep and ten meters in diameter, with an eye-watering aroma of bad eggs drifting up and out of the cavity and blowing gently away with the wind.

It did not take a genius to realize the harsh truth. All of the legion's officers, except for him, and most of what had been the First Cohort—the legion's most experienced troops—no longer existed. The anger of an unknown god came down from Olympus and had destroyed one and all. And in the process, possibly assuring the complete and total destruction of everyone who, at the moment, still lived on this cursed hill. Dawn was but only two hours away, and with the first light of a new day, the hills above their position infested with Rome's enemies would look down upon the middle of the valley and see what had been wrought in the middle of the night.

The enemy would come howling and screaming at them with blood lust in their eyes and the smell of victory upon them. Thousands of them. All sensing a great victory at hand if they but struck with overwhelming force before the sun lifted much higher than dawn's light in the morning sky. If the Ninth was not prepared, if not their position was compressed and strengthened somehow, if the men were not ready to *fight*, all would be lost. By noon every living soul on this hill would be dead. Consigned to the eight levels of Hades for the rest of eternity. A situation Decimus was grimly aware of but determined to contest the issue to his last breath.

The thin, hardened old veteran of a dozen battles, turned to face the many faces of his junior officers staring up at him, hungrily waiting for orders. He began talking in a commanding, but calm voice.

"I want the Second Cohort, Brutus, to take up position on the northern flank of the hill. Pull back from your original position and deploy halfway up the hillside and dig in. Crassus, take the Fourth and deploy directly behind the First. Draco, your Sixth will take the eastern slope. The Seventh will deploy directly behind you. The west slope ..."

A calm voice. An assured, experienced commander. And a plan. A plan delivered concisely, with little fanfare, and direct. Decimus' brown eyes did not waver as he looked into the faces of each of his centurions. Orders were given from an old soldier who had seen it all. The *Prefect* in his quiet calm, simply radiated self-confidence out to his men like some mystical lantern held up in the dead of night to light the way. No one knew if the *Prefect's* plan would work. In some respects, most of the centurions didn't care. There was a plan. There were orders given and expected to be carried out to the letter. Someone was in charge. Someone they knew and respected.

What more could a soldier ask for or expect?

Only the gods knew what would happen once dawn filled the sky with light.

What remained of the night was filled with the movements of legionnaires repositioning themselves on the hill first, followed by the sounds of men digging into the soil, and hammers thumping loudly onto stout wooden stakes as they tore down the ones set earlier in the day and repositioned them in their new defensive stance.

Decimus, with the silent Gnaeus beside him, kept moving around the hill directing men here and there. Even pitching in when a set of extra hands were needed to drive stakes into the ground or to throw up additional barricades of dirt in front of their positions. No one complained. No one slacked off. Not with the *Prefect* beside them in the dirt and grime working as hard as they were.

When the first gray shades of predawn began to lessen the darkness around them, everyone knew. They were ready. Ready for whatever might come.

III

7 A.D.
Dalmatia
The Dawn

F og. Long wispy lines of white fog clung close to the ground and hugged the high hills with a passionate embrace. Thick, yet alive, for it moved slowly, almost rhythmically, with the gentle breeze blowing from out of the West. Completely hiding everything behind its cool, icy curtain. A brooding entity all its own that held no love for the Ninth. Yet, in its own right, a visual treat he knew he would never forget.

He smiled grimly, gripping his *gladius* in one hand, and his curved, rectangular *scutum,* his shield, in the other. He would remember this day, this *fog,* until his dying day. He smiled, hoping that day would come many, many years away yet.

The one other note of interest about fog, however, he remembered again. It may hide what it covered, or what was behind it. But it *enhanced* sound manifold. Distorted it. Magnified it. In the process, distorting and magnifying the terrors in the mind of each and every soldier hugging this hill so desperately. He saw several of his younger soldiers visibly shaking in fear as they knelt on one knee behind their scutum and waited for what was to come.

He stepped among the young recruits and spoke to them all. Spoke to each with a word or two. Calm. Assured. As if he was talking to equals around the dying embers of a campfire. He knew his presence as an old and experienced legionnaire and commander of men, was sometimes all that was needed to assuage the fears from men's hearts. He remembered battles past when he was but a young legionnaire. He felt their fears. Their dread for what was to come. A calm voice, a sudden smile, a quiet word was like an elixir in the ears of the fearful.

Deep in the gray-white mist they heard the approach of their enemy. The clatter of shields and spears clacking against each other. The rumble of men shouting in Greek and Dalmatian, shouting to each other and further fueling their murderous fury. Horses snorting impatiently and nervously. And the blaring notes of horns. Dozens of them. Blaring out three and four note commands only the enemy understood.

And Decimus Julius Virilis as well. The old, scarred veteran.

He had fought the Greeks and Dalmatians before. Watched them gather in their assembled masses. Listened to the wings of their fabled spearmen in their bronze helmed phalanxes communicate to each other via the blasts of their many horns. He knew what was coming. And reacted accordingly.

"Cohorts! Shields up! Ready pilum!"

Like a bolt of lightning cracking across the sky his order shot out across the perimeter of the hill in an instant. Forty-eight centurions, the surviving junior commanders left standing after the devastating explosion, relayed Decimus' command across the hill with ruthless efficiency. Each centurion commanded eighty men. In a fully manned, fully equipped legion, each cohort's complement would be six centuries strong. Roughly four hundred eighty men per cohort. But not on this day. The *IXth Brundisi* landed on the shores of Dalmatia woefully undermanned. And now, with the First Cohort's demise, Decimus knew he barely had a little over three thousand men alive enough to face an enemy vastly superior in numbers.

Decimus, half turning to face the enemy, watched the swirling pattern of white mist dance before his eyes. Dance and slowly *evaporate* ever so minutely. But enough to see the first dim outline of the approaching foe.

"Pilum... now!"

The Roman pilum. A short throwing spear, more like a weighted javelin, designed to bury deep into the shield of an approaching enemy. Half of the javelin's length was the heavy iron head of the spear itself. Heavy, but made of soft iron. The iron soft in order to make it twist and bend out of shape in the shield. The wooden shaft was purposely designed to break off, leaving just the iron head buried stubbornly into an enemy's shield, thus making the shield too heavy and cumbersome to handle in battle.

One hurled pilum would not make much difference. But four hundred such weapons, hurled at the same time, created a deadly cloud of swiftly falling carnage to the front lines of the oncoming foe. Each legionnaire was armed with two such weapons. Curtains of falling death rained down through the fog on the unsuspecting enemy. Caught unprepared, not exactly sure where the Roman lines were in the fog, the sudden carnage of hurling death caught the Dalmatians by surprise. The explosion of surprise, rage, and pain from the collective mass of falling death onto invisible foes shattered the semi-quiet of the early morning with a cacophony of murder.

The enemy, being distantly related to the Greeks to the south, fought like the Greeks of old. With shield and spears lined up in large blocks, or phalanxes, of infantry which marched slowly and methodically toward the enemy like some gigantic, weighted mass of steel, blood, and sinew. A Greek phalanx was like the mailed fist of Zeus himself, encased in steel and bronze and weighing collectively a thousand tons, smashing into the frailty of yielding human flesh. It wreaked havoc and carnage whenever the blow fell.

For centuries, the Greek style of warfare was the queen of the battlefield. Only heavy phalanx meeting heavy phalanx could defeat this mode of destruction. Until, that is, the Greeks ran up against, centuries earlier, the fledgling martial fervor of Roman arms. Almost two hundred years earlier a Greek general by the name of Pyrrhus of Epirus, at the behest of a minor Greek colony residing on the Italian peninsula, invaded Italia and fought the Romans in a series of battles.

Pyrrhic victories. Costly victories in both manpower and material. So costly that, even though victorious, Pyrrhus' ultimate goal of building a new kingdom for himself on Italian soil quickly became nothing but a fading dream. Having won battles, nevertheless he lost the war. Because of those costly victories, Pyrrhus and his Greeks were forced to returned to the Greek mainland, where they eventually faded into the pages of history. And Rome began its unstoppable march toward greatness thanks to its martial fervor and unique style of warfare.

While others mimicked the style of the Greeks in making war, Rome fought differently. Rome fought with shield and swords. The *scutum* and *gladius*. But more than that, Rome believed in flexibility and organization. Forever adapting, forever modifying its method of organized murder, Rome was unparalleled in the ancient world in its adaptability. All one had to do was look at its weaponry. The fabled short sword, the *gladius,* came from Spain. As did the heavy javelins called *pilum.* The *scutum,* or rectangular shield, was a modification of the Greek round shield. Roman armor, called *lorica segmentata,* was essentially derived from a kind of armor worn by gladiators in the ring; gladiators and gladiatorial games, a cultural carryover from Rome's long dead ancient masters, the mysterious Etruscans.

But the true strength of the Roman legion was its unprecedented command and control of a legion and its subordinate formations within the legion. No other foe Rome would face in its five-hundred-year reign could match the maneuverability and resilience of a Roman legion. Not even the legendary phalanxes of Alexander's ancestors could carry the day against a well-led, fully equipped, and properly supported Roman legion.

And for many within the skeletal shell that was the Ninth, their belief and firm faith in the bloody reputation of the cunning fox that was Decimus Virilis was unshakable. They knew what lay ahead of them. The real work of fighting a battle was about to begin. Somehow, knowing that Decimus, "The Lucky," was in command, gave the men a sense of purpose, a surging sense of pride pounding in their chests. A sense of unrealistic invincibility.

IV

7 AD
Dalmatia
Hard fighting

When the attack came it was just as the sun's growing intensity began to burn off the fog hanging stubbornly in the morning air. The panorama of the narrow valley began to materialize out of the thinning fog, revealing both the rugged terrain of the valley, and the rectangular masses of enemy infantry dressed in their various assortment of individual armor. Dalmatian tribesmen were not nearly as wealthy as their Greek cousins. When one might be encased in the full armor of a Greek warrior, five or six others of his kinsmen might be wearing various forms of leather armor, or no armor at all. But all gripped in their right hands the Greek *sarissa*, the eight-foot-long Grecian thrusting spear made famous by Greek armies all across the Mediterranean basin.

The first assault came along the northern slope of the hill. The slope offered the easiest access up the moderate-sized hill overlooking the road which ran through the middle of the valley. Two phalanxes of infantry, each rectangular box of men composed of eight ranks of infantry, numbering perhaps a thousand total, began making their way down the road and toward the northern slope in a slow, determined dance of death.

Decimus eyed the approaching enemy, holding his curved shield close to his body with one hand and firmly gripping his sword with the other. The breeze crept down the length of the valley, blowing the fog away in its path, and played with the black horse-hair plum of his tribune's helm haphazardly. Shafts of sunlight cut through the evaporating fog, illuminating portions of the battlefield below, as well as segments of the legion's defensive positions. Bright columns of yellow sunlight moved across the terrain slowly. One such shift drifted slowly up the hill and momentarily illuminated Decimus and his position, along with his servant, the silent Gnaeus at his side, before drifting away. But in those few seconds when the gods gifted the tribune with their light of favor, for lowly and superstitious Roman and Dalmatian both, the image of a warrior bathed in light was stunning to behold.

Fifty meters away from the defensive perimeter's edge, the leading Dalmatian phalanx split in half, wide enough for a dozen horsemen to come galloping through, the riders whirling long ropes over their heads, each rope ending with the ugly mass of a grappling hook attached to it. They charged toward the wooden stakes driven into the ground just behind the low defensive trench the legion dug first when they began building camp. Decimus, seeing what was about to take place, stepped into the first rank of the cohort, his voice a powerful trumpet heard by all.

"First rank, pilum! Cut them down before they tear the palisades apart!"

Eighty legionnaires rose, lowered their shields, and hurled

their stubby javelins before stepping back and squatting down and locking their shields together in a defensive stance again. The air in front of the first rank turned partially dark as the cloud of falling pilum fell like rain onto the horsemen. The results, for the horsemen, were devastating. Eight of the bare-back riders fell from their mounts with multiple javelins buried into their chests and extremities. The remaining four had their mounts screaming in pain from the falling rain of death. They went mad from the pain, whirled on their haunches, and raced back toward friendly lines.

A cheer from the cohort, four hundred eighty voices full, rose into the clearing foggy morning with a raucous defiance. But the cheering did not last long. The first ranks of the Dalmatian spearmen came marching up to the rows of wooden stakes. With the sharp echoes of multiple voices repeating the same command, the enemy phalanx came to a sudden halt, round shields up to protect warriors in the second rank back to the sixth rank. The first rank, and most exposed spearmen, discarded their spears and began ripping apart the wooden palisades.

Decimus, hunched behind his shield, watched with a grim admiration. The commander of this enemy force *knew* the Ninth had not acquired its detachment of auxiliary bowmen. Without the century or two worth of bowmen—roughly eighty to one hundred sixty men pressing forward to hurl their deadly flights of arrows toward the enemy, the enemy was free to do as he pleased. Somehow the Dalmatian commander *knew* there was nothing his men could do to stop them from destroying the palisades without detaching a century of men or more to break the legion's defensive lines and step forward to contest the issue. Breaking the defensive lines of the first rank of the cohort was the last thing Decimus would do.

Soon enough the real work of a legion's life began when

Dalmatian spearmen came marching up the hill in mass and plowed into the first ranks of the defending cohort. The resounding shudder of legionnaire shields crashing into lowered ranks of hundreds of spears cut through the morning air with a terrible snarl of martial fury. Followed, soon enough, with the curses and screams of men fighting for their lives.

Hard Roman training of using scutum and gladius in close combat situations consumed each legionnaire. Working as a well drilled machine, the Roman line of legionnaires began their bloody work with cold efficiency. With shields covering their bodies the men in the first Roman line found gaps in the wall of spears in front of them or cut through the massed steel of pikes aimed in their direction. They slipped inside the line of steel and began hacking away at the enemy at close range. The gladius was designed to be a thrusting sword. Not a slashing sword. Finding gaps between the enemy's shields, Roman steel slipped in and wrought their bloody work. Soon the hill slope was awash in blood and falling bodies as badly trained Dalmatian spearmen fought valiantly with their superiorly trained foes.

For two hours the cutting and slashing of Roman steel with the Dalmatian mass of infantry was hot and fierce. The Roman ranks wavered and bent but never broke. The entire cohort pressed forward at times to lend support to their brethren in the first ranks of the formation. At the end of the two hours the ranks of the Dalmatian spearmen staggered, lurched back, and then broke entirely. Panic swept through the first Dalmatian phalanx and they fell back, dropping shields and spears, and turned to flee from the battlefield. Their disjointed withdrawal smashed head long into the second phalanx of spearmen directly behind them. Panic in their eyes and voices, the smell of a rout was like a disease which rapidly infected the second phalanx.

The officers of the second phalanx tried desperately to hold their men in formation. But it was for naught. More untrained Dalmatian tribesmen than seasoned soldier, they too turned and fled from the field as fast as their feet could carry them.

Again, from the voices of the legion, a wild cry of victory and defiance lifted toward the heavens. From the hills and forested slopes of the mountains surrounding the narrow valley the enemy watched in silence at the failure of their initial attack. Watched in hatred as the men of the Ninth raised their bloody swords, and their voices, toward the heavens in celebration.

Twice more the enemy marshaled its men and hurled themselves against the shields of their enemy. Bloody fighting. Cruel deaths. But both waves of Dalmatian infantry shattered like ocean waves breaking against unyielding rock and washed away into nothingness. Fortunately, late in the afternoon as the legion licked their wounds and watched across the valley floor at the gathering tide for a fourth assault, gray clouds filled with rumbling fury rubbed out the mountain tops surrounding them from view and began to descend into the valley. Within an hour a fierce rain filled with raw lightning and cracking thunder filled the air with a ferocity only nature could hurl at men.

The gods, being the pranksters they were, decided Roman steel and sinew had to endure the rawness of a wet, cold Dalmatian night without the comfort of a dry tent to dress their wounds, or hot food to calm their fears.

V

7 AD
Dalmatia
Reprieve

Decimus stood in the center of a large group comprised of his surviving cohort commanders. They were all bloody, their armor splattered with mud, each soaked to the bone from half a night's worth of fierce rain, with several wounded and in need of medical attention. But they all stood surrounding Decimus and listened tentatively to his every word. It was an hour before dawn. Thankfully the rain had stopped. But the hill was a quagmire of deep mud and dead bodies lying everywhere around them. In the darkness, high in the hills, the hundreds of brightly burning campfires of the enemy were all too visible for one and all to see.

"I have sent for help," he began, speaking softly, eyeing each of the cohort commanders carefully. "Two men familiar with this territory. Each sent off in a different direction. Both heading back toward Asa. Before we left the port, the legate informed us Tiberius was soon to follow with two full legions in his command. If we are lucky, and if the gods finally decide to smile upon us, he and his men will have landed and disembarked from the ships. If our men get through, and if Caesar can rally his troops fast enough, they will come sometime late tonight or earlier tomorrow morning."

"If our men reach Asa, sir."

"And *if* Caesar and his legions are there," a second Roman veteran grunted, scratching the side of his face with his commander's baton. "Too many ifs, if you ask me. Do we have an alternate plan if this one fails?"

Decimus nodded and turned to point to a smaller hill approximately a thousand meters away.

"We survive the day. If Caesar and his relief detachment does not rescue us by this time tomorrow morning, we retreat to that hill and set up our defenses. Nightfall we withdraw when the deepest part of the night falls upon us and we leave this valley. If we get past that second line of defense, the enemy can only attack us from one side and that's down the road. We can defend against that. A covering force can hold the valley entrance long enough for the majority of the legion to escape. I will command the covering force."

Cohort commanders, to a man, turned and stared at the dim shadow of a hill far off in the distance. No one offered a different suggestion. There were none to offer. Each knew their chances for survival dropped precipitously if they were forced to retreat. Instead, they silently prayed to their respective household gods Caesar would come with men to pull them out of this trap.

He saw in their faces their grim determination to hold this hill for one more day. Saw the determination *and* saw the underlying suspicion they might all die. He grunted, and spoke again firmly, with a note of optimism ringing in his voice.

"Many of you have never fought the kind of fight the Greeks are famous for. You tasted their style of combat for the first time yesterday. You survived. Greek spears sent against a well-placed defensive perimeter has limited opportunities. But the gods have given us a gift this night, my friends. The rain. Yes, the rain. This valley is one gigantic bowl of soupy mud. We sit upon a hilltop with steep sides leading up to it. Steep sides of bare earth turned now into slippery mudholes. Steep enough for a phalanx to ascend when dry. But a disaster for any kind of advancing formation to attempt when it's like this. It will be impossible for the enemy to mount a truly overpowering blow against us. They will try. They will push forward their bowmen to pepper us with their shafts. But the mud, and our defensive position, will stop them from sweeping us off this hill. Have faith in my words, men. We still live. As long as a Roman breathes, there is a chance for victory. Now go, tell your men what to expect. It will be a long day. But we will survive."

He watched them turn and move away. When the last man faded away into the night he heard the approach of Gnaeus. Half turning to nod to the silent man, Decimus looked up the hill at the gaping hole he knew was there.

"Do you believe in the gods, old friend?" he asked, bringing his eyes back to the old soldier who had been ever faithful to him.

The smaller, older man shrugged and then gestured with his hands. A few years back, while still serving as a legionnaire, Gnaeus had been captured by one of the many Germanic tribes in the far north. The Germans, always at war with Rome, were cruel and known for their cruelty. For some unknown reason they did not sacrifice him to their fierce gods. But they did cut out his tongue. Ever since then the smaller man had been Decimus' personal servant and confidant. He followed him from legion to legion, campaign after campaign. Since the loss of speech, he and Gnaeus had thought up a language unique only to themselves. A sign language which gave Gnaeus back not only his speech, but his wit and his caustic, rather rude outlook on life in general.

Watching the little man's hands, Decimus could not help but break into a smile.

"I doubt Jupiter would particularly care what part of his anatomy you'd like to stuff his lightning bolts into. But, on the other hand, if he actually exists, I imagine he really doesn't care what one Roman soldier thinks about him."

The balding, sharp eyed little man said nothing, but his hands move rapidly and eloquently. Decimus nodded in agreement.

"Yes, too many questions and not enough answers. Strangers appear among us and then, soon after they leave, the earth explodes. Coincidence? The wrath of the gods? But what if the gods are not involved in this tragedy, Gnaeus. What then must we conclude? Was this some unfortunate accident? Was the legion, and the legate's headquarters and the entire first cohort, just unfortunate victims who happen to be at the wrong place at the wrong time? Or are we to conclude something more sinister, more *deliberate,* happened here."

Gnaeus replied, pointing off into the dark.

"No, we do not have the time to investigate," the praefectus said, shaking his head. "Daylight is approaching and our friends up in the hills will soon come calling. First thing's first. We save the legion and then, if allowed, we will look into this perplexity more closely. But for now, put your armor back on and let us wait and see what surprises the Dalmatians have in store for us."

By midday the answer came with a resounding *silence.* The hours of waiting as the sun rose higher into the skies seemed interminable. In the early morning twilight, the men of the

Ninth counted the number of smoke columns rising out of the forest covering the hills. Columns of smoke marked the campfires of the enemy. Far, far too many. As time slipped by, Decimus, eyeing his men, moved from one position to the next and felt the strain of the waiting as much as his men. He, like his men, more than anything, was impressed with the blanket of silence shrouding the valley. There were no faint shouting of Dalmatian officers screaming at their men. There were no enemy horns lifting shrill notes into the early morning air. No clatter of arms of men marching into battle. The ground did not shake as Dalmatian cavalry gathered for an attack. Only silence.

Not even the sounds of birds chirping or insects crawling about. Nothing flew, except for the growing cloud of vultures circling high up in the heavens, patiently waiting to feast. It was as if all life, except for the Romans occupying this one lonely hill, mysteriously ceased to exist. As the sun approached its zenith in the clear blue skies, tribunes gathered around Decimus again, to a man each as worried as the next about the unnatural silence. Joining the group were a number of centurions, commanders of eighty men each, the backbone of each cohort when it came to keeping discipline and leading the men into battle. All stood quietly, their faces filled with worry and unease, and waited for Decimus to break the silence.

He did. With a soft grunt of amusement.

"If this is a battle, it is too quiet by half for my taste. It appears our Dalmatian friends have decided not to dance in the mud with us today."

"But sir," one of the bolder tribunes growled, shaking his head. "We should still be aware of their presence. The hills should still have campfires burning. We should see their smoke. We should be able to observe some kind of movement up in the hills. But my men have seen nothing. Heard nothing for hours."

The men and centurions nodded in agreement, their frowns becoming more severe on their hardened faces. Decimus, for his part, nodded in agreement as well. But he did not make a reply. He waited for others to comment. He did not wait long.

"I say this is some kind of trap," an old soldier by the name of Titus Flavius growled, pointing with his baton toward the south. "The only safe way out of here is through that valley entrance behind us. The one Decimus talked about earlier this morning. What if the enemy is waiting in silence up in the hills for the reinforcements which are coming to seal us in this valley? If that is the case, we will be surrounded. Cut off from the rest of the world and far outnumbered."

Some, but not all officers nodded in agreement. Most remained frowning but waited for Decimus to reply.

"Anyone else have an opinion?" he asked quietly.

"There is the possibility Caesar may be approaching with a sizeable amount of men. Perhaps the enemy's gods of war decided to roll the dice and they came up with a losing throw."

"Bah!" a different tribune said, spitting into the mud angrily before continuing. "It is far too soon for any of our messengers to have traveled the distance from here to Asa. Assuming they were not captured and killed beforehand. I agree with Titus. It's some kind of trap."

Everyone stirred uneasily and looked at each other nervously. Decimus, on the other hand, smiled and gripped the old tribune's shoulder fondly.

"Grendel, you have always been a fountain of optimism and good cheer which have inspired us all."

Grins and guffaws splashed across the faces of most of the officers in good natured relief. Even the dour faced Grendel, always the sour faced Grendel, smiled sheepishly and shrugged. Decimus continued.

"It is quite apparent to all of us. We need more information. I need six volunteers. Three men need to head up into the hills and scout the terrain. We need to know if the enemy are up there and waiting. Or have they left the valley entirely. The three other men will head south and explore the territory beyond the valley entrance. Is Caesar coming? Or are more of the enemy coming? We need to know.

The rest of us will remain on this hill. We will follow our original plan. Tomorrow morning, just before dawn, we will retreat to our next line of defense. Or, if the gods smile upon us and our scouts come back with the report that the enemy has left the valley, we will decide what our next course of action will be. While we wait for the scouts to return, tell the men they have permission to prepare fires and cook a hot meal.

Are we in agreement? Yes? Very well. Let us act like the Senate and how the people of Rome expect us to act. Dismissed!"

The officers snapped to attention, saluted, and hurried back to their respective commands. Six volunteers were found and sent off into the unknown. No one in the legion expected to see their return.

Except, of course, Decimus. Decimus the contrarian.

VI

7 AD
Dalmatia
The hole

The waiting.
 The burning sun. Thirst.
The constant demand from the officers to remain vigilant. To be ready.

Someone within the ranks grumbled to himself out loud. His comrades heard him. "By Jupiter's hot piss! Waiting here in the trenches killed more men than facing a hoard of screaming Gauls with only a bread knife in one's hand! Where's the fucking enemy?"

`And the debate started. Like a ravaging plague, it swept through the ranks. Huddled down in hastily dug trenches, shields partially protecting them from any random arrows falling from the heavens, the entire legion rank and file participated in the debate. How many hours could a man take waiting for an enemy to make an appearance? Had any legionnaire ever died of old age while waiting like this? In a twenty-year hitch in the army, how many hours did one sit on his ass and wait for something? Which method of death did you prefer? Being killed by a German axe man splitting your skull in half? Or sitting here like this, bored out of your skull, dying slowly from thirst and inaction?

The debate at times became quite lively. Entire cohorts debated with each other. Several times centurions waded in among the men and demanded them to talk less and be vigilant more. The men grinned, grew quieter, but soon resumed the debate with vigor.

Decimus passed the word down to quietly let the men have their fun. The talk kept men awake. Made the slow march of time pass more quickly. Possibly made them more vigilant. And more than anything, it made this hodge-podge collection of freshly grouped men blend together faster. Making them more like one. A unified command. A true Roman legion.

Decimus Julius Virilis knew how to command men. He had been doing it for a very long time. Even though he was a family member of the Julii family, he came from the common stock, the plebian side of the clan. Not a born patrician, or of a noble family, meant he entered the army as a commoner. He rose through the ranks like any other soldier. It took him eight years to become a centurion in the tenth cohort, the most junior of centurions in a legion serving in Spain. The legions of Octavius Caesar hardly ever stopped fighting. Octavius, now known as Caesar *Augustus*, brought to an end decades worth of Roman civil war when his armies defeated the forces of Anthony and Cleopatra. But although strife and warfare on an empire's scale ceased with their defeats, uprising and malcontent nations still required legions and men who knew how to command them.

Decimus, in his fifteenth year in the legions, caught the eye of his distant cousin, Octavius. Promotions came rapidly.

Assignments, both personal and secret to the Julii family were given to Decimus to perform. Occasionally Augustus sent Decimus out on temporary special commands. Special commands that required tact, yet decisiveness when the time came to act. And absolute secrecy once he returned. No matter the assignment, the plebian Julii performed brilliantly.

Now, in his last command before retiring from the army, Caesar personally gave him the role as third in command of the IXth Brundisi. No one could have imagined what would happen to the Ninth when he was ordered to report to the new legion.

Like all the men of the Julii in their later years, Decimus was losing his hair. His naturally curly brown hair was thinning at the top but not yet completely gone. However, the thinning hair accentuated the already high sloping forehead, creating the look of a deep thinker. The family resemblance to the Julii family was uncanny. It seemed to be common knowledge among patrician and plebian families alike that the Julii produced handsome men. Handsome men who were particularly adept at being both ruthless and calm in difficult situations. Some of the Julii were gregarious and perhaps far too arrogant for their own good. Some were reticent and shunned being seen in public. But there was no denying the fact the Julii produced men who were gifted.

Those who knew him well knew he leaned toward the reticent side of the spectrum. He did not seek honors. Did not wish to be surrounded by a sea of sycophants who constantly praised his every word. The thought of retiring and becoming a politician, of which many within the Julii family often suggested, was never seriously considered. But Decimus had one talent he wanted to explore further. He liked puzzles. Specifically, he liked the ageless puzzle of why humans preferred to be devious and deceitful in planning another's untimely demise.

The art of murder fascinated him. The reasons behind it. The implementation of the deed. The cover ups and disguises the culprit devised to make himself appear innocent. All of it. Tracking down the felon and revealing his identity gave him immense pleasure. Even more so if the murderer happened to be a person of wealth and high prestige.

Or, curiously enough, he found himself fascinated over the idea of committing the deed and getting away with it. What would it take to murder someone and remove the body from any possibility of being discovered? Or how could one kill someone and make it look like natural causes? How could someone hide in plain sight? Was it possible, in other words, to commit the perfect murder?

Caesar Augustus became aware of his talents soon after the two met. Octavius had a concubine whom he was immensely pleased with. She died mysteriously while living in her small villa just outside of Rome. He asked Decimus to look into it, and if there was foul play, to identify the culprit and bring him to justice.

It took him a little over a week to find the killer. After resolving the case successfully, Decimus found himself a new potential career. Augustus Caesar had many enemies— many who wished to see him dead. His older cousin needed someone who would be discreet and reliable in tracking those who wished to harm him and his family and resolved the issue quickly with as little recrimination as possible. Word spread quietly through the loyal ranks of Caesar's followers. With Caesar's permission, the heads of some of the wealthiest families in the empire sought him out and asked for his help.

Now, only months away from retiring from the army, Decimus knew what he would do in his retirement years.

But ...

On this day, this hot, steamy day on the hilltop, waiting

either for the enemy to attack, or a relief column to come into the valley to save them all, Decimus turned his attention to the gaping hole at the top of the hill and stared at it. Even now, hours after the horrible event, in the air he could smell an odd aroma. A smell which reminded him of rotten eggs. He was all too familiar with the smell. From years of campaigning in Greece, Thracia, and in the Grecian colonies along the Turkish coast, he knew of caves filled with this odd odor. Atop many of these caves were Greek temples. Temples dedicated to one god or another. The priestesses of many of these temples were known to enter the caves below to inhale the gas. Doing so made them hallucinate. In their hallucinations, the devout often told him, they talked to the gods directly.

Or, tragically, died from inhaling too much of the foul smelling odors.

He knew the gas could burn brightly, with a fierce heat, if enough had accumulated. He also knew it took but a tiny spark to ignite it. Narrowing his eyes thoughtfully, he half turned and looked at Gnaeus, the ever-present Gnaeus, and spoke.

"Find me Lucius Galba. If alive, bring him to me."

The little man nodded and hurried away. Decimus brought his attention back to the gaping hole in the ground and began slowly making his way up hill to the treacherous lip of the deep cavity.

Over six hundred men wiped out in one blow. The entire first cohort. About five hundred and twenty men. The legate and all of his staff officers. At least another thirty or more. Plus, the legion's medical team and slaves. All gone in one thunderous explosion. A reality Decimus found almost incomprehensible to grasp. Yet, there it was. A stark reality. Squatting down, eyeing the debris field of the deep cavity, his mind kept playing over and over again the image of the men leaving the legate's tent and disappearing into the night just before the nightmare happened. They were in a hurry. They did not want to be recognized. With heavy cloaks thrown over them, their faces hidden deep in their cape's dark hooded folds, the men left not more than four or five minutes before the explosion...

Left as if they knew something terrible was about to happen.

But how was this possible? Who could plot such a terrible deed? Were these men Roman? Or did they claim to be Roman allies assisting Rome in this nasty little war?

He growled to himself angrily and stood up. His mind was filled with questions and clouds of confusion. Not for a moment did Decimus believe this was some supernatural decree proclaimed by a god sitting high atop some mountain and looking down upon puny little creatures called man. Yes, he was a Roman. Yes, he knew his Roman comrades were, in general, very superstitious creatures. Glancing to his left, his eyes playing across the backs of his legionaries, he didn't doubt for a moment that most, if not all of his men believed nothing mysterious had happened. The gods were angry at the Ninth. They had been punished. The only question left to be resolved was whether the gods would allow them to live or not. They would know soon enough.

But he knew himself. He was not a superstitious man. He had asked too many questions. Questions about the gods. Questions which were answered in vague terms which offered no satisfactory answers. He had seen too much. Watched men's actions too long. Especially the actions of supposedly religious men. If there were gods, then the gods were incredibly capricious in their actions. If there were gods, the gods did not particular worry about fairness, or mercy, or honesty, or love. They acted like man in their every action. Greed, and intolerance, and deceit, and cruelty seemed to be the driving forces of both. If both acted the same, the question had to be asked. Why was there any need for gods?

'No.

He did not believe in the divinity of any religion. This terrible event happened because someone, somewhere, *somehow,* came up with a plan to destroy the Ninth. Or the legion in its entirety. Or someone in particular who could not, for yet unknown reasons, be eliminated through assassination in one form or another.

He paused, hearing behind him someone struggling to run up the hill in the mud, and turned to see one of his junior centurions approaching.

"Sir!" the young man said, sucking in air but remembering to salute. "The scouts sent out to find the enemy in the hills have returned. They're gone, sir. Apparently, they left sometime early this morning. A couple of the scouts said they found campfires still burning and pots filled with their morning meals hanging on spits ready to be served."

Caesar must be coming. Must, in fact, be very close to their position. Glancing to the south, Decimus' active mind wondered how the young Caesar had come so far, so fast, in such a short time.

"Very well. Inform the cohort commanders they can stand down the men. Tell them to rest the men for the rest of the day. If Caesar joins us soon, we'll break down the camp and depart with him."

"Very good, sir!" The young centurion nodded, saluted, and turned to depart.

A few yards away the images of the tough piece of leather called Gnaeus, and a second old soldier just as hoary, just as experienced and as cagey as his aide, followed at his side. Watching them ascending the hill, he observed Lucius Alba approaching with something in his hands.

Lucius Alba was the legion's chief engineer. All Roman legions were built with detachments of skilled artisans and specialty troops such as Bowmen from Thrace or Cyrene. Extra detachments of cavalry were usually horsemen from Gaul or Mauritania. The medical staff was either Roman or Greek, or Egyptian and Engineers who were skilled tradesmen built a legion's war machines, or built bridges and camp buildings, or planned and supervised a legion's camp while on the march. Anything that required the touch of a skilled carpenter, or the plans of a trained architect and engineer, a legion possessed. Lucius Alba had originally been a Roman architect. But for reasons only he could explain, he became a legionnaire. When the Ninth was coming together he asked for Alba personally.

"Praefectus," the bald man said, nodding to Decimus. "I've been wondering when you were going to start making inquiries about this."

Decimus eyed the man warmly but said nothing. Lucius Alba was a taciturn creature who knew how to keep his opinions to himself. The two had served together in a number of different legions all across the empire. They trusted each other. They shared a number of common traits. Both were astute observers of humanity. Both were naturally attracted to the odd and unique. Like, for instance, the massive explosion of hill tops.

"What have you there, Lucius?"

Gnaeus glanced at Alba's hand and as the balding architect stepped forward, he deposited the jagged piece of pottery into Decimus' open hand.

"I found this last night in the rain. Not in the hole, mind you. But some meters away."

"What is it?"

Alba grunted in amusement and stepped closer to answer.

"It's a pottery shard, Praefectus. One from a common clay pot used for storage in this part of the world. Any city, or town, or hamlet you might find in and around the hills and valleys of this land you would find hundreds of such pots. The local inhabitants store everything in them. Grain, wine, oil. Anything."

A set of delicate fingertips moved across the glazed outer surface of the shard. There were no markings of decoration in the glaze he could see. But the dark brown color of the shard's outer surface was pleasant to look at.

Not so on the concaved inner surface of shard.

"Ah, you've discovered my little mystery, Decimus. Feel the gritty, oily film? Good. Now, lift the piece to your nose and take a small whiff of its aroma."

He did not hesitate. One shallow sniff was all that was needed. A profoundly repugnant aroma filled his nasal cavities and made his eyes water. Quickly lowering the shard from his face, Decimus looked at the Roman architect inquiringly.

"It was the smell which told me everything, sir. I've only come across it once in my career. Ten years ago, I think. Serving in one of Caraccola's three legions sent to Judea to chase after Parthian raiders."

Decimus grunted, nodded, and looked at the shard in his hand knowingly.

"Greek Fire."

"Truly," nodded Alba grimly. "The genuine stuff. In the hands of someone who knows how to use it, it becomes a terrible weapon to behold. A horrific one if used against you."

Greek Fire.

From the fertile mind of a Greek alchemist, this diabolical concoction was created. A thick, dark liquid, with the viscosity of olive oil, it burned hot and bright whenever a flame touched it. It burned even hotter and brighter, and longer, if someone threw water on its ever-ravenous flames. Once lit, nothing could put it out. It adhered to any surface, be it steel or flesh, and burned until all of its dark evil was consumed.

The formula for Greek Fire was one of the most sought-after prizes in the empire. The brilliant mind who had invented it, no one knew. But it had been long ago—first used even before the time Alexander the Great conquered the Persians.

Decimus gazed upon the ragged looking shard again and frowned. The evidence seemed conclusive. The tragedy the night before was no accident. No judgement from the gods. It was planned, premeditated murder. A mass murder from someone, or from some group, who wished to kill Romans in herculean form.

"Anything else, Lucius? If you have anything, I wish to hear it."

The dry, craggy faced older man turned, and lifting an arm, pointed down at the bottom of the hole.

"Can't get down there now, Decimus. Too much muck and debris and too much water filling the bottom. But cast your eyes down at the water and watch. See the bubbles? This hill sits atop a large vent which sinks deep into the earth. The earth's fumes come up from the depths ceaselessly. Before the rains came, I climbed down there with a burning torch to examine the vent. I almost blew myself up doing it. But I did find something interesting. Someone used shovels and picks to widen the vent in the earth. I'd suggest what they did was to build a large cavern around the vent. The escaping gas filled the cavern, magnifying the explosion, along with the Greek Fire when the fuse was lit."

Indeed, bubbles rippled across the muddy brown water in the bottom of the hole without let up. He could smell the odor of rotten eggs easily enough. In his mind he visualized men, their faces hidden in shadows, a number of them, working hard to dig out the cavern and preparing the deadly trap. He even half glimpsed, in his mind, a dark form standing atop the vent, arms crossed over his chest, directing the men below in their dig. Decimus saw the image clearly. Saw everything clearly except the faces. The faces remained a mystery.

"Very good, Lucius. Commendable work. Do you have anyone in mind who might have the know how to do something like this? Perhaps a Greek scientist or engineer you might have heard about from your many postings in this part of the world?"

Lucius Alba frowned and shook his head. He knew many Greeks. He had heard of others who were very good in their work. Some of them hated Rome with a passion. But he knew of no one who would have come up with such a diabolical idea as this.

"This," the old Roman began, frowning, waving a hand dismissively toward the gaping hole, "doesn't feel like the handiwork of a Greek, Decimus. This is far more than that. This—this is not just hostility aimed toward Rome. This is a grand show of disdain. Of fury. Someone wanted to make a statement. Someone wanted to humiliate someone. Show them as being impotent. Even incompetent."

"In other words, this is the work of a Roman," Decimus muttered quietly, turning to stare down at the water-filled hole. "Or at least, someone very familiar with Romans. A very angry, determined, and obviously dangerous Roman."

VII

7AD
Dalmatia
Caesar

The Chosen One, Tiberius Caesar, riding at the head of two thousand Roman horsemen, thundered into the valley just as the sun slipped behind the high Dalmatian hills. Caesar, and all of the horses and men following him, were caked in mud from the hard ride up from Asa. Horses and men looked ragged and exhausted. But not Caesar. He looked determined, in command, and expecting a fight. In other words, he looked like what a Roman general should look like.

Entering the camp, he leapt off his mud splattered horse and landed on his feet, throwing up a wave of mud in the process. His fiery eyes took in the view of the gaping hole. As Decimus hurried through the gathering soldiery toward Caesar, it occurred to him Caesar did not seem the least bit surprised by the situation. As he stopped and saluted Caesar, the younger man turned toward Decimus, lifting a hand up to point to the hill, and stepped toward the older Julii.

"I came as fast as I could, cousin. I gathered all the horse up from the two legions disembarking in Asa and we hurried through the night, storm or no storm, to get here."

"A decision which probably saved our lives," Decimus acknowledged after stepping up and embracing the heir to the empire fondly. "The enemy fled into the night sometime early this morning. No doubt because they knew your force was approaching rapidly."

The handsome young man turned and stared at the gaping hole for a moment before returning his gaze back to the older Julii. Glancing to one side, Tiberius stepped forward, gripped Decimus' arm and moved away from those who might overhear their words.

"This is a disaster, cousin. A complete disaster. Somehow news has already reached Rome that the Ninth has been destroyed. Apparently rumors began to fly around the forum and in the temples even before the disaster took place. The moment I landed in Asa I was informed of the disaster. We met the men you sent out to find us a few hours after leaving the port. I find this whole affair most peculiar, Decimus. Most peculiar and most disturbing. Rome is already a jittering pile of raw nerves thanks to this rebellion. Rumors of a Dalmatian invasion fly around the city streets like a raging inferno. Now we have this disaster to solve."

"Come," Decimus said, frowning. "Let me show you the aftermath and what we have found already."

Both of the Julii men strode up the hill and peered into the deep hole. Tiberius Caesar remained silent as Decimus explained in detail the events which culminated in Caesar's timely arrival. The older Julii left nothing out of his report.

When he mentioned the discovery of clay shards which had at one point contained Greek Fire, Tiberius turned and faced the older man, a look of deep concern on his young face.

"Are you saying this was planned long before the Ninth even landed in Asa? A conspiracy of grand proportions? Is that what I am hearing, cousin?"

"The evidence suggests it, Caesar. This was an undertaking that required detailed planning and unwavering execution to pull off. I suspect dozens of operatives were involved. Both operatives from the enemy and from Rome. Your news of rumors circulating of the Ninth's demise even before the disaster struck suggests that."

"Frankly, this mess places my father in an untenable position, Decimus. The Sulla family is very powerful in Rome. They have never been great admirers of the Julii. It was my father's insistence that the younger Gaius Sulla be named the commander of this legion. A number of senators in the forum were furious over the decision and loudly protested the boy's posting. They said the boy had not earned the right to command a legion. Royal favoritism in awarding the legion to the Sulla family in the hopes of keeping the Sulla content has rubbed many powerful men the wrong way. Coming to grips with this debacle and finding those who planned this is of paramount importance.

"So here are your orders, cousin. Find those who planned this treachery. Run them to ground. Every one of them. Keep one of the cohorts in Asa and use them in any way you deem necessary in your investigation. But find them. Bring them to Rome for all to see. Prove beyond doubt they planned this. Begin immediately."

Tiberius turned and started to descend the hill. But stopping, he turned, and looked up at his older cousin.

"And Decimus, my father and I personally thank you for being the one man who could save the men in this legion. Father will agree with me, I know. You will be rewarded handsomely for your devotion and quick thinking. That, I promise you!"

VIII

7 AD
Dalmatia
The Port of Asa

The port of Asa was more of a fishing village than a true port. A clutter of stone cottages, an inn or two, a couple of rambling warehouses, and an ill-kept outer stone wall littered the rugged island strewn coastline of dark rock surrounding a deep-water bay. The bay itself was barely large enough for half a dozen ships to ride anchor in. Tonight, four heavy looking Roman *corbita* transports and two Roman navy *quinquerriemes* idly road the still waters of the harbor.

From the four *corbitas* columns of wide, flat-bottomed boats snaked their way across the waters to the various wharves, riding low in the water from men and material being off-loaded. By early tomorrow morning the transports would be gone, replaced by four more in a never-ending game of supplying an ongoing war.

The town itself was alit with hundreds of burning torches

illuminating the streets. The city was filled with legionnaires. Squads of soldiers, each armed with heavy clubs, roamed the streets and moved along idle soldiers standing around after leaving one of the town's two inns. Decimus, standing underneath a bright burning set of torches which lit up an intersection of two narrow streets meeting each other on the town's outer perimeter, eyed the city and the harbor for a moment or two and then turned to face the three soldiers standing behind him.

"We understand our orders?" he asked, eyeing the two centurions closely.

"Yes tribune," the two answered together. "Cletus will make inquiries about the strangers who entered our camp just before all hell erupted. And I will begin asking questions to various locals on who our bomb maker might have been. By the time you return to us we should have something for you."

Both centurions were hardened, experienced soldiers. They had served with Decimus before. He trusted them. They would be diligent in their efforts. He had no doubts they would dig up some interesting pieces of information which would help in the investigation.

"Very good," he nodded, looking at the men. "Gnaeus and I must take the remains of the legate back to his grieving family. Gaius Cornelius Sulla, the Elder, is a very powerful man in the Roman Senate. He has been making demands to know what happened to his son. Caesar thinks it would be wise for me to personally return his son's remains so a proper Roman funeral can be had. Perhaps, in the process of his grieving, the elder general might give us a hint as to what might have originated this terrible tragedy."

"But Praefectus, the contents of the casket you take with you does not contain the legate's remains," the taller of the two centurions pointed out, his voice filled with skepticism. "The explosion was so intense nothing was ever found of the legate, nor the men who died with him."

"True, Simon. We know the truth of the matter. I suspect even Gaius Sulla knows the truth. A wealthy family such as his will have spies everywhere. But the Sulla are tradition bound. The death of a son requires a formal Roman funeral. It is my hope offering the Sulla something to claim as their own so they can keep up tradition will be appreciated."

Both centurions looked unconvinced but said nothing. He almost smiled. He too didn't think this ruse would succeed. But Tiberius Caesar believed this gesture of condolences had to be done. And it had to be Decimus who brought the casket back to Rome.

"We will be in Rome for a week. Possibly two. If something is found which requires my immediate presence, send a fast courier at once. I am no more than a week's hard travel away. Otherwise, be discreet in your inquiries. I suspect the enemy lurks near. He knows we are on the hunt for him so do not be surprised if you find your efforts are met with some kind of resistance. Be wary, centurions. Be wary."

The two nodded, saluted smartly, and left Decimus and Gnaeus standing under the burning torches on the empty street. Gnaeus, his craggy old face filled with the warm light of the torches, used his hands to speak. Decimus watched and in the end, shook his head as he turned to eye the harbor below.

"The Sulla are no friends to the Julii, old friend. There is too much history between the two. Years of intrigues, treacheries, and failed promises. One of the richest families in the empire. A family with unlimited wealth to draw from and political clout which rivals any family in Rome. Yet, for the moment, they are not our enemies. At least, not that we know of. There is a strained neutrality the Sulla surround themselves in in relation to the Julii. The Caesars wish to keep this neutrality intact."

An hour later they were aboard one of the transport ships, standing on the curved stern of the sturdy transport, silently watching the men rattle out the thirty or so oars and dip them into the water. It was a slow, delicate process, requiring some skill for the crew to warp out of the compact harbor using only oars and straining backs for propulsion. It was not until they were well out from shore before the crew pulled in the oars and dropped the two large rectangular sails and set a course for the Italian peninsula.

Under the light of a full moon, Decimus stood by the stern railings of the ship, arms folded across his robed chest, and watched the wake of the ship and the receding shoreline of land. The brilliant white luminescence of the ship's passage through the wine-gray waters was a bright contrast to the gray mass of the sea surrounding them. A warm summer's breeze played across his face, ruffling what little hair he had left on the high crown of his head as his dark eyes gazed into the night.

At his feet, the ever silent but quite loquacious Gnaeus made his pallet on the ship's deck and laid stretched out fully and deep asleep. Behind him only a few of the ship's men moved about. Most had, as well, found their favorite spots to bed for the evening. By morning the eastern shore of Italy would fill the distant horizon.

Years of service given to the Julii had taught him one thing: Rome and power were synonymous. If a family wished to rise to the level of the Julii, or the Sulla, or any other powerful family, which controlled the empire's politics, the usurpers had to be ruthless, dedicated, relentless, and intelligent. If the killing of Gaius Cornelius Sulla, legate of the Ninth, was the opening act in a family's political move on the chessboard of Roman politics, he would agree it was both ruthless and dedicated. It took a certain level of bravura to come up with such a plan and actually carry it through. It bespoke of a certain level of expertise, backed by sufficient wealth to implement the deed.

But one question kept repeating itself over and over in Decimus' head. Was such a sudden and declarative move in the middle of a war yet teetering on the dice tables as to who won and who lost, an intelligent move?

Entertaining that one question was an invitation for others to etch deeper worry lines across his forehead. If a political move, why first attack and humiliate the Sulla? Of all the families to make a move on, the Sulla would be the very *last* family he would choose to attack. Gaius Cornelius Sulla the Elder was a man with a hard reputation. A prickly reputation which did not tolerate insults to the family, or to his reputation. It was a foregone conclusion the leader of the Sulla clan would use every means, every tool, he commanded to find the murderers of his son. No stone would be left unturned. No corner of the empire would escape his scrutiny. People were going to die in this search for his son's killer. The only questions were how many, and how many innocent victims might stumble in the way? Which made Decimus pause in his ruminations. Pause, and almost smile. The smile of a pit viper observing for the first time his next intended victim.

Perhaps he was wrong. Perhaps the legate's murder was an inspired stroke of genius.

What better way to roil the empire into a calamitous uncertainty than an attack on one of the most powerful families in the empire mysteriously and unexpectedly. The news of the near destruction of the raw legion had, by now, swept through the ranks of the nearest legions here in Dalmatia and on the peninsula. Rumors would be multiplying on a daily basis. Whispers of another civil war tearing the empire apart undoubtedly growing like a disease sweeping through the empire.

Glancing out at the moon lit waters of the sea, Decimus could feel the unease in his bones. The empire, under Octavius, had just now healed itself from decades of civil war. There was a reason why the Roman Senate awarded Octavius the title *Augustus*. It had taken Octavius most of his adult life to hunt down and destroy the group of Roman senators who murdered his paternal uncle, and adopted father, Julius Caesar on the steps of the Roman Senate. And years more to defeat the usurpers who claimed the right to rule the empire as their own.

He knew from experience, having spent a major portion of his own lifetime serving in the legions of Octavius fighting those very same usurpers.

But now the empire was whole. Unified under the rule of *Augustus* Caesar. The empire, under his rule, was healing itself from the decades of constant warfare. It was growing. It was becoming wealthy again. The very idea of another civil war sweeping across the empire would chill the very souls of each Roman family he knew. Therefore there was a need, an urgency, to find those who committed such a daring plan and bring them to justice as fast as possible. For the longer the issue remained afire with possibilities and innuendos, the certainty of calamitous times to follow could not be ruled out.

Turning his head to gaze toward the west, the old warrior and Roman tribune hoped Gaius Cornelius Sulla the Elder might have some idea on who might his enemies be. And how determined they were in destroying the Sulla name.

IX

7 AD
On the Via Flamina
Ten kilometers north of Rome

It had been a hard five days' ride from the port of Arminum south toward Rome. The Via Flamina was paved, one of the half dozen or so paved highways the Roman Senate and Caesar maintained diligently for the primary movement of the legions back and forth across the Italian peninsula. The travel had been brisk, with few interruptions. During the last two days neither Decimus nor Gnaeus observed many travelers. Lodgings at one of the several way stations along the highway had been easy to obtain. But both knew, from past experience, that a truly good meal and a hot bath could not be had until they reached the Inn of the Forest Nymphs in the small village of Castor, ten kilometers north of Rome.

Both rode their horses briskly all day long, each anticipating a good meal and a bath later that evening. As they dismounted from their mounts each felt the aches and pains of riding a horse, a mode of travel few legionnaires were familiar with, along with the inevitable march of old age catching up with them. Yet both men were alert as they unpacked their few belongings from the mounts and strode across the open space between the stables toward the inn. Each knew, since leaving Arminum, they had been followed. A single horseman kept position about a kilometer and a half behind them the entire way south, making no effort to speed up or slow down.

Neither said anything to the other, each knowing their companion was aware of the horsemen the moment they first mounted their horses and left the port city the day before. Years of campaigning together taught each man the value of the other. But, unpacking their horses, each waited for their mysterious traveling companion to eventually make his appearance in the inn's courtyard. As slaves led the tired, sweat stained horses toward the inn's small stables, both Decimus and Gnaeus stood around and waited for the rider to appear. Both accepted large stone goblets of wine from the inn's owner who came out with servants and greeted them as if they were old friends. Which, frankly, they were. The grinning, jovial owner of the inn was an old legionnaire who had served with Decimus years earlier in Gaul. Retiring from the legions, the balding fat man bought the inn from its previous owner, found a local girl to marry, and had a dozen or more children.

It seemed as if Decimus Virilis knew everyone who served, or had served, in the army. Perhaps it wasn't such an exaggeration. Twenty plus years as a professional soldier, serving in one legion or the other, from Hispania to the Levant, and from Germania to Egypt, introduced Decimus to many different men. After the civil wars, Caesar kept only twenty-eight legions of the fifty or more legions which faced each other across the battlefield to serve as the 'official' army. Most of the legions kept intact were legions loyal to Octavius. But in a show of unity, of forgiving those who fought against him, several legions which had been created by one or another of Octavius' challengers had been kept as well.

The inn keeper led Decimus and Gnaeus to a small garden patio littered with plain wooden tables and benches but shaded from the sun thanks to large Poplar trees providing a deep shade. In the middle of the patio a large fountain gurgled fresh water out of the marbled mouth of a small statue of Pan. Two or three individuals, fellow travelers from their appearance, sat scattered about, none paying any attention to the new arrivals. As they sat down, servants brought platters of freshly cut bread, cheese, and more wine, for their enjoyment. Relaxing in the cool shade from the hard ride from Arminum, they nibbled on the food and drank sparingly of the wine as they waited for the rider to make an appearance.

Not unsurprisingly for Decimus, the rider never arrived. Sipping the cool wine and eyeing the others who sat in the shade of the small patio around him, the tribune seemed to be completely at ease. But not so of the old piece of dried, tanned leather that was Gnaeus. Turning his head away from the road he had been diligently observing, he glared at the tribune, his hands suddenly gesturing angrily toward his benefactor.

"Our companion is a cautious man, Gnaeus. He does not want to make an appearance here in the inn because he does not want any witnesses who might be able to recognize him later on."

Gnaeus' hands flew again. Decimus, smiling, sipped wine and waited for the silent man to finish.

"Oh, but I do expect a trap, old friend. I suspect the attempt to silence our inquiries will come late tonight or early tomorrow morning about an hour or two before the cock crows. So we must be prepared."

Gnaeus, frowning, thought over Decimus' words and then quickly asked another question.

"I think he is working alone, Gnaeus. We've seen him several times from afar. But each time he's been alone. He's followed us since we've left Asa ten days ago. I doubt he has had time to make arrangements with anyone to meet him here. Not yet, at least. But after tonight, I would suspect otherwise. From here to Rome will be our most dangerous trek, old friend. It would be wise for both of us to sharpen our swords and keep them close to us when we retire tonight."

Gnaeus' hands flew again asking another question. Decimus, lifting an eyebrow in surprise, lowered his wine and chuckled with amusement.

"I had not thought of that, Gnaeus. Yes, our friend makes himself scarce because he may be afraid *we* will recognize him. Which, if true, suggests he may be someone from the legion. Hmmm, that possibility throws a whole new angle onto this situation. Perhaps we should not be so passive, my friend. Instead of waiting for him to make his move on us, we should consider the idea of quietly hunting our friend down and capturing him. What do you think?"

The tribune saw the man's answer immediately. Gnaeus preferred action over contemplation. It was difficult for the slightly older soldier to sit and remain quiet. Constantly moving, the hardy legionnaire was always cleaning, always repairing Decimus' equipment, always constantly in motion. Yet Gnaeus knew how to sit for hours absolutely motionless if and when it came to a hunt. Hunting either animal or man.

"Well then, it's settled," the tribune said, lifting his cup toward his servant in a salute. "We will set a trap for our friend. Lure him in and run him to the ground. Afterwards we will ask him a few polite questions. Just a few. And perhaps not so politely."

X

7 A.D.
One stroke past midnight
The Inn of the Forest Nymphs

For the rest of the day nothing out of the ordinary happened. The distant companion made no appearance at the inn, nor did any of the few travelers who stopped at the inn rouse Decimus' or Gnaeus' attention. Just a handful of travelers came, washed a day's worth of grime and dust off their faces and hands, drank some wine and rested a few hours, before departing in an unhurried fashion. The warm afternoon sun drifted slowly toward the sunset. Lanterns and candles illuminated the night. The innkeeper's plain, but sumptuous meal of breads, beef, cheese and wines were served to an inn full of local citizenry as well as the few travelers who remained.

A few of the local color remained to drink a few goblets of wine and discuss local affairs. None bothered the tribune or his servant as they sat at their table on the opposite side of the inn in seclusion. When, at last the local customers slowly emptied the inn, Decimus and Gnaeus rose from their table and drifted off to their room.

Neither prepared for bed. Instead, they laid their trap for the anticipated assassination attempt. Neither knew for sure if an attempt would be made this night. But both were convinced if an attempt was to be made, being only ten kilometers from Rome's nearest gates, it would be either this night, or early tomorrow morning.

As the night deepened and the inn's occupants retired to their beds, Decimus waited a few moments to make sure no one stirred in the tavern below before descending the stairs and finding his way out into the night. In the moonless night's darkness, he found a deep shadow close to the inn's small barn and knelt in the darkness. With his sheathed sword leaning against his shoulder, he began his vigil. Upstairs in their room, Gnaeus opened the windows' heavy wood shutters, offering a would-be assassin the perfect avenue of entry. The wiry old servant had, by now, used a set of pillows to make a large lump in the bed which, in the darkness, vaguely resembled a human body lying asleep. On the floor at the base of the bed, where a servant would naturally sleep, he made a similar disguise of a sleeping soul before slinking off into a far corner of the room. He kneeled, lying in wait for an intruder's deadly entrance.

Hours rolled by with a numbing slowness. The inn and its surroundings grew incredibly still. Both Decimus beside the barn, and Gnaeus in the inn, fought to remain awake. Their eyelids grew heavy. Yet motionless they remained. Years of army life had put them in situations like this all too often. Years of practice. Of knowing what would happen if someone fell asleep or made an unwanted gesture such as a soldier nodding off to sleep, his head dropping just inches in the process before waking up.

When the assassin finally appeared, just a moment or two after the stroke of midnight, he announced himself quietly in the night with the soft whisper of cotton cloth rubbing against cotton cloth.

Decimus heard the faint whisper near him. But in the blackness of the night he could see nothing. He felt a presence very close to him. Remaining completely motionless he heard the faint sound of a sandal stepping ever so gently onto soil, and then the sense of the assassin's presence evaporated into nothingness. Still the tribune did not make any overt movement that might attract attention. Very slowly, he turned his head to one side and then slightly upward to stare at the tiled roofline of the large tavern.

A mirage of darkness on darkness running across the edge of the tavern's roof flirted across his eyes. So vague, so ill-defined, the old tribune knew it could have been his imagination playing tricks on him. On the other hand, the image was shaped like a man bent down into a deep crouch, moving in rapid stealth toward the open window leading into his room just underneath the lip of the roof. Taking a chance of being heard, Decimus came to his feet, quietly drawing the cold steel of his gladius from its sheath, gripping it firmly in his right hand.

Pandemonium broke out instantly from above.

Decimus heard the bang of a stone pitcher of cold water crashing to the floor, soon followed by the unmistakable clash of cold steel striking against cold steel. Two distinct blows of steel falling on edged weapons, soon followed by a heavy weight, undoubtedly that of a falling body, smashing through the small wooden table beside the bed which had held the stone pitcher of water moments before.

The sounds of crashing furniture and smashing stoneware were enough to arouse the inhabitants of the inn, and especially, the sleeping mastiffs the inn's owner kept both in the inn and outside in the barnyard. Huge animals, these mastiffs. But unlike the army's canine corps, these were well fed and mostly docile. But roused from their sleep rudely, and sensing immediately something amiss, these giants with their massive jaws and sharp teeth broke into a torrid explosion of barking and howling. Their voices were both deep and commanding. In seconds within the inn the lights of several different torches lit up the tavern's interior. Angry voices filled the night. The sound of doors banging open clearly heard.

Decimus started running toward the inn's main entrance but slid to a halt in the tavern's yard when he saw something fly out of the window of his room and sail through the night air across the wide space which separated the inn from the inn's low barn. Instinctively he knew this was the assassin making his escape. He raced toward the barn, bare steel in his grip, just as a half dozen burning torches and shouting men filled the courtyard.

Plunging into the darkness of the barn's interior, sword in hand, he heard voices behind him of men hurrying toward the barn. Through the cracks and crevices of the barn's walls, the light of flaming torches and heavy lanterns sent shafts of light cutting through the darkness. But the blackness of the barn's interior was so thick Decimus could see nothing solid or discernible more than a foot away from him. Four steps deep into the barn and the tribune decided it was best to wait for reinforcements. In the blackness, the advantage was on the assassin's side. A knife blade, a stroke of a sword, even a poisoned dart would find him long before he knew his death was imminent.

Behind him men threw open the wide barn doors with a thunderous crash, filling the barn's interior with the light of a dozen torches. Lucky for Decimus the inn's proprietor and his servants entered so fortuitously. For the moment when the light of torches filled the corners and crevices of the dark barn, to a man, a dozen shouts of warning filled the night air. Directly behind the tribune, less than a foot away, the hooded figure was rising like a deadly ghost from out of the hay and dirt strewn flooring, a hand gripping the long blade of a knife. The knife lifted over the hooded figure's unseen head and was about to plunge into Decimus' back.

The sharp edge of the deadly knife never found its mark for just as the assassin was about to plunge downward the death-blow, two separate actions came into play which saved the tribune's life. First, Decimus instinctively twisted to one side the moment the barn doors were thrown open violently. The assassin's blade, sailing downward in a vicious thrust, glanced off the leather armor of Decimus' right shoulder and slid to one side. At that exact moment, two massive black forms of the inn's mastiffs sailed through the air, fangs bared, and smashed directly into the assassin's chest.

The violent collision of dogs and assassin threw the tribune to one side. Crashing to the floor he rolled on one shoulder and came back to his feet, sword still in hand, and turned to face his foe. But there was no foe present. Somehow the assassin slipped from the steel jaws of the mastiffs and disappeared into the darkness. Gone. Like the ghosts of Egyptian mummies in the depths of the lonely Sahara.

Immediately Decimus organized armed search parties and sent them out into the night in search of the assassin. For hours the countryside around the inn was lit up with bobbing torches of men searching everywhere. More mastiffs were found to aid in the search. The noise of dozens of search parties with their accompanying mastiffs was enough to waken the dead.

But nothing was found of the assassin. Nothing except for a faint trace of blood from where one of the mastiffs' teeth sank his long fangs deep into the man's flesh the moment the assassin's blade flashed toward the exposed neck of Decimus.

XI

7 AD
Before the walls of Rome
Late afternoon

Gnaeus slid off his horse gently, pain clearly written on his lined, deeply tanned face, and clutched his ribs with one hand. The scuffle with the assassin in the inn's dark room had been less than stellar for the middle-aged legionnaire. The moment the hooded figure appeared in the open window and hurled two knives straight into the bed where normally, the tribune would have been sleeping, he had launched himself toward the assassin. His intentions were to grapple the dark figure and hold him captive until help arrived. But the hooded figure was both incredibly strong and incredibly fast.

Steel met steel in the clash. But a sandaled foot caught the smaller Gnaeus full in the ribs, sending the small man flying across the room and smashing into the far wall. By the time he returned to the living the assassin was gone and sun was rising above the eastern horizon.

Decimus, lifting the leather water container off his saddle, walked around the front of Gnaeus' horse and handed the heavy container to the balding older man.

"Do you wish to stop, old friend? We can purchase food here from the local vendors and have lunch first. A small reprise before entering the gates of Rome will not hinder us any. Last night's festivities took a lot out of both of us, I confess. A nap would not be out of the question right about now."

Wherever there was a temple, there would be food vendors. The Temple of Fortuna was no different from the dozen or so other temples which littered the open spaces beside the various paved roads leading toward the city. Both men stood just a few yards away from the marble steps leading up into the small but smartly designed temple dedicated to the goddess. Less than two kilometers down the road was the large Porta Collina, the northern most gate in Rome's Servean wall. The temple's well-manicured grounds of bountiful shade trees and small gardens were littered with both weary travelers taking a small rest before moving on to Rome, or the city's devotees of the goddess who journeyed out of the city for a day's visit to the well-known temple.

Gnaeus, eyeing a particularly large tree which covered the ground beneath with a wide canopy of cool shade, looked back at the tribune and spoke with his hands. Decimus smiled and nodded in agreement.

"A cool glass of wine and some bread and cheese sounds like an excellent idea, Gnaeus. Watch the horses while I find a temple servant who will unsaddle them and give them a good rub down. I will then order lunch."

It did not take long. The temple's staff moved swiftly and efficiently when a generous monetary donation was offered to the goddess. As Decimus moved through the milling crowd toward Gnaeus he noticed slaves had already taken the horses away and a large picnic basket, complete with wine and freshly baked bread, had been spread out underneath the shade tree. Lowering himself slowly to the ground, the tribune grunted in pleasure when the balding Gnaeus handed him a large goblet of dark red wine.

"We grow too old for this, old friend. Too old. It is time we should be thinking about retirement and living the rest our lives out in our home on the Palatine."

A wicked grin of sarcasm stretched across the old legionnaire's face as he lifted a hand up and spoke rapidly.

"Bah!" hissed the smiling Decimus, shaking his head in mild disagreement. "I would not be bored living the life of a retired soldier. True, perhaps I might regret the intellectual demands of soldiering. I would have to find something to occupy my time. But the physical exertions of soldiering have taken a toll on me, on both of us I might add, over the years. We are not the young pups we were ten years ago, Gnaeus. Time, and old age, are catching up to us."

People moved constantly around them as they sat underneath the shade tree. The movement of travelers on the Via Salarna, both moving toward Rome and departing from the capitol, was a constant, though not excessive, flow of humanity. Like them, a number of people, mostly families, came to the temple to picnic and enjoy the beauty. Children of all ages played beneath the trees. Young couples, fresh in their love, strolled through the gardens. Weary travelers, dusty and suffering from the summer's heat, washed themselves at the small fountains and pools placed strategically in front and to the east side of the temple. Most were merchants with small wagons pulled by donkeys or oxen. There was a large group of tradesmen heading for Rome in the hopes of finding work. Soldiers were plentiful. Individually or in small groups, scattered throughout the temple's crowd.

And, as was true for all things Roman, thieves, pickpockets and cut throats mingled among the innocent. It was the latter which kept Gnaeus' eyes busy roaming the crowd.

Decimus saw his silent friend's wary eye and he chuckled amusedly as he cut slices of bread both for himself and Gnaeus. Handing the old legionnaire his slice, the tribune leaned against the tree and took a bite out of the bread before speaking.

"Relax, old friend. No harm will come to us while the sun shines and we are in the midst of so many. If nothing else, last night's affair suggests that our foe wishes to silence us quietly, without witnesses around to possibly point a finger at him. An assault in broad daylight would be an act of desperation. Our foe is far from being desperate at the moment."

Gnaeus eyed the tribune for a moment and then reluctantly nodded his head in agreement. Tearing a chunk of bread with his teeth from the larger piece of bread, he began chewing slowly, eyes still roving the milling crowd surrounding them. He trusted the tribune's judgement. Years of experience working and serving with the tribune had taught him one thing. Decimus Julius Virilis was, without question, the most intelligent man he had ever met. The man's brown eyes had this hypnotic trait of seemingly baring one's soul to him. You could not stand before him and lie to him and expect to get away with it. The tribune had this ability to know truth from fabrication. Even legates and powerful Roman Senators hesitated to say an untruth to the tribune.

And he knew everything. He could look at a soldier, or farmer, or a merchant and tell, just by looking at him, from what part of the empire the man hailed from. A smear on a man's toga. A scuff mark on a sandal. Perhaps the color of dirt on a man's sweaty forearm and the tribune knew. Knew everything he needed to know about the stranger in front of him.

The tribune was perhaps the best tracker in the army. He

could kneel and examine faint traces in the ground and know exactly in what direction the fleeing soul took and much, much more. A day old or a month old, it seemingly did not matter. The tribune could follow anyone.

But the truly uncanny talent the tribune had was his ability to find those who plotted and executed the murder of another soul. Murder, as everyone knew, was as common in a Roman's daily experience as it was for a Roman to drink strong wine. People disappeared all the time. One day they were there. The next day they were gone. Rumors circulated daily of someone finding a body hidden away in a dark crevice. Or worse. The dead found lying on the cobblestone streets of Rome as the first rays of a new day filled the streets with light.

The tribune found a hidden talent within him when, one day, he was asked to find and punish the perpetrator of the murder of a fellow Julii kinsman. This was even before the time Caesar sought Decimus' help in solving the murder of his concubine. He remembered the day vividly. Years earlier, when Caesar was still leading his armies in the field, he came to the tent of Decimus Julius Virilis personally and sat down with his distant cousin and asked for help. For Gnaeus, the memory was as vivid to him now as it was years earlier. Back then Decimus was the First Spear, the Primus Pilum of the First Cohort of Augustus' Legio *II Sabina*. The legion was in Hispania fighting Spanish tribesmen. The tribune, back then a centurion, had just been promoted First Spear of the legion's First Cohort when Augustus came to ask for his cousin's help.

A young Julii kinsman, a child of fifteen, was found with her throat cut and lying in a pool of blood in her own bed. A child whom Augustus loved gently and cherished deeply. Caesar demanded justice. Swiftly, and most importantly, discreetly. The child's father was suspected to be the killer. But no one knew for sure. Caesar gave Decimus full authority to investigate the murder and exact punishment on the guilty.

Decimus agreed to his cousin's request. The killer was apprehended. Judgement was exacted. The incident was never talked about within the confines of the Julii again.

But from that first instant, Decimus Julius Virilis found his true calling. Down through the years Decimus was asked by several powerful people to use his unique talent in solving a particularly horrendous murder for them. Caesar also used him upon occasion. Each case was resolved satisfactorily. His reputation grew.

Gnaeus' eyes drifted back to the sleeping tribune again. The day was hot. There was hardly a breeze stirring through the trees. The size of the crowd had considerably diminished as the day's heat increased. It was that time of the day where many wished they could sit down underneath a shade tree and nap. But as long as the tribune leaned against the tree and napped, there would be no rest for him. Gnaeus had that gut feeling they were being watched. Friend or foe, who knew? Of course, he suspected those behind the destruction of the Ninth were near and watching them discreetly. But there were others who wished to do harm to the tribune as well. Old enemies who never forgot the insults committed onto their person by the tribune's persistence.

A career soldier of Decimus Julius Virilis' talents did not march through life without making enemies. Numerous enemies with long-held hatreds waiting for the right time to strike.

Gnaeus remained vigilant. He wondered what the life of a retired tribune might be in a year from hence. He suspected the obvious. It would not be a quiet one.

XII

7 AD
The Egyptian Amulet
Late Afternoon

The tribune splashed water on his face and arms as he stood beside one of the temple's fountains, along with five or six other travelers who were also washing themselves, before stepping back and catching the rough cloth tossed to him by Gnaeus. Drying himself, he turned and walked back to the large shade tree. Tossing the towel onto the stack of bags and saddle ware lying on the ground, the balding Decimus turned and looked at his friend.

"Do you still have that amulet you found on the bedroom floor last night?"

The wiry old legionnaire nodded and reaching inside his tunic, pulled out something leather and stone and tossed it to Decimus. Holding it up by one hand the tribune inspected it closely, a frown beginning to pull the corners of his lips downward. Dangling before his eyes was a long piece of leather string with a carved piece of black onyx depicting a woman with a lion's head setting on her shoulders. A rather scantily clad woman in Egyptian dress.

"Know what this is, old friend?"

Gnaeus shook his head and eyed the dangling image with suspicious eyes.

"This is Menket. A Nubian goddess of war people in southern Egypt worship. A fierce, blood thirsty goddess she is, Gnaeus. "She who Massacres," is her reputation. I heard rumors there is a cult growing around her. A cult of assassins. Apparently, the rumors are true."

Gnaeus' hands moved, asking a question. The tribune grunted and nodded.

"Our intruder was indeed Egyptian. Did you note the weaponry he left behind? The daggers? Definitely Egyptian in design."

Gnaeus asked another question silently as Decimus tucked the amulet underneath his leather armor and turned to face the older man.

"Perhaps, Gnaeus. Perhaps. While I agree there appears to be an Egyptian connection, we cannot rule out the possibility that the murder of the legate and this attempt on my life are not necessarily related. I've served several tours of duty in Egypt, my friend, before we came to know each other. Years ago, I admit. But enemies were made. One of my assignments as an up-and-coming new centurion was to track down this assassin's cult. Over the weeks of my investigation, I faced growing opposition from the natives. People died. Both laymen and Egyptian priests of Menket, along with a few men under my command. In the end I found nothing concrete to prove the existence of the cult. I was reassigned to other duties."

Gnaeus hands flew.

"It happened years ago, Gnaeus. So yes, I find your observation most apropos. If the cult has selected me for assassination, why have they waited so long before attempting to silence me?"

Gnaeus was about to ask another question but stopped when the sound of horses, several of them, pounding up the Via Salarna distracted them. Turning to face the highway, both watched eight purple-clad Praetorian guardsmen turn off the road and ride into the gardens of the temple and come to a halt. Immediately one of the guardsmen swung off his mount and moved through the crowd, head dancing to his right and left. When he caught sight of the tribune, he moved toward him swiftly. Saluting smartly the young man, holding the rank of a Tesserarius in Praetorian Guards, glanced quickly to his left and right and then stepped close to Decimus.

"Sir, we received word about your encounter last night with an assassin. Orders came down we were to find you and escort you to your home. Word has come to us that possibly another attempt on your life is quite imminent. Caesar has ordered the guard to provide you with a bodyguard for the duration of your current assignment."

"What is your name, soldier?"

"Titus, sir. Titus Encimius, Fourth Cohort of the Guards. At your service, sir."

"Well, Titus Encimius. How did you know Gnaeus, and I would be here at this time of the day?"

The young equivalent of a senior NCO in modern times grinned and shrugged boyishly.

"A lucky guess, sir. My orders were to find you. But receiving them so late in the day, and knowing where you encountered last night's actions, I thought it would be wise to stop here first."

Decimus nodded and eyed the young Tesserarius' small detachment. Mostly young men, not too long in service in

Caesar's newly established Praetorian Guards. But experienced, nevertheless. The guard liked to pull experienced legionnaires out of various legions and assign them to the guard.

The Praetorian Guard was an old tradition in the Roman army. Originally the personal bodyguard of a legion commander, chosen from the sons of noble families whom the general knew would be absolutely loyal to him. Octavius Caesar had taken the concept and expanded it greatly. Now *Augustus* Caesar took the idea and created an entire legion, an extra-strength legion of the best equipped and most experienced men he could find, and had it permanently stationed in Rome. Its primary mission was to protect the nobility, especially the noble family who currently ruled the empire. Its secondary mission was to quell the all-too-frequent riots from one warring faction or another within the city and keep the city relatively safe.

"Dismount your men, Titus. Have them water their mounts at the fountains. We'll rest here for a half hour before we journey on. Send men to the temple and purchase some wine to quench the men's thirsts as well."

"Thank you, sir!" the young NCO nodded, holding a hand out and accepting the small bag of coins from the tribune.

The young officer saluted, whirled around on a heel, and moved back to his men. A quick command and the seven men dismounted and began leading horses toward the nearest fountain. Decimus and Gnaeus watched the men for a few moments before moving back to the wide swath of cool shade underneath the big tree. As they sat down in the grass the old piece of leather for a servant asked a question.

"Yes, news travels fast, old friend. But should we be surprised? My cousin has spies everywhere. I'm sure either he, or his personal secretary, have people watching our every move. But I admit, I would like to hear more about this imminent attack the Tesserarius mentioned. To be forewarned is to be prepared for any eventuality."

A half hour later Decimus, Gnaeus and their escort mounted up and began riding toward the city's Collina Gate just as the late afternoon sun began to dip behind the trees. Passing people hurried to the city on foot, no one wanting to enter the city at night. At least not individuals. Large carts and wagons, pulled by Oxen and horses, each wagon straining under the heavy loads with the needs of a city's daily consumption, began to lumber onto the highway and turn toward the city. The city did not allow wheeled transportation to enter the city during daylight hours. But at night the city's main thoroughfares were filled with wagons and carts, driven by men who knew how to handle the terrors of the night. No one in their right mind would dare to bother an old wagon master and his servants. Even the thieves and cut throats who came out like clouds of locust at night gave the wagons a wide berth.

But for individuals and families who traveled to Rome, entering the city at night was almost a death warrant for those who could not hire protection to escort them to their destination. The streets of Rome at night were extremely dangerous. With hooves pounding on the solid stone streets, the entourage of horsemen with the tribune in the lead swept through the fortified gate and continued unimpeded.

Down the long, straight road called the Alta Semita, Decimus and his escorts rode. It was perhaps the oldest street in Rome— so old it was said that before Rome became a city, the footpath, which traveled south to north, was established and already well used. When the city began to grow, this footpath soon became one of the city's most important thoroughfares.

Rome, under the rule of Augustus, was becoming a city of grandeur. The wealth of Augustus was converting what once was nothing but a minor regional city of brick and stone into an awe-inspiring city of architectural wonder. And a seat of unquestioned power. With Augustus bringing peace to the empire by finally eliminating usurpers who vied for the leadership of the senate, the city's populous began to grow and flourish. It was said now that perhaps the city's population was approaching a million strong. Decimus would not refute it. As evidence to sustain that assertion, all one had to do was look at the ever-growing number of temples being built.

Rome was a city filled with power and greed. But it was also a city of temples and piety. No less than six temples, large and small, the tribune counted as they rode down the paved street toward the Julian forums. Gods, both Greek and Roman, were honored with temples scattered throughout the city. But Romans did not stop there. Gods of all sizes and shapes found within the empire were worshipped in the city. Egyptian, Carthaginian, Parthian, from whatever far corner of the empire, somewhere in the city a devotee would find a temple they could worship in. And perhaps the greatest of all temples, the Temple of Mars Ultor, resided near the heart of the city.

The Temple of Mars Ultor. Mars the *Avenger*. Perhaps one of the most impressive architectural wonders Augustus Caesar personally financed and held an interest in. The crown jewel dominating one side of the new forum he dedicated to himself. The forum built beside the large Forum of Julius, the one built by his adoptive father, Julius Caesar, was the seat of power for the empire. Here the Senate would sit and vote on going to war or not going to war. Here the power brokers from the far corners of the empire would congregate and conduct their business daily. Here army officers, in mass, would formally receive their assignments on the steps of the temple and be sworn to uphold the power and will of the Roman Senate.

Decimus and his escorts rode past the entrance to the

forum and began the ascent up the Palatine Hill toward his small house. The Palatine, one of the original seven hills of Rome, was dotted with large and small domiciles, each individual architectural jewels only Roman power could sustain. The homes of both Caesars were here. As were the homes of the majority of the Julii. As the tribune reined up and then slid off his mount, he glanced across the hill and saw the flickering of lights from the lanterns which lit up the gardens surrounding Augustus' home. He smiled. He knew his older cousin better than anyone. If anything, the elderly ruler believed firmly in one old saying he had learned a long time ago...

Keep your enemies close to you, and your friends and relatives even closer.

XIII

7 AD
Caesar's Chief of Spies
Caius Lucius

Decimus sat on a stone bench of carved white marble in the small gardens of his house eating cheese and a freshly baked loaf of bread for breakfast. Across from him, sitting on another stone bench, were two other old friends—army veterans whom he employed as servants. One was called Rufus. The other was Hakim. Rufus was of good Roman stock, a city boy from Capua. Hakim was from Numidia. Tall and aloof, he was almost always silent. Yet the man could ride a horse with the natural ease of one who had lived with horses all his life. He was also a talented tracker. There was no trail he could not follow. A talent Decimus had used often.

Rufus, on the other hand, with his severely hooked nose and brooding dark eyes, had a talent he too could claim. Pick pocket, thief, ruffian or procurer of rare things; however one decided to describe the small man, Rufus could procure it.

Silently and efficiently. Another talent the tribune found quite valuable to possess.

Gnaeus stepped out of the house and into the gardens carrying a plain wooden tray with four stone cups and a large jug of wine. Walking across the stone path between two well-manicured beds of colorful flowers, he set the tray down on the table in front of Decimus before sitting down himself and signing.

"Yes, it was a bit cramped, space wise, with the men sleeping in the gardens. And true, we are pressed in feeding everyone this morning. But we'll correct them. Hire a few servants, a chef in particular, to prepare our meals. Give him a budget that will feed twelve or more men adequately. You do know someone who may be available here in the city, don't you?"

Gnaeus signed. Of course, he did. Several excellent chefs, in fact. If available, the one he had in mind would be here early this afternoon. Tonight's meal would be far less Spartan than this morning's breakfast.

Decimus nodded, turning his head to listen to the sound of two guardsmen talking softly to themselves on the other side of the wall surrounding the gardens. With eight Praetorian guardsmen keeping watch on the house and its immediate surroundings, the possibility of a visit from the Egyptian assassin seemed remote. But that did not mean another assassination attempt might not happen. Servants of the Goddess Menket, the one of several Egyptian Goddesses of War, would not stop in their mission to kill unless death itself claimed them. Caution and clarity of attention were called for until the assassin was apprehended and interrogated. *If* he was apprehended and interrogated.

His attention was diverted toward the house when the

young Praetorian Tesserarius emerged out into the sunlight and approached.

"Sir, there is a person who wishes to see you in private. A very important person, I might add."

Decimus heard the note of urgency in the young man's voice. Nodding, he rose from the marble bench and followed the young soldier into the house. Standing in the middle of the dining room was a small man dressed in rags, or what at first appeared to be rags. Decimus pressed his lips back in a barely perceptible grin and softly dismissed Titus Encimius.

He waited for the young officer to leave them before saying anything. Eyeing the remarkably unremarkable older man in front of him, Decimus again had to admit Caesar's chief spy was amazing to behold.

Caius Lucius was, perhaps, the most uncommonly bland looking creature in the empire. Somewhat smaller in stature compared to the tribune, with shaggy brown hair uncombed and unkept, a big nose, and brown, red rimmed eyes, there was not one feature the man possessed which one might remember of his existence the moment he left the room. Not even his clothing. But what, in Decimus' mind, truly made the man fascinating was the ability the official spy for Augustus Caesar had of completely re-inventing himself.

Today Caius Lucius was a beggar. A street beggar which filled the city's streets yet were completely dismissed by every passer-by. The man even had that certain aroma which made one of a more genteel birth turn aside and hurry along, holding a perfumed scarf to their nostrils and dismissing the creature from thought as quickly as possible. Tomorrow Caius Lucius could be a Roman Senator, regal and imperial in look and decorum. Or he could be a poet: effeminate and sweet smelling with layers of perfume wafting from his robes. Whatever persona the man wished to take on, the man's facial and physical stature changed as well. Caius Lucius never looked the same in his chosen persona.

The spy's ability to disguise himself was a rare, precious gift. But the man had other attributes which made him a rare jewel as a spy. The spy was, without question, extremely intelligent. Intelligent and patient. He was also ruthless. Rumors circulated throughout the empire of people, from all ranks, disappearing and never to be seen again by loved ones. If his cousin ordered someone to disappear, and disappear permanently, the task was given to Caius Lucius.

He suspected he knew why the chief of spies had come calling disguised as a beggar. Stepping to the dining table, he poured wine from a plain looking stone carafe into two stone glasses and handed one to the smaller man before lifting the other up for himself.

"Greetings, Caius Lucius. It has been some time since we've crossed trails with each other."

"Greetings Decimus Julius Virilis." The spy nodded, lifting his glass in a gesture of silent respect. "It has been indeed a long time since our last sharing of the grape. But, like times before, it seems each of us are working in parallel paths toward the same goal and compel us to meet."

"The Fates are fickle bitches, old friend. Not even the gods know what tapestries they weave for each of us. All we can do is endure. Endure and wait."

The smaller man laughed softly in amusement before sipping his wine. Eyeing the tribune, he mused himself by quietly recollecting all the years he had known the military man, this cousin to his employer, and how the man rose up from the ranks in a spectacular fashion. Decimus Virilis was, in some respects, much like himself. Skilled, ruthless, and doggedly persistent when assigned a task. The tribune was a natural leader of men and, to be quite frank, uncommonly lucky. The stories he heard of the tribune leading men into battle were the seeds of legend. The recent disaster of surviving the decimation of the nearly destroyed legion being but one example. By rights, after seeing a third of the legion destroyed in a gigantic explosion, and then immediately attacked by hordes of raging Dalmatian rebels, the tribune and every remaining survivor of the legion should have been hacked to pieces.

But the tribune did not die on that Dalmatian hill. Nor had the severely mauled legion been swept from the hill and sent packing off to the darker regions of Hades. Much to the astonishment of many.

That's why his men named him Decimus Virilis. *Virilis* for manly luck.

Without question the tribune was incredibly lucky.

"How may I help you in your endeavors, Caius Lucius?"

"Caesar has been called to Germany. He left this morning. But he has asked me to drop by and fill you in on some background history of the Sulla family which might help you in your investigations. Technically, my task is tangential to the problems you face. But aspects of both of our investigations touch in places. Caesar, as we both know, prefers us to work separately. But whenever investigations mingle with another, he wishes us to, shall we say, coordinate our efforts."

"The patriarch of the Sulla family," Decimus concluded, eyeing the smaller man with interest. "Gaius Cornelius Sulla the Elder."

"Precisely," nodded the spy, silently asking the tribune if he may refill his wine glass and receiving a barely perceptible nod. "Caesar is considering sending Sulla back to Egypt as the legate of Upper Egypt. But there are issues that must be worked out before this happens. My task is to settle the issues."

Egypt. The word rang in Decimus' ears. Another connection to Egypt. Somehow all mysteries seemed to return to Egypt.

"May I inquire as to what issues have arisen which require your skilled touch?"

Caius Lucius poured wine into his glass and smiled the sly, wicked grin of a fox about to enter a hen house. Lifting the heavy stone glass from the table he turned and faced the tribune.

"No one knows Caesar is considering Sulla for the post, except now for you and me. But in the last year, in Egypt, stirrings of unrest have begun to grow. Apparently, rumors have begun to circulate that a divine creature of some sort is about to return to the Upper Nile. With her return, the yoke of Roman rule will be overthrown. My task is to track down the source of these rumors and make a decision as to whether rumors whispered in taverns and dark alleys may have some basis of truth behind them."

"Caius, are you saying these rumors may have started here in Italy and spread across the sea to Egypt?"

The spy eyed the taller tribune for some seconds with a bland, unreadable mask for a face. He lifted his glass and sipped the excellent wine. The tribune was noted for always having excellent wine available in his house. But Caius Lucius wasn't thinking about the wine. He was looking at the tribune and shaking his head in admiration.

"How do you do that, Decimus? How do you snatch from out of the thin air a theory I've been working on for weeks? But to answer your question. Yes, my sources both here in Italy and in Egypt inform me the rumors began here and traveled there. What concerns Caesar, and thus concerns me, is this. The rumors have been growing slowly for a year now. But Caesar wasn't considering assigning the post to Gaius Cornelius Sulla until about a month ago. This coincidence, if it is indeed a coincidence, puzzles Caesar."

"And my cousin is uncomfortable with coincidences," the tribune put in, frowning.

He waved the spy over to a couch as he sat on one himself and eyed the ceiling for a few seconds in deep thought. The master spy, for his part, reclined on the couch, stone glass in hand, and kept quiet. He watched the tribune's open, honest face with some interest. Everyone knew the tribune somehow communicated with the gods. The gods apparently loved this dedicated, ruthless soldier. They protected him. They whispered into his ear the thoughts of others. It was the only possible explanation which made sense on how this man, this strange Julii kinsman, knew so much of the thoughts of others.

When Decimus came out of his thoughtful musings, Caius was unsurprised at the words which followed.

"So who, old friend, do you suspect is the source of these rumors within the Sulla family?"

The spy lifted his head slightly, rumbled in amusement, and shook his head in admiration. The gods must have spoken. He suspected the tribune already knew the answer.

"Seventeen years ago, Sulla was the legate in Upper Egypt. He had the arduous task of putting down a revolt of the natives led by the priestesses of some arcane Egyptian goddess. In the process of subjugating the natives, his forces captured the head priestess of this goddess. A woman by the name of Shebet. This creature had a young, very beautiful eighteen-year-old daughter by the name of Hatshepsut. Hatshepsut had at the time, a child of some five years in age.

"My sources tell me Sulla took one look at Shebet's daughter and fell madly in love with her. Swept her off her feet. Wooed the girl until she agreed to marry him, even gladly adopted her child as his own in the process. He even agreed to spare his new bride's mother from her death sentence. You see now how our two investigations merge at this point."

Indeed, the tribune did. The child of Hatshepsut was a boy. A boy adopted into the family of Gaius Cornelius Sulla. The boy grew up to become Gaius Cornelius Sulla the Lesser. The commanding officer of the ill-fated *IXth Brundisi*.

Eyeing the innocuous looking spy for a moment, a hundred different thoughts rolled through his mind at the same time. Decimus cleared his throat and sat his wine glass down on a table.

"What of the priestess Shebet. What happened to her?"

"No way of knowing," Caius Lucius replied. "She seems to have disappeared off the face of the earth the moment Sulla released her. I'm told that, after she stepped out of the gates of the prison, various people saw her trekking out into the deep desert. That was the last time anyone saw her."

"You think Hatshepsut is the source of the Egyptian unrest?"

"I am saying nothing at the moment, tribune. I am investigating. I can tell you that over the period of the last few weeks the Sulla household has received a number of different guests who have just returned from Egypt. Most of them have been military couriers one would expect a general like Sulla to receive. A few have been, shall we say, more mysterious in nature."

Decimus eyed the smaller man silently. Waiting.

"Merchants, Decimus. A number of different Egyptian merchants have come and gone from the House of Sulla. What makes them mysterious, in my eyes, is the fact that, as far as I know, Gaius Cornelius Sulla has very few business dealings in Egypt. Sulla's wealth is enormous. Mainly found here in Italy and in Spain. But merely a pittance in Egypt."

Crossing his arms in front of him, a hand came up and a

finger began moving back across the tribune's lips slowly as his mind dived deeper into the problem. For a few moments the two men occupied the room in silence, one waiting for the other to break the silence. It was Decimus this time.

"I have something to show you, Caius. Wait here for a moment."

When he returned there was something in the tribune's hand. A trinket he dropped into the waiting palm of the spy. Caius Lucius eyed the object with curiosity, recognizing its importance immediately, as Decimus related to him how he'd come into possession of the thing.

"Egypt," the tribune said at the end. "Everything points to Egypt. It is like no other connection can exist for us to explore, don't you think? All suspicions lead to Egypt and the Goddess Menket."

Caius Lucius heard it. An odd note in the tribune's voice. Eyes shot up to stare into the man's face intently.

"What I am saying," Decimus began, seeing the look on the spy's face, "is this. Gaius Cornelius Sulla is perhaps the second or third richest Roman in the empire. Certainly, as powerful as any Roman patriarch has ever been if we exclude our patron protectors in the process. For a man with such power and wealth, his enemies must be legion in number. Enemies almost as powerful as Sulla himself."

"Are you saying someone is trying to politically assassinate Sulla by insinuating this Egyptian connection to his wife as well as the attempt on your life?"

"I am saying, old friend, we must tread carefully. We must eliminate all possible motives until we come to the one, no matter how incredulous or impossible it may sound, who fits all of the facts that we know."

"Agreed, tribune. I heartily agree. I have no desire to accuse the wife of Sulla with any crime unless I have overwhelming, positive proof to back them up."

"Early tomorrow morning I am to present the remains of Sulla's son to him personally. I hope to question him, with discretion and respect, on whom might be capable of such a horrendous plot to destroy an entire legion. Perhaps I might have an opportunity to ask some questions about the Egyptian connection as well."

"Good. Good," the spy nodded, smiling. "Now how do you propose we coordinate our separate investigations in achieving our shared goal?"

"We already are working our various avenues of inquiry, Caius. I will continue to work on the assumption that Gaius Cornelius Sulla the Lesser was intentionally murdered by person or persons unknown, while you continue to ferret out the connections which might exist between Egypt and the Sulla family. I might add, the task of possibly tracking down our mysterious assassin, and discovering who he may be, and where we may find him might be of paramount interest to both of us."

"It will be done." The spy nodded. "I'll begin inquiries immediately."

"Discreetly, old friend. Discreetly. We do not want to frighten off those who wish wicked retribution to shower upon the innocent. At least not before we are in position to capture them."

Caius Lucius smiled. Wickedly and conspiratorially.

"If anything, tribune, I am the epitome of discretion and subtlety. It will be as you command."

XIV

7AD
Rome
The House of Sulla

The fame, and wealth, of the Sulla family were well known. As was Gaius Cornelius Sulla's reputation of being a conservative traditionalist. A fierce *true Roman,* as he called himself. One who did not tolerate fools or incompetents. Decimus knew the family well enough. Twice he had served as a centurions in one of Sulla's legions and knew, from personal experience, how garrulous the patriarch could be.

Pride and garrulousness ran in the family. Ninety years earlier, Sulla's ancestor, Lucius Cornelius Sulla burst onto the political stage of the Roman Senate in all his terrible fury. Roman history was a long trail of bloody rage perpetrated by arrogant, and many times, quite insane dictators. Filled with war, strife, revenge and retribution. And in this centuries-long dialogue of power and bloodletting, Lucius Cornelius Sulla's exploits sat at the very pinnacle of those who were the most diabolical.

It was the general Lucius Sulla who gathered his armies and first marched on Rome to settle old political scores. In setting this example, not only did Sulla accomplish the precedent of Roman legions pledging their loyalty to their generals instead of to the Senate and the People of Rome, but he also opened the door for the next sixty some odd years of civil war which almost tore the Roman empire into shreds. He also was the first to implement the devastating political expediency called *proscription*. The act of coming to power and immediately proscribing, or listing, off one's enemies and executing them without trial or ceremony. Long lists of Roman citizens died. And with their deaths, their wealth, lands, and titles stripped from the surviving family members and awarded to Sulla.

The Fates, as every Roman knew, were devious creatures who relished playing pranks on those who presumed to be more powerful than the gods. In regard to Lucius Cornelius Sulla and his heirs, when the elder Sulla was in power, he held in his hands the power to destroy the Julii family long before the Julii rose to such stellar heights. Julius Caesar, as a young man, was a name rumored to have been proscribed on one of Sulla's lists. He was to be hunted down and destroyed. Only daring and audacity saved Caesar's life.

Today, the irony was Octavius Caesar, called the *Augustus*, and the adopted son of Julius Caesar who ruled the empire held *in his hands* the power to either honor or condemn the entire Sulla family in infamy.

Decimus, wearing his best armor, polished and glistening in the early morning sun, stood a few meters off the paved Via Latina and watched the eight Praetorian guardsmen brush the dust off their parade armor and make some last-minute adjustments before assembling into a tight, disciplined looking unit. Each man had over their breast plates the leather harness which held the small round disks of gold, bronze, or silver. Each projected a face of one of the Julii heirs. Each disk a medal for some valor earned on a battlefield.

No one became a Praetorian unless he had served in one of Caesar's twenty-eight legions. Each guardsman was a decorated veteran. Several of the men had three disks, called *phalerae* adorning their breastplates. The rest had at least two each. Titus Encimius, the unit's commander, had three round disks, plus a bronze armilli wrapped around his right bicep. The armilla, or arm band, was another decoration of valor awarded to a brave soldier.

Even Gnaeus, the silent old legionnaire, stood near the tribune dressed in his finest uniform. His leather harness draped over the polished breast plate held three phalerae attached to it. Two bronzes and one silver. Around the man's right bicep was a bronze armilla.

Decimus, the twenty-year veteran, and currently the de facto commander of the Ninth, was no less decorated. The leather harness riding on his breast plate contained five round phalerae. Two gold, one silver, two bronzes. Adorning his right arm were two armillae. One gold and one bronze. But the truly impressive decoration was the thin gold crown, a *Corona Aurea*, riding on his forehead. The gold crown indicated to one and all he had stood over a fallen comrade in the face of battle and had saved the man's life.

When the tribune appeared in front of his men earlier that morning the eight Praetorian guardsmen stared at the balding officer in silent respect. Every one of the younger men had heard of the name of Decimus Julius Virilis. The man was, frankly, a legend among the legionnaires. But to stand in front of him and see the years of service the tribune had faithfully given the Imperator was awe inspiring.

Silently, Decimus nodded to the young Tesserarius. The young officer barked a sharp command and the purple-clad guardsman instantly snapped to attention. Eyeing the men critically, the tribune said nothing as he wheeled around, standing in front of the small unit, and began marching toward the sprawling country estate of Gaius Cornelius Sulla. The men behind him followed immediately. A hundred meters in front of them the legate and his entire family stood in the sun, dressed in their finest togas and silks, and waited for the military unit to approach.

It was apparent the elder Sulla was suffering. His skin was as white as the virgin white and purple-trimmed toga he was wearing. The older man's eyes were red rimmed. And he seemed to be leaning ever so slightly to his left. The legate, now completely bald, looked a hundred years older compared to the last time Decimus had spoken to him. A hundred years older and as close to being one of the living dead as could possibly be imagined.

The legate stood some two meters in front of the large entourage of relatives, patrons, and priests who had come to witness this solemn occasion. Directly behind Sulla, dressed in the soft, pale green robes of a woman, stood the small figure of his wife. Hatshepsut. A shawl of the same color as her toga covered her head and a thin veil of translucent green partially hid her face. One hand held the veil to her face. But there was no way to hide the woman's beauty. Big, almond-shaped brown eyes stared at the approaching tribune and his escort. The one visible hand was the light mocha color of someone from the heat of the Egyptian desert. She was much younger than her husband. Even though she was in her mid-thirties, her husband was in his late sixties and ill.

She was, Decimus remembered, the daughter of a priestess who worshipped an Egyptian goddess of war. A very cruel and bloody goddess of war.

Coming to a halt directly in front of the old legate, they slapped their heavy leather sandals onto the ground at the same time; the tribune and the men behind him threw up their right arms in unison in the typical Roman salute.

"Hail, Gaius Cornelius Sulla. I am Decimus Julius Virilis, tribunus militum, and Praefectus Castorum of the Legio IXth Brundisi. Regretfully, legate, I am here to officially inform you my commander, and your honored son, Gaius Cornelius Sulla the Younger, recently passed away while commanding his legion in hostile territory. Augustus Caesar has asked me to convey to you his sincerest condolences for the loss of your son. He has also asked me to personally return the remains of the general to you and your family in the hopes your son will be duly honored and laid to rest as is the custom of your ancient and venerable house."

The elder Sulla seemed to waver but steadied himself as a Praetorian guardsman stepped up beside the tribune, carrying in his arms a large and expensive looking red funeral jar, and snapped to attention. Sulla's red eyes gazed down at the pottery and tried to say something. But words would not come. Instead, nodding slightly toward Decimus, he half turned to look at the entourage behind him. Two priests dressed in the robes of the temple of Mars Invictus moved forward solemnly and slipped the red pottery out of the grip of the guardsman and returned to their stations behind the legate in a slow, respectful cadence.

Sulla, head bowed, one hand rising to cover his forehead, turned and looked briefly at his wife before walking away. He retreated to his villa, the large entourage waiting for him splitting open to let him enter his home. When he disappeared from view, Decimus turned to look at the veiled woman.

"My husband has been devastated by the loss of our son, tribune. But he has asked that you and your men remain and participate in a funeral dinner we have prepared. He has also asked me to invite you to his private study for a short interview. He has questions about our son's demise."

She had a soft, whispery voice. Her Latin was excellent. But it held just a small lilt of the exotic that the educated women of Egypt somehow cultivated in their voices.

"I am yours to command, Madame."

"Commander," she whispered again, this time looking at the young Praetorian officer. "You will find refreshments and chilled wine in the gardens. Please, join us in our celebration of our son's short life."

Decimus nodded to Titus Encimius and the young man dismissed his men with a short command. A slave stepped forward to guide the guardsmen and Gnaeus to the gardens while Decimus remained and waited for the dark-complexioned wife of Gaius Cornelius Sulla to escort him to the general's private study.

Entering the dark interior of the sprawling villa, the tribune was instantly impressed in three quite unique discoveries. Just inside the house a slave stood waiting for him and his mistress, in his hands a silver tray possessing two large, ornate silver goblets of wine. Hatshepsut took one of the goblets and handed the other to Decimus with her own hand. As she did, he saw the beautiful woman look up into his face and smile a very sad, pain-filled smile.

"My husband has asked that you first taste the wine before you join us in his study, tribune. He says you are somewhat of a connoisseur. He seemed to remember you had a fondness for a particular vintage of a foreign origin. He hopes this meets your approval."

The tribune's first discovery was the wine itself. A very rare

Spanish vintage said to have disappeared a decade ago. Years earlier as a young, freshly minted centurion, he discovered the wine from a small vineyard situated on a mountain slope overlooking the western sea. One sip of the dark wine sent him twenty years into the past, feeling again that unexpected delight of tasting something only the gods themselves might have consumed on Mount Olympus.

His second discovery was even more impressive. The wine, excellent as it was, was even more tasty because it was ice cold. The bottle of wine had been chilled in snow. Snow, here just outside the walls of Rome, in late summer. There was, at this time of the year, only one place to find snow. Only the high peaks of the northern Alps still retained its crystalline whiteness. But to transport snow from there, almost four hundred kilometers away, made it an impossible task to complete. And costly. Infinitely costly. Yet the old general did just that. Demanded, and paid for, this rare wine to be chilled in snow.

The final discovery further impressed the tribune in the wealth and power of the Sulla clan. Sipping the wine, just inside the foyer of the villa, Decimus' eyes drifted down toward his sandaled feet and beheld the mosaic tiled floor.

The majority of the floor was black tile. But in the center of the floor was a light purple colored roundel. A large circle which took almost half of the foyer's floor space. Around the outer rim of the purple circle were eight faces. Eight life-like faces of the last eight male Sulla heirs in vivid color. So vivid, so life-like, he stepped back in respect. To stand on one of the general's distant ancestors seemed almost an act of insolence.

An artist, or artists, of superb talent had spent hundreds of hours in creating the mosaic masterpiece. It was a stunning visual delight to gaze upon. A visual delight which bespoke of the wealth of the Sulla clan.

"Gaius brought in glaziers from Cappadocia to do this

floor. It took them a year to complete it. I remember having to shoo little Gaius away and not bother the workers. He was only nine years old then and constantly bothered them as they worked."

Her eyes watered when she mentioned her son as a boy. But she refused to cry. Smiling quickly, she stepped to one side, lifting her free hand to point the way to the general's study.

"Shall we go in now? I am sure my husband is eager to speak to you."

Gaius Cornelius Sulla stood in the middle of the large study, back turned toward the study's entrance as he faced the opened doors leading out into a different part of the estate's sprawling gardens. The room was wide and spacious with one wall filled with hundreds of niches, each niche filled with scrolls. Sulla, the tribune knew, was a vociferous reader. Authors and poets from all over the world resided here in his study. Silently Decimus gazed upon the large wall of knowledge and felt a pang of jealousy.

In front of the wall of knowledge was a large desk of intricate design. Its top was cluttered with papers and maps and four or five wax tablets. Even from this distance, standing on the other side of the room, Decimus noticed one of the maps was a detailed geographical study of Southern Egypt. The land where the woman standing beside him hailed from.

"Gaius," Hatshepsut whispered softly, stepping toward her husband and gently laying a hand on his right arm. "The tribune is here as you requested. I shall leave you two to discuss matters."

"Eh?" the elder Sulla grunted, coming out a deep reverie and turning to face his wife. "No, no. Stay, Hattie. Stay and hear what Decimus must report to us. He was your son more than he was mine."

The elder wrapped an arm around the shoulders of his

younger wife and kissed her gently on her forehead before separating and turning to face the tribune. A little color returned to the man's cheeks. His eyes, still red from grief, nevertheless was filled with intelligence and determination.

"Decimus, under any other circumstances, I would embrace you as a comrade and old friend. We have served together in two legions. I have valued you and your astute advice on numerous occasions. I was pleased when Caesar picked you as the Ninth's Camp Prefect. If anyone could mold and hold together a raw legion it would be you. I told Gaius to value your wisdom. I hope he complied with my wishes."

"Indeed he did, sir. Often."

An outright lie. The younger Sulla had gone out of his way to separate himself from the more experienced officers surrounding him. Especially separating himself from the one person designated to be the legion's primary training officer. The Camp Prefect in any legion was that man. Of tribune rank, recently promoted up from the centurion rank of Primus Pilum, or First Spear of a legion's First Cohort, the Praefectus Castorum, or Camp Prefect, was a hardened, twenty-plus year veteran who had risen through the ranks the hard way. Such a veteran knew how to command men. Knew how to command a legion. Knew every aspect of the daily life of a legion. Knew, and faced, countless enemies over his twenty-year career as a legionnaire.

Decimus had been the Primus Pilum of *Legio II Augusta*, based in a Spanish city called Bracarta in northwestern Spain. The Second fought the forever warlike Cantabarii who resided in the mountainous regions of northwest Spain. Hard fighting, much like what would come to the Ninth Brindisi when confronting the Dalmatian rebels in their mountain strongholds. The ever-astute elder Caesar, knowing the Ninth would be raw and commanded by young, inexperienced officers,

DEATH BY GREEK FIRE

commanded him to leave the *II Augusta* and travel to Brundisium on the southeast coast of the Italian peninsula and become the one officer in the new legion who knew how to command.

Eyes closely watching the elder Sulla, he stood respectful, still holding the heavy silver goblet of wine in his hand and waited for the legate's next words. He knew what they would be. The general would want, in detail, exactly what happened which killed his son and badly crippled the Ninth to near destruction.

"Caesar sent me your written reports on the Ninth's struggle. Frankly, I'm surprised anyone survived. An entire hillside blew up? And a rebel army attacked you immediately afterwards? Incredible. Simply incredible."

Both husband and wife were staring at Decimus. The general painted a neutral, unreadable mask on his face. His wife, Hatshepsut, had tears streaming down her cheeks and staining the veil covering the lower half of her face.

"Your reports were concise, precisely written, clear up to a point. But my gut tells me you left out critical pieces of information. I want to hear the truth, Decimus. I want to know everything that happened that night. Tell us every detail. Do not let our emotions inhibit your words. Begin from the beginning of that night's events."

Decimus complied with the order.

He began at nine in the morning. On the march up from the port city of Asa. Usually about this time in the morning the legate would command the legion's engineers to ride ahead and find a suitable camping site the legion would fortify and pitch camp on. Because each camp required hours of work in proper preparation. Wide, sloping trenches around the perimeter of the campsite had to be dug. Sharpened wooden stakes filling the trenches and back slopes of the trench had to be erected.

And there was the camp itself. The ground had to be staked out, the stakes indicating where each of the six cohorts and the attached specialty units would pitch their tents.

Because it took so long to properly fortify a campsite, a typical legion marched for only half a day. The rest of the time was spent constructing their overnight stay. But on this day, hours before the disaster, Gaius Cornelius Sulla the Younger did not order the engineers forward to find a suitable plot of ground. The young legate knew where they would camp. In the lead, the young general led the legion straight to that ill-fated hill.

"This was not in your official report, Decimus."

"Indeed, sir. I did not think of this oddity until after I wrote my initial reports and sent them off to Rome. It was a couple of days later before I thought of this."

The elder Sulla grunted, glanced at his wife, then returned his attention to Decimus and told him to continue.

Decimus went on with the day's details. He described the rugged mountainous terrain. He described the on-again, off-again rain that plagued them during the afternoon hours' drudgery of preparing the camp. He mentioned scouts being sent out and coming back reporting no sign of the enemy's presence. He went on and described the evening hours passing by without incident. He described the hillside suddenly coming alive with thousands of campfires burning brightly when they became aware the enemy was near. And then he came to the time he stepped out of his tent to begin the tour of the camp's perimeter. When he came to the part about seeing a group of army officers and a hooded figure leaving the general's tent just moments before the explosion, the elder Sulla lifted a hand up to stop him.

"These officers. Who were they?"

"I have no idea, sir. There was not enough light to see their faces. Only one hid his face with the hood of his cloak. Those whom I saw I did not recognize."

"Did you find out later their names?"

"Initial investigations led nowhere, sir. Soon after their departure the entire hilltop went up in a gigantic explosion. After that came the fighting. Intense fighting for several hours. When Tiberius Caesar came to our rescue and the rebels fled the battlefield, we were ordered back to Asa, and I was given orders to return to Italy and return your son's remains to you. But I assigned officers to make inquiries while I am here. I should have a full report when I return to Asa."

Sulla nodded, frowning, and motioned to Decimus to continue his narration.

XV

7 AD
In the House of Sulla
The Curse

He did not spare them from the harsh details. Decimus described the horrors of the explosion. The devastation of the camp. He described the exhortations he and the remaining centurions bellowed out in the night rallying the dazed men and throwing up ad hoc defenses just before the rebels attacked. He described the fighting. Noted how, at first, the enemy seemed so intent on swarming over their position and killing them all. Finally, he described how the fighting slackened, then melted away altogether just as mysteriously as it had begun not more than two hours before Tiberius Caesar and his column of cavalry rode into camp all covered in mud.

For several long moments husband and wife stood shoulder to shoulder in silence staring at the tribune. Outside in the gardens, faintly, Decimus heard men's voices. Too far away to hear what they were saying. But hearing the rumble of a number of different voices. A warm breeze infiltrated into the study, ruffling softly the papers and maps on the general's overburdened desk. Decimus, standing before Sulla and Hatshepsut, waited for either to recover their wits and say something. Yet, in their eyes, he saw the silent horrors which played in their imaginations at what had taken place that night on some nameless Dalmatian hill.

It was Sulla who broke the silence. Turning to his wife, he laid a hand on her shoulder, the color gone from his face again, and spoke in a harsh whisper.

"So. It has come to pass. Your mother's curse and Mars' wrath have come to pass as she promised it would. You know what this means, my dear."

"I do not believe in curses, my love. I certainly did not believe my mother could ever communicate with the gods. I still do not. We must be realists. There must be another explanation. A logical one which explains the death of our son."

"General," Decimus spoke up, finding himself most curious about the short exchange between husband and wife and wishing to know more. "I am not finished with my report. May I continue?"

Withdrawing his hand from his wife's shoulder, Sulla faced the tribune and nodded curtly. For his part, Decimus reached behind his back and pulled something out of his belt before stepping forward to reveal what he held in his palm.

"After the last rebel assault, and just before Tiberius and his cavalry arrived, one of the remaining engineers informed me he found something of interest deep in the pit the explosion carved out of the hilltop. He found this."

Both Sulla and Hatshepsut stepped forward and gazed down at the object in his hand. It was the piece of pottery shard.

"I do not know about curses, nor the wrath of the gods,

general. But I know a premeditated act of murder when I see one. Someone planned this disaster. Someone took the time to find a hill riddled with small caves filled with a noxious, flammable gas. They took the time to dig pits deep into the caves and they filled these caves with clay pots filled with Greek Fire. Somehow, they ignited the Greek Fire, which in turn ignited the noxious gas, creating a stupendous explosion.

"A diabolical mind planned this, general. An evil creature intent on harming both one of the legions of Rome and, if I am not mistaken, your son in the process."

Sulla staggered back, clutching his tunic with white knuckles. Both Hatshepsut and Decimus reached the man's side just before he collapsed. The general whispered in a strained voice to help him over to a couch where he could recline in comfort. As they gently lowered him onto the couch, they both heard the head of the Sulla clan whispering under his breath, *"It's true, it's true. The curse is true."*

The dark eyed woman whispered to Decimus to stay with the general while she ran to find the doctor. She was gone for a good hour. In that time, the elder Sulla seemed to sleep. But fitfully. Waking himself several times from terrible dreams. Yet, lethargic, he fell asleep again and again. When Hatshepsut returned, she had with him a thin man with startling white hair carrying a heavy leather bag. The little man hurried to the general's side and began feeling the man's forehead and loosening the general's toga. Hatshepsut, surprisingly, stepped back from her husband and gripped Decimus' arm and led him out into the gardens.

"You must understand, my husband is a sick man. For the last three months, long before this current tragedy occurred, he has moped around the house and thought of nothing else except my mother's curse. When news came that Gaius died in that horrible explosion, I thought the news was going to kill him. It may yet. We can only wait and pray for a miracle."

The tribune turned and stared into the study. Slaves had arrived carrying large bowls of water and fresh towels. The doctor was soaking towels and then laying one after the other across the general's bare chest and neck. Apparently, the general did indeed have a fever.

Looking back at the woman beside him, brow furled thoughtfully, he broke the silence as gently as he could.

"Madame, tell me about your mother and this curse she laid upon you and your husband."

Tears welled up in the woman's eyes and streamed down her face. A hand covered the veil around her mouth as she sobbed silently. Turning from Decimus, she walked to a marble bench and sat down slowly, still sobbing yet trying desperately to regain her composure. The tribune followed, sitting down beside her and waited for the Egyptian beauty to speak.

"Seventeen years ago, as a child of twenty, that man in there swept into my life and carried me away to Rome. He was tall, handsome, powerful. But most of all, he was kind. Kind to me and kind to my son, who was nine at the time. The first man ever to show me kindness. Like the silly child I was, I fell madly in love with him. And I still am, tribune. I'm still madly in love with him."

"You were the daughter of a priestess named Shebet, were you not?"

"Yes," she replied, using part of her toga to wipe tears from her eyes. "Which made it even more remarkable, if you think about it. His sudden coming into our lives. His insistence that I marry him. His obvious love for me.

"Mother was a priestess of the goddess Menket. A wicked, terrible god. Full of wrath and fury. For years mother was the leader of the resistance movement dedicated to the one goal of throwing off the Roman chains of servitude from all of Egypt. Gaius captured her and threw her into prison, breaking the resistance movement in the process. She was condemned to die. But Gaius, showing the depth of his love for me, pardoned her and gave her freedom back to her. She was freed but exiled from Egypt. The last time I saw her alive was when she and a few of her followers mounted horses and rode off into the desert."

"That was seventeen years ago and just before you married the general?"

"Yes." The still beautiful woman nodded, wiping tears from her eyes again. "So long ago."

"Madame, if I may ask discreetly, were you not a follower of Menket as well? Did you not protest to the general on your mother's banishment?"

For a few seconds Hatshepsut sat on the bench beside Decimus and remained silent as she stared through the open doors of the general's study and at the general being administered to by the family doctor. On her face, or what he could see of the face, Decimus saw infinite sadness fill her lovely countenance. When she spoke at last, she spoke in a whisper filled with pain.

"I loved my mother, tribune. But I hated her as well. I hated what she had become. She was insane. Filled with a hatred all things Roman. She would scream in rage at anyone who voiced an opinion that Rome was too strong, too wealthy, to defeat. She even tortured and killed those who resisted her in her efforts to raise an army up and fight the Romans, claiming the goddess herself demanded such retribution."

He paused for a moment, hesitating to say the question on his mind, but asked anyway. "Would perhaps, the natural father of your child, be one of those whom your mother sacrificed?"

In silence she wept again, her body wracked with spasms of agony as she used both hands to cover her face. For an extended period of time Decimus sat beside the woman and waited for the daughter of an Egyptian priestess to purge herself of the pent-up emotions she had for so long held in check. As he sat beside her his eyes took in the actions and administration of the general's doctor working on the slumbering figure lying on the couch in his study. When, finally, Hatshepsut drained herself of tears and remorse, she lowered her hands and sat up, turning toward Decimus in the process.

"So long ago. I was so young. He was almost twenty. Nothing more than children, really. The two of us. But we were madly in love. I became pregnant and he went straight to mother to ask for my hand in marriage. His father was a wealthy desert chieftain. He promised mother we would live in luxury for the rest of our lives. But mother, already deep in her madness and fury toward Rome, wouldn't have it. She knew Anwar's father was an ally to Rome. Were actually good friends with Gaius. She condemned Anwar and her father as traitors to Menket. She whipped up her followers in a murderous frenzy and Anwar and his father were sacrificed to the goddess.

That's when I began to hate my mother, tribune. Until that time, Rome was nothing but a name and a far-off empire I had little interest in. But after Anwar's death, and especially after little Gaius was born, I began to learn everything I could about Rome. That's when I began to secretly correspond with my husband about my mother's madness."

"You became the general's spy and that's how the two of you met?"

She nodded, using the side edge of her hand to wipe tears from her cheeks. Staring into the study at her unconscious husband she continued with her story.

"A year it took. A year for Gaius and me to set up a trap we knew my mother could not extract herself from. A year living with that horrible woman. Watching her sink deeper and deeper into her madness."

Frowning, the tribune leaned back against the cold stone of the bench with folded arms across his breastplate. A hundred different thoughts, a hundred different questions, ran through his head. Two in particular demanded answers. But before he could ask them, he felt Hatshepsut slide an arm under his and grip it with both hands fondly.

"Gaius says you are touched by the gods, tribune. You have a gift for finding the unknown. And maybe for talking directly to the gods?"

"I do not talk to the gods, my lady. I have this malady, much like the one Julius Caesar had, but not quite as severe. He had the shaking disease, and as you know, we Romans think that is a malady that is given to us by the gods. I am not quite as unfortunate. Sometimes I develop a fever that makes me delusional. Apparently, I see imaginary people and talk to them. I am fluent in several languages, a natural gift since childhood. When I converse, I converse in the language of whatever the imaginary character speaks."

"Ah," the woman nodded, her voice soft and gentle and understanding. "You Romans are a superstitious lot. Far more than we Egyptians. No doubt when you go into these fevers your servants think you commune with the gods? Perhaps even frighten those who do not know of your sickness?"

"Yes, quite true, my lady. Fortunately, these fevers are very rare. And I am aware when they are soon about to grip me. There are methods, unpleasant methods, which can push back these ravings if the situation calls for it. I've been blessed in the respect that a fever never incapacitated me in my career."

Hatshepsut nodded absently, still gripping the tribune's

arm in hers, and stared into the study watching the doctor. It seemed so natural. Not as a signal for a possible sexual encounter, but as an old friend sitting beside and appreciating an old friend. For several moments, both sat in silence and watched the lessening urgency of the physician's administrations on the general.

The silence ended when Hatshepsut inhaled deeply and slowly exhaled. An act of relief in seeing that her husband had pulled through this crisis and still lived. When she spoke, she spoke with the soft voice of a woman filled with ancient wisdom.

"Gaius told me you saved his life once. Something about being present in the general's tent late one night when assassins entered with the intent to silence him?"

Decimus sat back again on the bench and grunted in surprise. So long ago! He had forgotten the incident completely. But indeed, assassins from the cult of Menket infiltrated the Roman camp as they campaigned out deep in the desert and attempted to kill Sulla as he tried to sleep. It was chance, pure luck, he entered the general's tent moments before the assassins struck to make a report.

Menket.

Assassins.

Exactly like the one who attacked him only a few days earlier. Strange and odd connections in this affair all linked to Egypt and something which happened seventeen years earlier. Decimus envisioned a long, thin arm of an ancient, wrinkled old sleeve of a priest's robe, hand exposed, pointing an ancient and arthritic finger of suspicion to this woman's mother.

Shebet.

"I sense your mind is troubled, Decimus. No doubt you have questions to ask. Do not let me stop you."

The tribune paused as the physician stepped out of the

study and walked toward them, wiping hands on a fresh towel. In a deep voice he informed Hatshepsut the crisis had passed, and her husband was on the road to recovery. But he hinted the general could not endure another revelation of bad news. He needed rest and solitude. And the loving attention of his wife.

Hatshepsut came to her feet, kissed the physician gratefully on the cheek, and promised the general would rest comfortably, secluded from all the outside world, for a fortnight or more. The doctor said he would remain overnight and monitor his famous patient, and then strolled back toward the study. The general's wife watched the doctor re-enter the study before turning, looking at the tribune, and sitting down again close to him.

"You had questions you were going to ask me, tribune."

"Yes," Decimus agreed, nodding. "Three come to mind."

"And they are?"

"If you hated your mother so much, why did you ask the general to rescind her death penalty? Is your mother still alive, after all these years, and is she again rousing unrest among her followers in Egypt? But most important of all, what was the curse she placed upon the general and, I presume, with you as well."

She sighed, leaned against the backrest of the bench, and closed her eyes. For a few seconds she remained perfectly still, quietly summoning strength, and then answered softly in her lightly accented Latin.

"I did not ask my husband to save her, tribune. Gaius gave her life back as a wedding present to me. A gesture to show his true love. I told him I loved him dearly for this act of kindness, but it would someday come back and haunt us. As we now see, my words were prophetic."

A single tear slid down the veiled woman's cheek as she

stared at her sleeping husband. But, inhaling deeply, she let the breath out slowly and continued.

"We have heard of the unrest in my homeland. Gaius has taken great interest in the growing reports of civil disturbances. As to whether mother could be involved in them in any way, I ... I really can't say. It has been seventeen years, tribune. Seventeen years. When Gaius released mother from prison, she was forty-two years old. She was banished into the desert never to return to Egypt. If she survived that ordeal, she would almost be sixty years old today. Maybe she is alive. Maybe she is the source behind the unrest. I don't know. But if someone can live off hatred, use hatred as a food to survive on down through the passages of time, I would not be surprised if all this could be laid at the feet of mother."

"But you have not been in contact with your mother?"

"Certainly not," Hatshepsut answered, shaking her head. "She cursed us, Decimus. She laid a hex on my husband and I which we could never break. A curse which guaranteed there would be no forgiveness. For any of us."

"What was the curse, fair lady? Tell me in exact detail. Leave nothing out."

"It was nothing, really. Just the ravings of a half-crazed, bitter old woman who saw with her own eyes her only child falling into her lover's arms. A lover who happened to be her most bitter enemy."

"The curse, Hatshepsut," Decimus continued to press, determined not to leave the general's residence until he heard the old woman's exact words to her daughter just before disappearing into the desert. "What did your mother say? Tell me exactly the words she uttered to the best of your ability."

The woman sobbed, wiped tears streaming down her cheek, and clasped both hands tightly together before answering.

"I remember exactly what she said, tribune. Exactly. She sat on a horse, just after being released from prison. She and a few of her followers were about to ride off into the desert. She turned to look straight at Gaius and me. She looked at us with that terrible stare she awarded to all she wished to destroy and said, 'I curse your house, Gaius Cornelius Sulla, and all who take your name and use it as their own. In time, not too far in the future, your only son will be awarded a great honor in his early youth. It will be his last. Soon afterward, great general, you will be cut down and rendered into dust. To be tossed into the four winds by an avenging hand. The winds will carry you away and your house will be forgotten. Forever. This I promise, general. This is the promise Menket has given to me. This the promise the gods I worship, and the gods you worship, have sworn to me will come true.'"

The woman beside him slumped forward, throwing delicate hands to her veiled face and succumbed into a spasm of silent tears. Eyes narrowed, Decimus wrapped an arm around the tormented woman and pulled her close to him. She did not resist but sank deeper into her spasm of tears. Several long minutes rolled by as Hatshepsut wept in silence. But as he comforted her in a fatherly fashion, the tribune's mind was an explosion of contradicting thoughts.

What did her mother's words mean? *This the promise the gods I worship, and gods you worship, have sworn to me will come true.* Had Shebet called in the wrath and power of other gods when she cursed Sulla and his new wife? Roman gods? He could see her summoning up the dark images of Anubis, the Egyptian god of the Underworld, to assist Menket in her revenge. But Roman gods?

There were, in his opinion, no nation or race more sanctimoniously religious than a Roman. Either plebian or Patrician. His countrymen were well aware of the gods of their forebears.

As well as the gods of those whom they conquered. Rome was filled with the temples of gods. Every Roman city, in just about every Roman conquered territory, were equally riddled with the temples of hundreds of different gods.

But hand in hand with a deep devotion to the gods also came the deep, unfathomable, and quiet visceral conviction in religious superstitions. A powerful force residing deep in one's soul which had the power to make a grown man bathed in rational thought become in less than a heartbeat— a panicked, unthinking creature of the night. A creature in human form so drowning in their superstitions that the slightest sound, the sudden movement of a fly, or even the snapping of a single fallen limb in a forest, would send thousands fleeing for their lives.

Decimus knew. He witnessed it personally. Observed half a Roman army simply dissolve into a fleeing mob of mindless trolls deep in a German forest. Germanic tribesmen surrounded the army. It was twilight. German clansmen, their faces and bodies painted in outrageous schemes, brandished massive long-swords and war-axes as they came out of the deep shadows of the forest. Like ghostly wraiths, they screamed and blew on large horns, falling upon the left flank of the army.

Panic ensued. The massacre began. The legion almost destroyed. But the remaining cohorts stood firm and fought hard all through the night and well into the morning. When daylight finally penetrated the gloom of the deep forest the legate in command gave the order for the legion to withdraw. He still remembered the sights and smells and visceral emotions of climbing over mounds of dead Roman legionnaires who'd fled from the enemy and were slaughtered mercilessly.

It was that incident, so many years earlier in his career, which made him a skeptic. A non-believer. He accepted the idea religion was a powerful force. It could fill a man's heart and make him a hero. But more likely than not, it also could drain a man of all reason, of all intellect. Converting him into a slobbering Cretan fleeing from the unknown. Incapable of defending himself or anyone around him.

And the reality was he knew Gaius Cornelius Sulla. A true Roman patrician. A traditionalist. A devout follower of Mars Pater. Mars the *father*. There was no Roman more devout in his religion. Or more superstitious.

XVI

7 AD
Rome
The physician, Aulus Nervanus

Hatshepsut finally regained her composure and stood up. Turning to face Decimus she tried to smile but failed. Decimus stood up and took a step closer.

"Madame, what did you mean ..."

She lifted a hand up to stop him from asking the question, shaking her head in the process.

"I, I cannot say anything else about it. I must go to my husband's side and be with him until he recovers. Thank you for being here, Decimus. Thank you for returning our son's remains to us. Your presence here in our house makes both the general and I feel safer."

She tried to smile again, her dark brown eyes glancing up into his, and then turned and hurried into the study and sat down on the couch beside her sleeping husband. She took one of the general's hands in both of hers and lifted it to her breast.

The white-haired Sulla stirred a little on the couch, and then fell deeper into sleep.

He felt an unease stirring in his chest. The mention of the curse and the *other gods* set off quiet alarms in his mind. Turning, walking deeper into the gardens, he followed the soft murmurs of the family and followers who were now gathered around tables filled with food and wine as they celebrated the life of the recently fallen. Finding his men, Gnaeus turned and handed the tribune a full goblet of wine, lifting a questioning eyebrow at the same time.

"The general is incapacitated. He became ill as we talked about his last time of service in Egypt. He admitted that, while in Egypt, the mother of Hatshepsut, a priestess of the cult of the goddess Menket, placed a curse on the two. When I mentioned my desire in knowing the curse Shebet imposed on them, he grew quite ill and had to be reclined upon a couch in his study. A doctor was summoned. How ill he is I am not sure. I think we need to find out. But first, I must speak with Titus Encimius."

Gnaeus tilted his head toward the young Praetorian officer standing in the middle of a few men talking quietly among themselves. Decimus stepped toward the group, caught the eye of the young Tesserarius, and motioned him to approach.

"Sir?"

"Delegate four men to remain here in the general's home. Tell them to be alert and prepared for trouble. Send a man into the city and to the nearest Praetorian unit HQ and have them send a squad of men here immediately. The general needs protection. Tell the unit commander the order comes straight from Caesar if he makes a protest."

"At once, sir."

The young man saluted, heeled around, and hurried off. In moments, one of the guardsmen was moving rapidly away from the tables and hurrying off to the city. Decimus, turning to look at the crowd, eyed the gathering for some time until he saw a person he was hoping would linger long enough for a glass of wine or two. He moved toward the gathering.

Turning to intercept the older, small man, he silently offered the doctor his untouched goblet of wine and smiled.

"Doctor, a moment or two of your precious time, if you don't mind."

"Hey? Oh, why thank you good man. A glass of chilled wine sounds perfectly marvelous right about now."

The doctor took the goblet and lifted it to his lips. Taking a deep swig of the cold liquid, he lowered the goblet and smiled.

"Goodness how does money speak when in the hands of the rich! Chilled wine, tribune. At this time of the year. I have never tasted anything so divine!"

"Fortune's smile has resided in the general's house for a very long time, doctor."

"Ah! Indeed, indeed. Now, tribune. How may I help you?"

"I am Decimus Julius Virilis, and at the present, I am on assignment from Caesar himself. There are a few questions I would like to ask you about the general and his health. Discreetly, of course."

The doctor, bushy eyebrows and all, rolled his face up into a frown and shot one of the eyebrows up over his forehead. Eyeing Decimus intently, the doctor hemmed and hawed for a moment, stepping from one foot to the next, and then shrugged.

"Tell me truthfully, tribune. You have concerns for the general's wellbeing?"

Decimus paused for a moment, surprised at the older man's question. Nodding his head, he answered in a quiet voice.

"I am convinced his life is in imminent danger, sir. I've assigned guards to stay here in the house, with reinforcements soon to arrive. Now, if you will, why did you ask such a question?"

The doctor ran a hand through his thick crop of unruly white hair and half turned to eye the large villa as he answered.

"This house has been filled with a sense of impending doom for the last six months, young man. Ever since the son left to take command of his legion. The general's health has been slowly declining. Declining for no apparent reason."

The tribune nodded, and frowning, gripped the older man's arm gently and pulled him away from anyone near enough to overhear their conversation.

"You perhaps know of the curse placed upon the family?"

"I have heard something of it, yes. Indirectly, of course. A word mentioned here or there. Whispers among the general's staff."

"What have you gleaned from these indiscretions?"

The doctor willingly followed Decimus deeper into the gardens. Gripping the half-filled goblet of wine in one hand, the doctor seemed almost relieved he was talking to someone as equally concerned about the general's health as he was.

"I know this. The general returned from the Temple of Mars Pater, the family's own temple the general's ancestors built just down the road, about two weeks before his son left to take up his command and relapsed into a deep sleep the moment he entered his study. So deep of a sleep his wife thought the general had sank into a coma. I was, of course, immediately summoned."

"Your prognosis?"

"There was nothing physically wrong with the patient. For his age, he was as fit as a Sheppard's set of panpipes. Whatever frightened the general, however, was severe enough to shake him profoundly and force his mind to repair itself with several hours of self-imposed sleep."

"The general had been frightened?" Decimus echoed. "Over what?"

"That I cannot say," the doctor said, shaking his head and lifting the goblet of wine for another sip. "But I can say this. Just as I arrived to see the patient, in a bronze dish on the general's desk I saw smoke rising from the ashes of something recently burned. Perhaps a letter, or a note, or possibly a map. I know not. But I have wondered if it had anything to do with the general's condition. It seemed quite odd to me at the time."

Tribune and doctor stood together eyeing the general's home for some seconds. Finally, to break the silence, the doctor shook his head, frowned, grunted and glanced at Decimus.

"I need more wine, tribune. A cup for yourself, perhaps?"

Decimus nodded as both men turned and walked back to the gathering assembly of kinsmen and clients. In silence both men poured wine into their respective cups and, gripping them casually, began walking away from the tables again.

"This Temple of Mars Pater. Is it close by?"

"Less than a kilometer down the road. A small temple built by the Sulla family. It sits atop the Grotto of Mars Primus. There's a small cave where a legend says Father Mars raised his sons, Romulus and Remus. Quite picturesque. With a small staff of priests. Apparently, the Sulla family's patrons frequent the temple often, along with the passerby's off the highway, of course."

Several more seconds rolled by in silence as each man sipped his wine and sank into their respective thoughts. For his part, Decimus drifted a glance or two at the small, shaggy haired doctor, and almost smiled. But turning, taking in the full view of the villa again, he asked another question.

"How long have you been the family doctor, uh..?"

"Aulus Nervanus, at your service, sir. And to answer your

question, I have been the general's personal physician ever since he was a young boy. More than thirty years."

"Indeed," Decimus mused, lifting an eyebrow in curiosity. "Were you, by chance, with him in Egypt when he met his lovely wife?"

"I was indeed. For the general, it was love at first sight. Fell head over heels in love with the young lady the moment his eyes first fell on her."

"Hatshepsut reciprocated in her love for the general?"

"Oh, without question!" Aulus Nervanus nodded emphatically. "The girl was playing a desperate game of intrigue against her mother. Her life was in immense danger. When she and the general met for the first time it was as if the gods on Olympus sealed their fates together for eternity."

"Perhaps they did, Nervanus. Perhaps they did," Decimus mused thoughtfully turning to look back at the house. "Did you by chance meet Hatshepsut's mother? Shebet?"

"Once." The doctor nodded, frowning. "While she was in prison. I was asked to examine her. To make sure no permanent injuries had been absorbed when she was captured."

"Your impressions of the priestess?"

Aulus Nervanus turned and looked up into the face of Decimus Virilis and shook his head in a negative fashion. The doctor's face was painted with a mask of genuine concern. Concern and fear. Concern and fear, even after all these years since serving in Egypt.

"Decimus Virilis, I am not a person who generally believes in the idea people are born good or evil. I do not believe the gods much affect the lives of we mortals. But I will say this. The hour or so I spent in examining this woman was an hour of my life I will never forget. I saw evil incarnate, tribune. Living, breathing, evil radiating out of this woman with such an intensity it was as if it could envelope you and sink into every pore of your body if you were around her too long. I will be quite candid. I feared for my life when I was with her in her cell. Genuinely feared for my life."

The words were intense. Deeply powerful. Without question as genuine as anything ever uttered. Fear still filled the doctor's soul. Fear dwelled in the man's eyes. Aulus Nervanus truly believed the mother of Hatshepsut was a monster. A monster in the service of the bloody goddess of war, Menket.

"You believe she is still alive," he said, eyeing the doctor.

"I do," the doctor answered immediately, nodding. "Evil of that quality does not die, Decimus Virilis. Not naturally, at least. It is, in itself, a strength that fuels the will to live. The living body is nothing but an inanimate vessel for this kind of evil to occupy. If the vessel dies, it simply moves into the body of another faithful servant. I fear Shebet is near. I can almost feel her presence myself. I fear for both the general and his wife, and for myself as well. Having once been so close to this creature, might I have become infected and might, one day, be her next vessel to reside in?"

"Why did the general release her if she was the monster you portray her to be?"

"I cannot explain it," the doctor grunted, shaking his head in disbelief and looking down at his sandaled feet. "The news came to me Sulla released Shebet and banned her and her following from Egypt. But of course, soon after she was released, the rumors began to circulate."

"Rumors?" Decimus echoed with interest.

"Rumors about a squad of Sulla's best killers sent into the desert to track Shebet and her followers and kill them when they were far enough away no one would ever find their bodies. The general was no fool. He knew a danger when he confronted one. There was no way he was going to allow this creature or her followers to live. He wanted, however, to make sure his new wife never heard of her mother's demise."

"Did they succeed in their mission?"

"My sources tell me the unit sent out to do the general's decree were never seen again. They left to track down their intended victims. They never returned."

Shebet was alive. Evil incarnate. Still alive after seventeen years of absence. If true, she was undoubtedly the driving force behind the destruction of the Ninth. She also would be the death of Gaius Cornelius Sulla and Hatshepsut. The curse was specific. A great tragedy would befall the only son of Sulla and soon after Sulla himself and those who loved him would die as well.

Obviously, for those who believed in it, the curse was quite real. The question he needed to answer was simple. How do you break the hold of a curse firmly believed in the minds of the superstitious?

Smiling, Decimus turned and looked upon the craggy face of the doctor.

"Aulus Nervanus, it has been a pleasure to meet you. You have given me much food for thought to ponder on this case. I hope we will someday meet again."

The old man smiled and shook hands with Decimus. He stepped back as Decimus strode back toward the general's villa. But the tribune took only a few steps before halting. He turned and eyed the doctor again.

"Give my compliments to your employer, Aulus Nervanus, for being so open with me. Tell him someday I will repay him in kind."

"My employer, tribune? The general?"

"Your employer, Caesar's master of spies, Caius Lucius. How long have you worked for the talented man, doctor?"

A look of sly cunning whipped across the old doctor's face then and quickly dissipated into thin air before he spoke.

"Long enough to deny any knowledge of such a man, Decimus Virilis. But what, if I may ask, suggested to you I might know this Caius Lucius you speak of?"

"Openness, my good doctor. Your willingness to openly talk about your patient's innermost details to a complete stranger. What true devotee of Asclepius would do such a deed? Except you were warned I would find you and have this conversation. For that, I offer my fondest salutations to both of you."

The shaggy haired doctor smiled knowingly and lifted his goblet of wine in silent salute. Decimus, nodding, made his way back to the villa. As he watched the powerfully built tribune enter the general's house, he sighed softly before lifting the goblet of wine to his lips.

Yes. It would be a long night tonight. His written report would be long and detailed. Something the master spy always insisted.

XVII

7 AD
Just outside Rome
The Temple of Mars Pater

Aulus Nervanus was correct in his assessment of the Temple of Mars Pater. The temple sat atop a small, boulder-strewn hill just off the Via Latina. Poplar trees, stunted and twisted, clung to the hill between the tumbled rock and boulders, partially hiding the narrow mouth of the cave at the base of the hill. But the temple itself was visible to all from the highway. Now, in the early evening light, torches lit the way up the narrow path to the temple. It was a small temple, classic Greek in design, featuring three Dorian styled marbled pillars per side of the rectangular building.

But what caught the tribune's interest were the two life sized statues flanking the four steps leading up to the temple's portico. On the right was a statue of Mars, helm slid up over the brow of his forehead, holding in his right hand a spear, staring down at his feet where two small children, Romulus and

Remus, were happily playing. On the face of the god was not the image of a terrible god of war in his full war-like fury. Instead the god was smiling. Smiling and looking infinitely patient as his children laughed and played around his sandaled feet.

To the left of the steps was the image of a goddess. Not the goddess Venus, the goddess of love and beauty whom most Romans believed was the wife of Mars. This time it was the almost forgotten goddess Nerio, a very ancient goddess of war and valor, who looked to her right and at the figures of Romulus and Remus playing with the look of an adoring mother on her soft white marbled face.

Romans, as superstitious as any, chose their own variations and interpretations of their gods. The Sulla apparently preferred the old, classical interpretation of Mars. That being a father-protector of his people more than that of a god of war, with a war-like wife who was the embodiment of all the variations of patience and valor.

Decimus, with the silent Gnaeus just behind him, stepped onto the wide portico of the small temple and were met with two snarling faces of bronze wolves staring at them underneath large burning torches. The wolves were life-like in every detail, but much larger than a typical wolf. They seemed to be crouched, ready to strike, their long fangs bared, every muscle in their bodies taut and visible underneath their coats of fur.

One male, one female. They bracketed the wide double bronze doors of the temple, facing the steps leading up to the portico. In torchlight, being so massive, they were terrifying creatures to behold in the night's gloom. But, interestingly, appropriate. The wolf, as everyone knew, was sacred to the cult of Mars. The stark contrast of Mars the Father watching Romulus and Remus playing around his feet, with the loving Nerio at his side at ground level, contrasted with the gigantic bronze wolves snarling at anyone who dared to enter the temple, would be both unnerving, yet thrilling, to any follower of the fierce god.

Both Decimus and Gnaeus eyed each other in silence for a moment before leaning into the mass of one bronze temple door. Entering the brightly lit temple the two walked between the ranks of statues depicting Mars in all his different variations. Between the statues were marble pedestals lifting from the dark marbled floors, each pedestal littered with ancient, rust stained weapons and armor. Bolted into each pedestal were bronze plaques detailing the deeds of one Sulla or another and describing the defeat of the foe who dared to stand before them.

Down the narrow aisle between the statues of Mars and the triumphs of the Sulla clan the two moved reverently. A few steps down the aisle was all it took, however, for their eyes to fall upon the truly spectacular display depicting the power and wealth of the Sulla family. A wall of carved ivory trimmed in gold. The entire back wall of the temple was a mural depicting Mars kneeling on one knee beside the fallen form of a Gaul. Mars gripped with one hand the shaft of his famous spear buried deep in the Gaul's chest. The dead warrior lay on the ground, one hand gripping the spear shaft just above his heart, the other splayed out across the ground.

On Mars' head was his famous upraised helm of solid gold. Around his waist a wide belt of pure gold. Torchlight falling upon the carved ivory gave off a soft glow of luminescent light which seemed to animate the whole scene before them. Mars looked as if he would stand up at any moment and pull his spear from the Gaul's chest. The dead warrior looked so lifelike one could not help but believe he had, only seconds before, breathed his last breath. The gold radiated a yellowish glow which seemed to fill the air with its rich color.

Neither man could pull their eyes away from the wall. It was a stunning piece of artwork. Seconds rolled by in silence, each one too engrossed in the visual feast before them to even contemplate uttering a word.

But their rapture was destroyed, with unnerving efficiency, when from out of the darkness to their right, a deep voice uttered three words slowly, distinctly, mournfully. Sounding ever so much like the three peels of a funeral gong rolling across a courtyard announcing the death of a great lord.

"Decimus Julius Virilis."

Tribune and servant, startled, visibly jumped and reached for their swords. Decimus had his half way out of its scabbard before stopping his hand. Gnaeus, sword drawn, standing slightly in front of Decimus, glanced at the wall to his left and pulled from its bronze holder a burning torch and held it high over his head. Taking a half step forward, he threw flickering light into the darkness.

The light revealed a ghastly sight.

Lying on the floor, slumped against the wall of the inner sanctum, legs splayed across the polished floor, the temple's chief priest leaned against the wall with both hands folded across the front of his once very white robe. The priest's blood stained the robe's entire front with a dark black color. A sea of blood covered the floor underneath the dying priest.

Decimus moved to the priest and knelt to one knee. Gnaeus moved behind the tribune and held the torch high overhead so torchlight could fully illuminate the scene around them. It was grim to behold. Someone had gutted the old priest with a sharp blade. Slicing open his stomach with a killing blow the perpetrator knew would take hours before death claimed its intended target. There was no help for the priest. Death would eventually claim him and drag his soul down into the dark reaches of Hades.

"She came an hour ago," the priest hissed, grimacing terribly as pain filled his face. "A monster with a woman's body but with the head of a lioness. She and her men. Killed us all they did. Took my brethren down into the grotto below and slaughtered them. But the monster said I had to stay. Had to stay alive until you appeared. A message for you, tribune. A message from the goddess herself."

Another wave of pain swept through the dying man's body. Gently placing a hand on the old priest's shoulder, the only comfort he knew he could offer, Decimus waited for the old man to continue.

"She told me to tell you this: *You are too late. The gods have spoken. She has seduced Mars himself and convinced him this is the way it must end. Only foolish mortals defy the wrath of Mars and his Consort.*"

A monster hidden in the image of a young woman's body but adorned with the head of a lioness. Menket. Here in Italy. Hunting her sworn enemies. Now with the aid of Mars himself, if one wished to believe this nonsense. With a hard set in his face, he knelt silently and waited for the old man to die. One last rattling breath and life left the old man's body. Rising to his feet Decimus was about to say something to Gnaeus, but the excited shouting of one of the Praetorian guardsmen stopped him.

"Sir! Sir! Hurry! You must see this! Hurry!"

He and Gnaeus ran out to the night filled portico of the temple. One young guardsman stood on the steps and, just as Decimus and Gnaeus appeared, lifted a hand up and pointed toward Rome.

A little over a mile away, lifting high into the night sky, the angry light of yellows and oranges of a gigantic fire plume rose straight up into the heavens. The flames twisted and turned and shot higher into the night in their destructive dance, topped by a towering pillar of billowing smoke. It too filled with glimpses of fire and burning matter as it lifted violently up into the moonlit night.

The Sulla estates were burning. A stupendous funeral pyre filling the night air with angry light. Illuminating the countryside with death and destruction. Without saying a word Decimus leapt off the portico and mounted his horse. His escort followed him as he whipped his horse around and galloped off toward the inferno.

XVIII

7AD
The Sulla Estate
An Angry Goddess

The scene of destruction was staggering to behold. The entire villa was ablaze, burning with an incredibly hot fire which seemed to grow in its intensity with each passing second. So hot even the trees and shrubs in the gardens surrounding the villa exploded in a loud clap of thundering flames. Acrid smoke swirling around the gardens made it nearly impossible to breathe. Bodies of servants and patrons of the general littered the grounds as Decimus reined in his horse and leapt from his saddle all in one motion.

The dead, intriguingly, were the victims of sword thrusts and deadly arrows. Not the blackened, shriveled remains of those dying from flames. Somehow not surprised, Decimus, sword in hand, began marching toward the part of the villa yet intact, followed by Gnaeus and the three remaining guardsmen. With luck he hoped he would find the general and

Hatshepsut yet among the living. But three steps toward the villa and he came to a halt as six men in black came running out of the flaming home and straight at him.

The six masked men, swords in their hands, fell upon Decimus and his entourage with a fury. The fighting was intense and bloody. Steel clashing against steel, the screams of men being cut down where they stood. Blood spurting out suddenly, hot and salty to the taste as it splashed against their armor. The typical carnage of a desperate swordfight all too familiar to the tribune and his entourage.

Six black clad figures dropped to the ground covered in their own blood. Blood dripping from his blade, Decimus stepped over his opponent and hurried toward the villa. Entering the house, he and his men hurried toward the general's study as flames and crashing timbers inched their way toward them. But there was no general, no wife, in the study. Motioning his men to follow him, the fire now eating into the walls of the study behind them, Decimus led his men toward the nearest exit.

Behind them the heat of the inferno was unbearable. They needed to move before the heat itself made them faint away. But into the night, a few steps away from the house, Decimus came to a halt and stared at the figure in front of him.

She stood in front of a magnificent black mare. A horse as tall as the figure standing in front of her. But the figure, that of a young woman dressed in the traditional garb of an Egyptian princess, with the head of a young female lion atop her shoulders, stood motionlessly twenty paces in front of Decimus and his men and stared at the tribune.

The goddess Menket.

She was alone. Just holding the reins of her horse behind her, staring at Decimus. She seemed unconcerned that standing before her were five armed Romans in blood splattered armor, with swords which had already tasted battle drawn and waiting for the command to attack. Decimus, nodding, gripped his sword and took a step forward to challenge the goddess. But the sounds of hooves forced him to halt. A dozen black clad figures rode up in mass and reined in front of the goddess. With a wall of followers and horse flesh between the goddess and himself all he could do was motion for his men to halt. One of the figures on horseback yelled in Egyptian, turning in his saddle and pointing off into the night. A second later the dozen horsemen rode off in the opposite direction, taking with them the exotic creature of the goddess into the inferno lit night.

He silently watched the horsemen disappearing into the darkness. But, not hesitating, he glanced at his men and told them to follow him. Quickly they moved away from the villa just as the walls of the large home came crashing down, throwing up thousands of burning sparks in the process.

From the city two complete contubernium, sixteen Praetorian guardsmen in total, came hurrying down the road in formation. The officers in the detachment yelled orders and the men broke down and hurried toward the fiery pyre, searching for any survivors and dragging them away from the hungry flames. A centurion came marching up toward Decimus, the light of the fires glowing against his polished armor and saluted smartly.

"Sir! We saw the flames and came as fast as we could. Is the general safe? How did this disaster happen?"

"I have not found the general. For the moment we can do nothing, centurion. Find any who yet live and pull them to safety. After the fire has subsided, I want you to drag all the bodies from the ashes and lay them side by side so they can be inspected. Perhaps the general's body will be discovered then."

"Sir!"

A quick salute and the centurion retreated toward his men. The inferno howled and screamed. Flames climbed toward the heavens. Smoke drifted across the countryside for miles surrounding the estates. Decimus stood on the other side of the Via Latina and watched as the villa and its surrounding buildings burned relentlessly.

The fires burned all through the night. Several times during the fierce blaze, groups of soldiers threw water onto the flames in an effort to limit the destruction. But whenever water touched the flames, the flames grew even hotter and more violent. There was nothing to do but watch the entire estate burn to the ground. It was well after sunrise before the flames subsided. Hours more until the ashes and debris became cool enough to search for bodies. By late afternoon Decimus' wishes had been completed. On the far side of the estate, away from the Via Latina, a long line of bodies lay on the scorched ground, shoulder to shoulder, in one grim display of human carnage.

Among the dead was the young Tesserarius, Titus Encimius and the four guardsmen Decimus left behind to protect Sulla and Hatshepsut. Also lying among the dead were eight black clad, black masked assassins who had been part of the raiding party. But search after search among the ruins failed repeatedly in their attempts to find Gaius Cornelius Sulla the Elder and wife, Hatshepsut.

"This is a disaster!" Caius Lucius exploded, for once losing his control and allowing his anger to boil over. "An Egyptian cult stages a violent raid on a patrician's estate just outside the gates of Rome itself and kidnaps the general and his wife before disappearing off into the night. Impossible! If I had not seen this with my own eyes, I would have laughed in someone's face and called them delusional. How could this have happened, Decimus?"

Decimus gazed into the frustrated face of the master spy,

who had hurried from some unknown corner of Italy, arriving at the smoking ruins of the general's estates two hours after sunrise, and eyed the little man quietly.

"Can't you see it, Caius?" the tribune answered, a hand sweeping across the destruction around him. "This, all this. The destruction of the Ninth. The attack on the villa. The abduction of the general and his wife. All of it. All of it nothing but three strokes of a master plan."

"A master plan?" echoed the spy, anger draining from his face and confusion replacing it. "What master plan? A plan conceived by whom? Surely you don't believe an ancient Egyptian madwoman like Shebet could do something like this? We have yet to prove that she even lives. For all we know she may had died years ago out on some god forsaken sand dune. But assuming she is the wizened old bitch she has to be now, surely, she is not capable of planning and executing something like this. Is she?"

Decimus smiled thinly as he strolled slowly down the long line of the dead with Caius Lucius following in tow, with the silent Gnaeus bringing up the rear. The spy's words indicating doubt began to drift into the man's thinking. He was a Roman. He was Caesar's spy. He knew the dirt and the secrets of most of the patrician families in the empire. Like Decimus, he knew the madness, the lust for power, which could grip the minds of many. Madness did not preclude genius. In many instances, the enemies of Caesar were both quite mad and maddeningly brilliant.

The tribune stopped unexpectedly, frowned, and turned toward one black clad body and studied it for a moment. Kneeling, he gripped the man's black mask and ripped it off and gazed upon the dead man's face for some seconds before speaking.

"I have seen this man before. Gnaeus, do you recognize him as well?"

The piece of dried leather and sinews stepped around the spy and stood beside Decimus and eyed the body. A hand came up and quickly signed. The tribune grunted, nodded in agreement, and rose to his feet.

"As I suspected. One of the Egyptian conscripts from the sixth cohort. Half of the sixth were Egyptian conscripts. Well played, I'm afraid. Very well played indeed."

"What was well played?" Caius Lucius asked, following Decimus as the tribune began his walk down the long exhibit of the dead.

"Our mastermind recruited and inserted practically an entire cohort of Menket followers onto the rolls of the Ninth even before the legion was officially designated as a new command."

"What? Impossible!"

Decimus smiled again thinly, glancing at the spy, before kneeling to rip the mask from the face of a second black clad assassin. Another Egyptian's lifeless face stared up into the tribune's eyes. Looking up and at Gnaeus, Decimus waited for only a second before the tongue-less legionnaire nodded in agreement. Rising again to his feet, Decimus turned and stared directly at Caius Lucius.

"Tell me the truth, old friend. Do not vacillate in your answer. I need to know. Who was to originally command the Ninth Brundisi?"

Caesar's spy narrowed his eyes at Decimus, then looked to his left and his right to make sure no one was within earshot of their conversation. Frowning, he ran a hand across his lips, then looked at the tribune again.

"Sulla the Elder was supposed to command the Ninth. The plan was the newly created Ninth, plus one Spanish legion and one from Gaul, plus accompanying auxiliaries, would push into Dalmatian territories from the southwest while Tiberias and his six legions would invade from the north. It was the elder Sulla's plan. He suggested it to Augustus and Augustus agreed."

"But something happened to change the plan. What?"

"The uprising in Egypt," the spy retorted, almost whispering. "It is far worse than we originally thought. The Spanish and Gaulish legions, along with the auxiliaries, were diverted and shipped off to Egypt. Sulla was to board ship and follow the next week. He was convinced his son was ready to take command of a legion and persuaded Caesar to give his son the Ninth. Caesar, wishing to keep the elder Sulla an ally, readily agreed."

Decimus' eyes clouded over in deep thought as he turned and faced the dead lying on their backs in the grass in a long, gruesome display of Roman violence. Caius Lucius, noting the look on the tribune's face, scowled and turned to look at Gnaeus.

"It is so irritating when he does this. It's as if he shuts out the entire world. What in Hades is he doing?"

Gnaeus lit up a wolfish grin on his darkly tanned face, shrugged elegantly, then lifted a hand and tapped one finger to the side of his forehead. A silent gesture which said eloquently: *The tribune was thinking. We mortals can do nothing else but wait patiently for the man to return.*

"Bah!" Caesar's spy grunted, shaking his head and starting to turn away. "When he comes out of his trance, tell him I've sent word out to all the ports and fishing villages to be wary of groups of strangers seeking passage to Africa. The navy has been alerted as well. If the general and his wife are here in Italy, we will find them. I will be in Rome if he needs me for anything else."

Striding away firmly, the chief of spies' face revealed a

scowl that threatened the life and happiness of anyone who crossed his immediate path. With relief Gnaeus watched the dangerous man mount a horse and turn it around toward the city. Sighing softly, Gnaeus never could convince himself to fully trust Caius Lucius. One could never trust the unblinking eyes of a pit viper—either the one who slithered across the sands—or the one who walked on two legs. Turning his eyes toward the motionless form of the tribune, he waited for his master to return to the living.

XIX

7 AD
Rome
The Day After

The Praetorian officer stepped into the small garden, brightly polished armor gleaming in the sunlight, the plumed helm of a centurion tucked neatly under his right arm and stood rigidly at attention. Eyeing the officer, Decimus concluded the young man was, perhaps, twenty-two or twenty-three at the most. Sitting himself down on a bench, a large stone table in front of him, the tribune eyed Gnaeus, sitting to his right, and his other ex-legionnaire servant, Rufus, sitting on his left. He smiled, lifting an eyebrow curiously.

"Another one? So early in the morning?"

"Apparently so, sir." Rufus grunted, frowning, as he twisted around and glared at the purple-caped officer. "It would seem Caesar wishes to keep you alive for as long as possible. Why, I haven't a clue."

Decimus lifted his head and laughed. Laughed easily and

without the least bit of rancor. Rufus, the oldest of his followers, and a superb thief, had a pattern of speech which constantly got him into trouble. How many times he had come to Rufus' aid, pulling him away from the wrath of a superior officer for speaking his mind, Decimus could not count. It was not that the experienced legionnaire meant to insult anyone, especially his superiors. It was just the way he spoke naturally. But on the other hand, if there was a piece of information needed which had to be worked out of a reluctant witness, or if there was an item the legion needed in order to function better in the field, Rufus became a very useful tool. Or if, for instance, an artifact had to be absconded in such a fashion as to be assured no one would ever know how it disappeared, Rufus was the man for such a job.

Gazing upon Rufus fondly, still chuckling, Decimus glanced at Gnaeus and nodded. The darkly tanned leather piece of muscle and sinew stood up and motioned the young officer to approach.

"Sir!" the optio yelped out loudly after marching briskly up to the table and snapping to attention and saluting at the same time. "Tertius Germanis, Optio of the second Praetorian century, of the Fourth Cohort, 'Caesar's Favored,' reporting for duty. Sir!"

In any Roman military formation, either Roman legion or the Praetorian Guards, or the city's new Vigiles, a newly implemented group of men Caesar created to fight fires as its primary mission and combat common street gangs ravaging Rome as its secondary mission, operated efficiently with a multi-layered command structure. Even the new Cohortes Urbana, a second group of law enforcement officers who were to stem the tide of organized crime in Rome, had officer ranks woven into the fabric of command in each unit. Tribunes, centurions, optios, tessararius, were the officers. Centurions being the backbone of any military unit, commanding approximately eighty men to create a century, with eight to ten centuries, to create a Roman cohort. An optio was his second-in-command within a century.

Tertius Germanis was the second-in-command of the second century of the fourth cohort of Praetorian Guards. The first major promotion for an up-and-coming junior officer rising through the ranks of the army.

"Welcome to my home, Tertius Germanis. I understand you have brought a new detachment with you?"

"Two contuburnia, sir. Sixteen good men waiting for you to command."

"Your orders?"

"To protect you and your household from any possible harm, sir. To assist you in any way your investigative needs in and immediately around the city of Rome. Orders, I might add, handed down to my commanding officer directly from the Imperator himself, sir."

Imperator was an honorific title Octavius Caesar accepted from a grateful Senate after he ended the many wars ravaging the empire. Like his adoptive father, Julius Caesar years earlier, Octavius refused to accept the crown of Emperor to be placed on his brow. Both Caesars, both father and adopted son, knew the animosity which would be generated if the title Emperor was bestowed on them. For Octavius, it had taken years to end the incessant fighting powerful patrician families vied with each other to ultimately control the Senate and the empire.

Imperator was a title awarded to a particularly successful Roman general. The title awarded the general almost unlimited power. But not the absolute supreme power an Emperor would command. Both Caesars, astutely aware of Roman politics and Roman politicians, believed an enduring peace could be forged and maintained if neither crowned themselves Emperor.

"Bivouac your men on the hillside behind the garden walls,

Tertius Germanis. Tell them to rest during the day. Tonight, we may be hunting in the streets of Rome, and I wish to have fresh legs and alert eyes with me if we do."

"Sir!" the young optio snapped, saluting, before pivoting and marching out of the gardens.

Decimus watched the young officer disappear through the garden gate and eyed the young man thoughtfully, before returning his attention back to the two men sitting at the table with him. Both Rufus and Gnaeus were watching him. Each with a face suggesting they had questions to ask.

"Yes, yes, I know gentlemen. Both of you want to know about this hunt. Well, consider the situation we have ourselves in at the moment. Consider what has taken place in the last month. A madman attacked and almost destroyed a Roman legion single handedly. A planned attack, cunningly set in place, aimed directly at the superstitious hearts of the average Roman soldier. Inflicting upon each and every soldier the wrath of Mars himself who hurled his mighty spear at the legion. His anger causing the explosion which ripped apart the hilltop the legion's legate and entire officer staff occupied.

"An act of madness, my friends. Sheer madness. But a statement as well. A declaration. This madman did not want to just destroy the legion. No. No. He wanted to specifically destroy one person in the legion in such a way all the world would know. He wanted the world to know, the Imperator to know, of his hate and anger for this one man. He wanted to show the entire world his genius and power. And what better way to do it than to blow up an entire hilltop just before thousands of Dalmatian rebels swept across the remnants of a shattered legion and put them to the sword."

Rufus and Gnaeus looked at each other, their complexions growing pale, their eyes filled with concern. They waited for the tribune to continue.

"Now consider the madman's next move. Even more audacious than the first. Practically under the very nose of Caesar himself he organizes and leads an attack on the estate of Gaius Cornelius Sulla and kidnaps both the general and his wife while men burn down the villa and murder most of the general's kinsmen and followers in the process. All this before help can arrive, mind you. Planned, set into motion, successful, and disappearing into the night all in one magnificently executed military operation. Genius, my friends! Sheer, malicious, insanity-laced genius!"

Again, Rufus and Gnaeus eyed each other, caught in the wonder of the tribune's words. But this time, when the two returned their gaze toward their mentor, Gnaeus lifted his hands and asked a silent question.

You say this is a madman who committed these heinous acts. You know who this creature may be?

Decimus smiled shrewdly at his silent companion and shook his head *no*.

"I have my suspicions, Gnaeus. And I may have misled you somewhat when I used the term *madman* in describing this genius. It could very well be a woman. The old priestess, perhaps. Shebet may still live. And quite capable in conceiving and executing such a plan. Until we find more proof and capture someone alive who might shed some light on this creature, we cannot be sure of anything."

Which is why we hunt tonight, eh? To find someone and capture them alive so we may question them.

"Rufus, I have a job for you," the tribune said, looking at the master thief. "Somewhere in this city is an enclave of followers who worship the goddess of Menket. Undoubtedly, they have gone into hiding. I entertain thoughts we might even find our assassin friend among them. If so, we may be in luck. He will possibly have much information to reveal to us. Find them,

Rufus. Observe them. Send word back to me their location. But under no circumstance are you to intervene in any way. Do you understand?"

"Concisely, tribune. If they are here, I will find them."

The tall, thin man rose from his bench, saluted in a slanderous, insolent fashion, and hurried off into the house to gather his things. Gnaeus, a look of worry itching across his rough features, watched Rufus as he left before turning back to face Decimus, hands flying in the sunlight.

"I know, my friend. A dangerous mission." The tribune nodded, looking serious as well. "But Rufus has proven himself time and time again in such missions. We cannot control our fates, old friend. When our tapestries of our woven lives come to a completion, we die. But until that time comes, we serve the wishes of Caesar. And hope we live to see another day.

But come, Gnaeus. We must find Sulla's family doctor, this Aulus Nervanus. I have more questions to ask him before we hunt."

XX

7 AD
Rome at midnight
The Old Krone

Aulus Nervanus practiced medicine in the Forum Julius in the elegant Basilica Julium, a three-floored building filled with government offices and small shops. Many in the city considered the building to be one of the most beautiful creations Julius Caesar ever commissioned to be built. On any given work day the basilica was a thriving beehive of people coming and going, with many of these same people being some of the wealthiest and most powerful in Rome.

The Forum Julius was, as was the Forum Augustus which sat right beside it, at the heart of Rome itself. In the narrow confines of the forum was the Temple of the Divine Julius on one side, with the temples of Castor and Pollux on the other, along with the smaller, much older Temple of the Vestal Virgins next to it. The three founding strengths of the Roman Empire: Roman law, Roman Government, and Roman Religion all compressed into one forum for everyone to witness and participate in.

Decimus was impressed the good doctor could afford office space in the basilica. He knew the rent was absurdly high. But it only confirmed his suspicions that Aulus Nervanus had a very successful, and very wealthy, practice of medicine. The man had no less than three office spaces, interconnected, on the second floor of the crowded basilica. And apparently, observing the crowd who sat in a long line of chairs in one of the spaces, he commanded a staff of assistance and junior physicians as well. As he approached the doctor's offices he had to twice stop and greet Roman senators who had, over the years, served with him in one legion or another.

But eventually he, along with Gnaeus, and three young Praetorian guard escorts following, approached the offices and was immediately met by a worried looking Nervanus. He rushed out and reached for Decimus' right arm to grip with both hands in desperation.

"Have you found the general and his wife, tribune? Are they alive? Please! Please tell me they are alive and in your safe hands again. Please!"

"The search continues, doctor. We believe they are still here in Italy. Most probably somewhere close to Rome. All the ports are being watched. Ships are being searched. We will find them."

"But will you find them alive? That is the question," the doctor replied, a look of genuine dread on the man's face. "But why are you here now? Am I a suspect now in the general's disappearance?"

The basilica's heavy crowd moved about them so close the corners of togas and capes briefly touched all six standing in the middle of the hallway. Eyes darted their way. People overheard scraps of their conversation. Far too many curious Romans were finding themselves staring at the doctor and the five men who surrounded him and were inching closer to hear more.

"Is there a quieter place here in the basilica where we can go and talk in private?"

'"Impossible!" the thin little man returned, snorting out a bark of laughter and shaking his head. "But if you have time, we can walk across the forum to the temple of Julius. On the portico are benches we can sit down and talk and at the same time observe the entire forum in the process."

"An excellent idea."

Surprisingly, the doctor was a brisk walker, setting a pace which swept them out of the basilica and into the forum in quick time. The forum, although populated by a large group of onlookers, businessmen, street merchants, and politicians, nevertheless was not overly crowded close to midday. The sun threw its hot gaze down from a cloudless blue sky, the day's heat radiating off buildings and the plaza stones beneath their sandals. Hardly a breath of air stirred. People moved in the forum with the firm step of one wanting to get out of the sun as rapidly as possible. No one paid attention to the small group cutting across the forum and marching straight to the marbled steps of the Temple of the Divine Julius.

The temple set upon an almost two-meter-tall stone base, lifting the entirety of the temple above the level of the forum impressively. Stone steps led up from the forum to the upper level of the base, and after a short walk, marbled steps at each end of the temple's portico led up to the columned portico itself. A portico thankfully consumed in a deep shade overlooking the forum.

Nervanus, not hesitating, turned to his left and walked to the end of the portico where a large empty stone bench invited Decimus, Gnaeus, and the doctor to sit in relative comfort while the three guards took up positions a few feet away which blocked off that portion of the portico the doctor and the tribune occupied.

"Isn't this a fascinating view, tribune? Fascinating and instructive. I often come here over my lunch hour and sit, eating cheese and bread, drinking a little wine, and watching the people below. So invigorating! So enlightening!"

Both the tribune and Gnaeus took the time to look out and survey the panorama before them. Directly in front of the temple's base a tall column of stone rose up into the clear sky, towering over the forum. Atop the column the over-sized form of a bronze Julius Caesar, dressed in the cuirass of a Roman legate, looked down upon the forum regally. Across the way was the white columns of the Basilica Julius glowing underneath the bright sun. Impressive indeed.

Again, the thought crossed Decimus' mind what he was seeing here was the true power of Rome. Roman law. Roman politics. Roman religion. Carved out of the savagery which afflicted most of the human race. Providing a momentary reprise of culture and civilization for those who no longer wished to be savages. Maintained by the power and might of Roman legions.

Deep in his soul Decimus felt that stirring. That uneasy churning in the stomach which hinted of something he knew to be illusionary. Culture and civilization were the illusions. The true illusions. Savagery and chaos the reality. Mankind's basic instinct, its most powerful driving force, was that of a savage beast who warred against everything new and different. And what Mankind feared the most were ideas. Ideas and ideals. In other words ... change. Mankind feared change.

If one wished to be *civilized* and to enjoy *culture*, one had to *learn*. To *change*. In the beating hearts of every savage was this dichotomy. The desire to change. And at the same time, the desire to destroy. Wolves, fangs bared, each tearing away into the soul of Man. To remain a savage? Or to bathe in the warm light of culture and knowledge? Or to remain the snarling wolf cloaked in the darkness of a bloody beast? Which wolf would be the stronger?

Each soul had to make that choice. One wolf or another had to be nurtured. The other condemned.

Decimus made that choice long ago. He was a Julii. He, like Julius Caesar and Augustus Caesar, believed in the power and grandeur that was Rome. Not just in the military might which was Rome, as formidable as it was under the Caesars. No, he believed in the idea that Rome offered to the world the best chance yet to bring the knowledge, the strength, and the commitment to convert the world's savagery into a more enlightened era.

There was a chance, as slim as it may be, to create a better world. Julius Caesar envisioned such a world almost sixty years earlier. And died because of it. Died in front of the hall of the senate, died from the hands of the senators themselves, because he dared to articulate a new Rome, a new vision, of what the world could be.

With Caesar's death, savagery prevailed. Savagery, in the guise of brutal civil wars, sweeping across the empire for almost forty years. Untold numbers of innocent people died. The empire almost collapsing into chaos. But in the end, miraculously, Octavius Caesar triumphs. The educated, urbane, astute observer of both man and culture, rose from out of the muck of savagery and conquered the savage beasts who wished to destroy everything. He did not do it alone. Along the way he somehow converted the hearts of a few of the savages to turn on their natural instincts and fight on his behalf. In the end the gods smiled upon him. In the end culture and civilization was restored.

But there was, out there in the proverbial night, the beating hearts of savagery still waiting ... and anticipating the time when they could strike again. To push back that time of darkness, to confront the fangs of the savages yet living, Caesar needed wolves of his own. Wolves with long fangs, dripping in blood, guarding the perimeters of civilization.

He was one of those wolves. Early in his career Octavius Caesar came to him and asked him to do the dirty deeds, the savage reprisals, which kept the chaos at bay. It was a job someone had to do. Only a few had the cunning, the predilection, the steel in one's heart to do it properly. It required a certain kind of intellect. A certain quality of savagery. A relentless drive to get the job done Octavius knew his distant cousin had in abundance.

Decimus accepted his fate. Agreed to be that certain dark wolf. The imperator's mailed fist.

Here he sat. On a bench on the portico of the Temple of the Divine Julius. Seeking information which would help him find, and destroy, the wolves who came slinking out of the night and into the open light of civilization with the intent of bringing chaos and savagery back into the world.

He turned and looked upon the face of Aulus Nervanus.

"Some time ago something happened in the Sulla household which changed the dynamics of the family. News was brought to them from Egypt. News which, I suspect, brought a large measure of fear into the heart of the general. And to Hatshepsut. News, my dear doctor, I suspect you know more than you have revealed. A point of interest I find most disconcerting."

The compact, trim little man grinned nervously, using the corner of his toga's right sleeve to wipe the beads of sweat off his large forehead. He looked away from the tribune and sighed.

"Just before the talk of trouble in Egypt began, I was sitting here one hot afternoon eating grapes and taking a respite from my patients' constant complaints. Sometimes even physicians get tired of hearing people whining all the time. Anyway, I was sitting here and that's when I saw them." The doctor frowned, beginning to sink into his own thoughts. But Decimus was in no mood for the good doctor's eccentricities.

"Saw whom, doctor?"

"What? Oh! Yes, yes. Of course. I was sitting here looking at the forum. It was a particularly hot day, and the forum was almost empty. But I saw the general's wife and her son walking briskly across the forum, heading for the basilica, on some official business. They were almost to the middle of the forum when a voice rang out loud and clear. A woman's voice. So loud even I could hear it. She spat out Hatshepsut's name as if she was spitting out a cup of poison. The general's wife and the young Gaius Sulla stopped, turned, and ... my word, the most astonishing reaction! I thought the young woman was going to collapse dead away the moment her eyes looked upon the creature!"

"Describe this creature, doctor."

"Well," the doctor began, twisting around on the bench, frowning, glancing apprehensively at the tribune. "I really didn't see a face. She was a heavy framed, short woman. An old woman leaning on a large wooden staff with both hands for support. She was wearing a shawl which covered her shoulders and her head. She had a very difficult time walking. A terrible limp which required the walking staff. She came hobbling up behind Hatshepsut and the young Sulla slowly. She had two men attending her. Dark complexioned young men. Men from the desert."

"Men from the desert," Decimus repeated, narrowing his eyes suspiciously. "You accompanied the general to Egypt. Were these men from Egypt?"

"Once," Aulus Nervanus answered, nodding. "With the general some years back. The general's last command. He took me along as his personal physician. We were in that god forsaken hot country for two years. Two horrible, horrible, years."

Decimus almost smiled. Egypt was a country you either found interesting or you detested it to the very core of your being. Apparently, the doctor was of the latter persuasion.

"You said the general's wife looked startled when she turned to look at this person. Tell me more."

"Oh, not just startled, tribune. Not just startled. She looked as if she had been stabbed in the heart. She threw up both hands to her breasts, dipped on one knee dangerously, and grabbed her son's arm for support. I seriously thought of coming off this bench and rushing to her aid. I didn't because Gaius Cornelius the Younger gripped his mother and pushed her behind him, confronting the old krone and her two followers. A most heroic gesture. The younger acted like a true Sulla. A true Roman. Most impressive."

Decimus frowned and glanced at Gnaeus. The old legionnaire spoke silently.

Shebet? Here? In Rome?

Decimus shrugged and brought his gaze back to the doctor.

"What happened next, doctor. Be precise, if you please. Leave nothing out in your impressions. Even the most innocuous action or gesture might be of paramount importance."

"Hatshepsut was definitely terrified throughout the encounter. From this distance, I could not hear what the old krone said. But she was the one who spoke to both mother and son. Twice I saw her extend an arthritic hand from out of her shawl and point a long finger toward the lady. When she did, the Lady Sulla would step further away from the krone and covered her face with both hands as if something terrible had been uttered."

Words spoken in anger. Perhaps the promise of imminent death approaching. Death for both Hatshepsut and the general. But what of The Younger? What was his reactions?

"Young Sulla stood between mother and the krone. His hands rolled up into balls of fists. Interestingly though, now that you mention it, I got the impression whatever was said to upset Lady Sulla was not directed toward Gaius Cornelius the Younger. I cannot say for sure, of course. The conversation was too far away for me to overhear. But it was odd. Quite odd watching the confrontation."

"Odd? In what way?"

Aulus Nervanus frowned, scratched his nose with an extended forefinger, cleared his throat, and twisted around on the hard stone bench before answering.

"When the krone first approached Lady Sulla and her son, the creature began speaking angrily. Her anger quite plainly aimed toward Lady Sulla. The young Gaius at first took up the stance of a son ready to defend the honor of his mother. But the more the old krone spoke, you could see quite plainly young Gaius changing. He slowly began to relax. His fists, the stance of his frame, changed. By the end of the hidden creature's monologue, the young Gaius was standing in front of the old krone like that of a student listening to his venerable old tutor. Strange. Most strange. And then, of course, there was the way the confrontation ended which captured my attention."

A flash of irritation swept across the highbrow of Decimus before disappearing. Irritation at the doctor. These revelations should have been told to him hours earlier. If they had, perhaps the general and his wife would have survived the attack on their villa. But Decimus said nothing and waited for the doctor to continue. He had his suspicions about why the physician had remained silent until now. Suspicions revolving around the rivalry he had with Caesar's master of spies.

"The confrontation ended, tribune, with the Lady Sulla turning and running off toward the basilica, hands to her face, weeping visibly. But the krone, the krone stepped closer to young Gaius and reached up with an old, deformed hand and gently touched the young Sulla's cheek. Much like a grandmother might do to her young grandson. Quite remarkable! She touched the young Sulla's cheek for only a second or two. But then she turned and limped away. Her servants following in her wake."

"What was Sulla's reaction?"

"Nothing," the doctor answered, shrugging. "He allowed the old lady to touch his cheek, making no move to resist in the slightest. When she turned and began to move away, he stood as if frozen in his tracks and watched the woman and her servants for some seconds. When they moved out of the forum he turned and hurried after his mother."

Decimus grunted, sat back on the bench and folded arms across his chest. Staring out over the forum, his mind raced along avenues and paths unrelated as to what his eyes were taking in. His mind was replaying the doctor's words as he tried to imagine the encounter between Hatshepsut, along with her son, and Shebet he witnessed days earlier. For several long minutes he sat still. Gnaeus, long used to the tribune's peculiarities, shrugged eloquently when a nervous doctor glanced at him questioningly.

"I ... I must go. I have patients waiting for me," Nervanus said, rising from the bench.

Gnaeus gently laid a hand on the doctor's shoulder and shook his head and silently mouthed the word *wait*. Aulus Nervanus sat back down, growled something unintelligible under his breath, and turned toward the tribune. Fortunately,

Decimus unfolded his arms, sat up on the bench, and cleared his throat.

"Just a few more questions, doctor, and then you may return to your practice. Tell me, did you encounter the old hag again, or perhaps either of her servants, later on?"

"No," the doctor said firmly, shaking his head. "Not the old krone. But *maybe* one of her servants during the attack at the villa. He was sitting on a horse issuing orders to the men attacking the villa. When he saw me staring at him, he wheeled his horse around and rode away. He did not look pleased I recognized him."

Decimus nodded, silently confirming a suspicion he was entertaining, before speaking again.

"Finally, doctor, why did you not tell us of this incident earlier? Or do I really need to ask such an obvious question."

Aulus Nervanus smiled warily, eyes narrowing, as he quickly glanced at the three Praetorian guards standing in a file, blocking a portion of the temple's portico, from the few souls who came to worship at the temple.

"You do know my employer is a rival, do you not? He sees you as a genuine threat to his advancement through the ranks in Caesar's service. I suspect it is a friendly rivalry. But to be honest, I'm not sure. Nevertheless, I was told to answer all of your questions honestly and truthfully. But not to offer any additional information. Nor clarify any answer I made unless you specifically asked for clarification."

Decimus smiled, glancing at an obviously irritated Gnaeus, and back to the doctor.

"Thank you, doctor, for your honesty. I suspected as much. You may return to your patients. We will not be bothering you any longer."

Aulus Nervanus came to his feet, took two steps toward the

nearest flight of stairs leading down from the portico, then stopped and turned to peer at the tribune again.

"I would advise caution, tribune. In the line of work you and my employer are in. I doubt fealty and honor are considered to be of paramount importance. And friendship goes only so far. Watch your back, Decimus Julius Virilis. Watch your back."

With that the doctor hurried down the steps and descended to the forum. Decimus and Gnaeus watched the little man hurry across the deserted Forum back toward the basilica. When the doctor entered the large building and disappeared from their life, the silent Gnaeus looked to the tribune.

"Come, old friend. We have an assassin to catch. Perhaps the gods will smile on us tonight and give us a break we need to find the general and his wife."

XXI

7 AD
Rome
Death in a tenement building

The city of Rome rolled across seven hills, filling the valleys between with magnificent structures and awe-inspiring forums. Wide streets, built only as a Roman engineer could build them, filled the city between its walls with swift, easy access to any part of the city. Rome, in the time of Augustus Caesar, was one of the largest cities in the world. People from all parts of the known world, from even the far reaches of the Land of Chin, came to Rome to marvel at its wonders and gawk at its beauties.

But there was another part of Rome very few people wished to acknowledge. The Rome of the poor and discarded. The Rome of the maligned and unwanted. The sick and the dying. The criminal side of Rome with its roving gangs and crime-filled back alleys. Into this dangerously fertile night

Decimus, Gnaeus and Rufus, along with eight of the Praetorian guards, were going to descend into in search for an assassin.

"I found a nest of Egyptians clustered together in an apartment building on a street called The Street of Dreams," Rufus offered soon after arriving back at Decimus' small villa just as night was giving birth. "The street is two blocks south of

the Emporium. One end of the street runs into the Tiber. The other opens into a maze of streets that lead you north toward the Circus Maximus. A small temple dedicated to the goddess Sekhmet is nearby."

"Sekhmet?" a young Praetorian officer who would be attending the night's hunt asked, looking clearly confused. "I thought we were looking for the temple of Menket."

"For many, the two goddesses are the same," Decimus answered patiently. "But they are not. Sekhmet is an Egyptian goddess of war. Menket is Nubian. From the far south of Egypt. Over the years the two deities have merged into one. At least, for the majority of Egyptians who live in the cities, they have merged into one. Not so for her followers who live in the desert."

Decimus' dark eyes turned back to Rufus.

"Any signs of activity from this nest you describe?"

"Indeed," the talented Rufus nodded, grinning evilly. "Every one of them seemed to be quite agitated. They've stationed men up and down the street as lookouts. Men are down on the wharves at the end of the street waiting for something, or someone, to arrive by boat."

Or perhaps waiting for a boat to arrive so someone of importance can leave, Gnaeus signed quickly.

"My thoughts as well, old friend." Decimus nodded, turning his attention back to the young optio. "Half of your men with us. The rest on guard around the house. Tell your men there will be fighting tonight. But first we must approach the street and this apartment building unseen and undetected. We leave in thirty minutes."

"Sir!"

The young man saluted, pivoted, and almost ran out of the villa in his eagerness to get his men ready. Decimus, Rufus, and Gnaeus watched the young man hurry off, each with smiles on their hardened, lined faces. They too had once been young. Young and foolish. But that had been long ago.

"Rufus, tonight, no matter what happens, we must capture one of these men alive. Find Hakim and take him with you. After Gnaeus, myself, and the guards enter the building in search of whoever is in there, pick one of the fleeing Egyptians and bring him back here. Perhaps if we are lucky we will find someone who can enlighten us on where we might find the general."

"It will be done, tribune."

Rufus nodded and left Gnaeus and Decimus standing alone in the villa's small library. The wiry old piece of leather that was Gnaeus snorted, shook his head, and walked over to a small table where a carafe of wine sat on an old Celtic-designed silver serving tray. Pouring wine for the two of them, he turned and handed a glass to the tribune.

"Wine? Before a night's worth of action?" Decimus quipped, lifting an eyebrow in surprise. "This is something new. Are you growing old, my friend? Changing spots on me, perhaps."

Yes. As you have often told me, Decimus. I am an old dog. Yet I can still learn a few new tricks. But what about you? If we survive through this ordeal and bring this mission to a close, do you still intend to retire from the army?

Decimus tasted the wine, lowered the glass, and smiled.

Retirement. To be truthful, he had not thought of his impending retirement in quite some time. His advancement to the rank of the Ninth's camp prefect, was usually the reward given to an old professional soldier who had worked himself up through the ranks and was about to leave the service. He was a freshly minted broad-stripped Patrician. A nobleman of some importance within the hierarchical society of Rome. Financially, he was relatively well off. Years of service with one legion or another had partially helped achieve financial stability. But more, the secret missions he accepted and pursued on behalf of Octavius, missions he agreed never to reveal to anyone, greatly enhanced his retirement benefits.

So, yes. Yes, he was going to retire after this mission was completed. He would become a civilian. Free from military or political whims. Free from military commands. Free from the constant campaigning. The constant clash of arms in some far-off godforsaken land. Free from intrigue and assassination. Free from rivalries and political jealousies.

He would be free. He would become his own man.

Gnaeus gave a rude snort, slammed his empty glass of wine onto the table, and glared at his benefactor with a mask of complete disgust as he whipped his hands around in an angry retort.

Bah! You old fool. Neither one of us will last three months idling around doing nothing. We will become like the two old cronies living down the street. Mindless fools with nothing to do but spend money on whoring and drinking. I tell you, both of us will go mad. Stir-crazy, completely bonkers. We will be at each other's throats within a fortnight. You know I'm right. You damn well know I'm right.

With that he turned and, head down and shaking it with disgust, left the tribune alone in the room. Standing in the middle of the library with a look of sheer amazement at the brutal honesty Gnaeus hurled in his direction, Decimus stood speechless. And then, as he lifted his glass of wine to his lips, a broad smile of amusement played across his lips.

Of course, the old soldier was right. He always was.

It was a precisely executed military exercise from the very start. Pairs of guardsmen, disguised as laborers, left the confines of the tribune's house as the evening approached, taking up pre-arranged stations in the alleys and narrow streets leading toward The Street of Dreams. By the time Decimus, Gnaeus, and the young Praetorian optio approached the street two hours before midnight everyone was in place. The trap had been set.

It was child's play for the wily old Gnaeus to take out the young Egyptian lookout stationed in the alley Decimus, and his group chose to approach The Street of Dreams. The young boy of perhaps eighteen or nineteen never heard the smaller, wiry ex-legionnaire's approach from his rear. Nor did he feel, until hours later, the blow to his head Gnaeus imparted on him with the handle of his sword. In the darkness of the alley the dried piece of leather that was Gnaeus struck. There was the sharp crack of a skull meeting a hard object, a soft 'umph' of the young lad's lungs exhaling in surprise, and then the muted sounds of a Gnaeus catching the falling body of the lad and laying him gently onto the alley's stones.

Decimus, Rufus, Hakim and the optio stepped over the slumbering lad lying in the alley without comment and approached the mouth of the alley. Leading the way, the tribune leaned against the wall of one old tenement building and bent forward to peer into the street. To his left, the street ran straight and true down to the Tiber. To his right he saw the small Temple of Sekhmet tucked in between two apartment buildings perhaps a hundred meters away. The street itself followed the incline of a small hill and disappeared over its crest. Both sides of the street were walled-in by various apartment buildings and warehouses.

The tenement building occupied by the Egyptians lay directly opposite of the tribune's position standing in the alley's entrance. It was four floors of cheaply built masonry. From the many open windows were the various urban markers of a building filled with sweating, marginalized immigrants. Flower pots, drying clothes, and people sat in the windows in an effort to catch a cool breeze. The building was noisy. Mothers hollering at their children. The rumble of men's voices arguing. All this in Egyptian. Familiar with the language, Decimus stood in the darkness of the alley and listened for a few minutes. When he had heard enough, he addressed his men.

"There's someone of importance in there. But not the general and his wife. They're calling him, 'The Guest' and, 'The Priest.' It sounds like they are afraid of this person. I don't know what floor he lives on. We need to find out before we enter."

"I can do that," Hakim whispered softly in the darkness. "I know the language and the customs. I can enter the building, knock on the door of the apartment manager, and ask if there are rooms available. I'll mention I'm a follower of Sekhmet and we'll get into a conversation. If he is a true Egyptian he'll want to talk for hours about his family, his life back in Egypt, and about whomever lives in the building. It should be easy."

The tribune readily agreed. Hakim nodded, turned, and disappeared into the darkness of the alley behind them. Ten minutes later all heard the *clop, clop, clop* of a walking stick slapping down onto the stones of the street in front of them. Peering to his right, Decimus saw in the darkness an old man, leaning heavily on a wooden staff, making his way down the street toward the tenement building. It was Hakim. Where he obtained the staff was a minor mystery. Decimus wasn't surprised. The man had a gift in being extremely resourceful. He had proven his resourcefulness over and over in the years he'd served the tribune. It didn't matter where he found a wooden staff this late in the night on some back street in Rome. All that mattered was Hakim was approaching the tenement building, walking and acting like a very old, and very tired, immigrant in search for a place to rest his weary body.

As the tribune observed from his vantage point, he noticed one of the men sitting in the window on the second floor turn his head and watched Hakim moving toward the building. After a few moments the figure left his sitting position and disappeared into the interior of his apartment. Moments later, just as Hakim stepped out of the street and onto the curb directly in front of the steps leading up toward the tenement's entrance, two men stepped out and folded arms across their chests, blocking the entrance in the process.

One of the men bluntly told Hakim to keep moving on. The building was filled with occupants. Hakim, the old man, used one hand, gesturing eloquently as he spoke making his case. He was very ancient. He was tired. He had been sleeping in the streets for the last month. Just that morning he heard of a building filled with the followers of the old goddess living here on this street. Shebet, they said, had come to Rome. Being one of her first followers, hearing news that his priestess still lived, he hoped he could serve her one more time while he still breathed.

The scowling face of one of the men seemed to soften in the torch light which illuminated the tenement's front entrance. He turned and spoke a few words to the other man in a voice too low for the tribune to hear. The other man snapped his head toward his partner and muttered a few words angrily. But, turning to look again at the old man standing on the curb in front of them, his arms unfolded, and he silently jerked his head forward, indicating to the old man to go ahead.

Hakim nodded and, with the difficulty of the ancient, climbed the four steps leading up to the tenement's main door. Following the scowling man, Hakim entered the building, with the younger man following behind. Decimus watched in silence. When Hakim disappeared into the building he spoke softly, telling the three men behind him to make themselves comfortable. They would be waiting for Hakim's return.

Everyone, including the tribune, sat on their haunches and leaned against the building wall, buried in the blackness of the alley. Long years of experience taught each man how to wait in silence. Even the young optio sat in the darkness and waited with stoic ease. It came naturally. A legionnaire's life required one to accept the old adage all armies seemed to live by. The 'hurry up and wait,' command army officers seemed to live by.

The Goddess Fortuna smiled upon them that night. Hakim and the two who escorted him into the building appeared in the doorway. Both of the younger men followed Hakim down the steps and continued following him as the *clop, clop, clop* of the old man leaning on his wooden staff began making his way up the street. Decimus, watching the two men behind Hakim talking quietly among themselves, realized Hakim told the landlord he had to retrieve some personal items he left behind him before he could return. The landlord assigned the two men to go with the old man and help him bring his possessions back with him.

Grunting to himself, the tribune stepped back into the alley and turned to Rufus and the young Praetorian officer. Without saying a word, he motioned the two to retreat in the same direction Hakim had left them earlier. They were to remove the escort from Hakim's side. Silently and without bloodshed. They bled into the darkness and were gone in the blinking of an eye. Ten minutes later the three of them returned to the alley.

"Sir, news. In the building are seventeen families of Egyptians. They occupy the first three floors. But the fourth floor is off limits. No one goes up there unless they are escorted by a priest of Sekhmet. But sir, here is the startling news. Shebet occupies the fourth floor. But she is dead, sir. Dead, mummified, and waiting for transportation back to Egypt. The whole building is in mourning."

"Dead," Decimus echoed, frowning. "And mummified already?"

It took days for priests to properly mummify a person of high rank. If Shebet was dead and mummified, she died long before the attack on Sulla's villa. If so, it raised one alarming question. Who was the figure disguising themselves as the Goddess Menket during the raid? Was there another player in this conspiracy no one was aware of?

"The landlord said the priestess died soon after confronting her daughter and grandson in the forum. She had long been sick. Some kind of wasting disease. Her body is scheduled to be transported to a ship sometime tonight."

"What of the assassin? Any word about him?" Decimus asked, staring at the tenement building directly across from him.

"A very high-ranking priest arrived some days ago. He is to escort Shebet back to Egypt. But he had other orders as well. Orders which had to be completed before he could return home."

"And they were?" the tribune asked, flashing a grim smile in the darkness at Hakim. "Wait a minute, let me guess. His other assignment was to eliminate one, if not two, disbelievers who have been the enemies of Menket for some time."

"Indeed sir." The tall legionnaire nodded. "But the ship is leaving tonight. The high priest must have completed his assignments."

"Perhaps Hakim," the tribune grunted, his voice a soft, hesitant whisper. "Perhaps. How many armed men are in the building now?"

"Very few, from what I could gather. Most of the men were involved in the raid on the general's house last night. They have not returned yet. They're expected back sometime tomorrow."

Gnaeus, who had been standing close to the alley's opening keeping watch on the street as Decimus and Hakim spoke, glanced down the street and then, hurriedly, pulled on the tribune's arm. Gnaeus pointed down the street. Peering around the corner of one of the buildings creating the alley, Decimus saw what had so animated the silent Gnaeus. A large boat, filled with legionnaires, holding burning torches over their heads, was rowing straight toward the wharf. In the middle of the boat, his face illuminated by torch light, stood Caesar's master spy: Caius Lucius.

Men, waiting for the barge which would transport the mummy of Shebet down river and to a waiting ocean-going ship, began running madly up the street, screaming at the top of their lungs that soldiers were coming. Their voices were loud and clear in the still night. Almost immediately women and children began running out of the tenement and disappearing down dark streets and alleys.

"With me!" Decimus snapped loudly, drawing his sword and emerging out of the alley at a dead run.

With the tribune in the lead, the men behind him pounded across the street and pushed their way through the streaming mass of women and children trying to escape before the soldiers arrived. Entering the building, two young men tried to block their way with swords and daggers. They were cut down swiftly. Finding stairs which led to the top floors above, they began fighting and clawing their way up to the top floor. The building was a madhouse as women were screaming, children wailing, and old people fled for their lives. Disregarding the noise and those trying to flee, Decimus and his men pushed on, finally stepping onto the fourth floor, swords in hand, expecting to fight at any moment.

But the tribune and his comrades met an eerie, unnatural silence as they stood at the top of the stairs on the fourth floor. The long hallway was dimly lit. Only a single candle, at the far end of the hall, provided any light. Behind the candle was a large open window. A window filled with darkness. On either side of the hall were doors indicating four apartments. The doors were closed, and no sound could be heard emanating from any of the apartments.

Decimus, his men clustered around him, paused standing at the top of the stairs. Underneath their feet, on the floor below them, they heard men's voices. Roman voices, yelling for those still on the floor to fall to their knees and surrender. Seconds later the sound of sandal clad feet, along with the clanking and ringing of armor accompanying it, pounded up the steps. Four burly looking legionnaires, in full combat gear, joined the tribune's small group and saluted.

And that's when she stepped into view at the other end of the hall.

Menket.

In the splendid white linen robes of an Egyptian priestess. The golden mask of a lioness head sitting on her shoulders turned to the left naturally, as if it was not a mask at all, but a genuine lioness, smiling toward the gathered Romans. In her right hand was an Egyptian Khepesh, a distinctly unique curved sword of very ancient design. But this one was made of steel, its blue blade reflecting candlelight, and very long for a typical weapon. The goddess turned and faced the gathered Romans, the lips on the lioness' face widening as if offering a silent invitation to her enemies.

The four legionnaires accepted the challenge.

With a roar they charged toward the goddess, two at a time, their shields coming up in unison. Fully armed, shields in one hand, swords in the other, each man felt confident of his abilities to cut down the lone enemy in front of them.

"Stop! Decimus screamed, stepping forward and reaching for the soldier nearest to him.

Too late.

The goddess struck. Struck with amazing swiftness. She allowed the four soldiers to reach halfway down the hall before she moved. But she moved with unbelievable swiftness. She took two long, powerful strides and leapt into the air. Her entire body turned in midair as she walked two more steps across the right-hand side of the corridor wall before landing directly into the middle of the four legionnaires. The tight formation of Roman soldiery stood no chance. One of the leading soldiers tripped and fell on his shield. As he started to fall to the floor the curved blade of the Khepesh flashed from right to left. The man's head, cut clean from his shoulders, sailed over the cluttered mass of humanity and rolled to a stop in front of the tribune's feet.

The remaining three lasted another four seconds. Blood, violently hurled through the air, splattered the walls of the hallway and flowed in deep pools across the floor. Four legionnaires, cut to pieces from a curved blade which moved with amazing speed, dropped to the floor, leaving only the bloody form of the Egyptian goddess standing upright in the middle of the dead.

The terrifying image of a bloody lioness smiled at the tribune and his men just before she turned her back toward them and strolled leisurely down the hall, kicking the small table and burning candle to one side. Leaping onto the sill of the open window she turned and stared at the tribune as her voice drifted down the long hall.

"We will meet again, very soon, my love. And when we do, I shall embrace you and you will become my adoring servant. My adoring servant for all of eternity."

As if frozen to the floor, Decimus and his men watched as the goddess tossed the bloody sword onto the floor. Spreading her arms slightly toward the tribune, she smiled and fell backward into the night, disappearing altogether from view.

Men came pounding up the stairs behind the tribune. A dozen legionnaires with the master spy in the lead. They came to a halt, shouldering past the oddly idle tribune and his men and stared at the bloody carnage which littered the hallway in front of them all.

"Mars' wrath! What in Hades happened here?" Caesar's spy hissed, staring incredulously at the blood-soaked walls and hallway before turning to glare at Decimus.

But the anger in the spy's eyes changed the moment he looked at the tribune. Decimus was standing motionless. All of his men were motionless. None could speak. None could move a muscle. Only their eyes could move. Like living statues all five men stood in the hall, surrounded by the spy and his soldiers, and remained absolutely still. Alarm filled the spy's face as he witnessed the tribune's immobility. Lifting a hand, he gripped Decimus' shoulder in concern. The moment he gripped the tribune's shoulder, he watched the eyes in Decimus' skull roll up in their sockets and disappear just before collapsing to the floor.

Vaguely, Decimus remembered falling. He remembered

several pairs of hands grabbing him and lifting him up into the air. He thought he heard a man screaming. After that came the dreams. The nightmares.

Of lionesses hunting in the night-filled desert. Of a bloody Egyptian Khepesh flashing into view, covered in blood and brain matter, rising and falling in an unending montage of murderous lust.

XXII

7AD
Rome
Lying in bed

Slowly, in rolling waves of pain and an intense thirst, consciousness returned to the tribune. At first awareness of feeling immensely thirsty, Decimus realized he was awake and forced his eyelids to open. His vision was blurry. His throat felt like dry sand. His tongue felt like someone had stuffed a wooden spike into his mouth. But, blinking eyes to clear his vision, he became aware of the fact he was lying in bed and the blurry image of a face hovering over him was that of a physician: Aulus Nervanus.

"Ha. You have decided to return to the land of the living!" the balding doctor beamed, a wide smile on his lips as he sat down on the reclining couch beside his patient and reached for the tribune's wrist to check his pulse. "I'm sure the god Hades will be most displeased to hear of your return."

"My, my men?"

"Some are awake and recuperating. The others are still balancing on the line between the living and the dead. Only time will tell. I must say, tribune, for a while I thought you might not return to us. Your brush with death was far too close to my liking. Far too close!"

"What happened?" Decimus whispered hoarsely, a hand coming up to lay across his pounding forehead. "And is there any water?"

"Here. Drink this," a second voice spoke up. A voice he recognized.

Caius Lucius.

The physician lifted Decimus' head up slightly, holding the small bowl of water in his other hand to the tribune's lips. The cold water sliding down his throat was deliciously invigorating. His vision began to clear. The pounding headache between his temples seemed to lessen in intensity. Pushing the doctor's hand away from him gently, he took a deep breath and twisted his head around to see his immediate surroundings. To his surprise, he found himself lying on a couch in his own bedroom.

"What happened to my men and me? How long have I been unconscious?"

"I am not sure, tribune. But what I think happened to you is called *The Curse of Menket*," Aulus Nervanus began, standing up and turning to look down at Decimus. "I heard about this when I served with the general in Egypt years ago. You were poisoned, Decimus Virilis. Some Egyptian alchemist long ago discovered how to take the poison from a rare desert scorpion and turn it into a fine powder. Throw the powder into a victim's face or prepare it in some fashion where the powder is inhaled, and one of two results will happen. Either the intended victim will die of asphyxiation, or, in a non-lethal dosage, it temporarily paralyzes the victim for several hours."

"Menket paralyzed us?" Decimus echoed, turning his head to the master spy. "Why paralyze us when she could have just as easily killed us all?"

The spy glanced at the doctor and then back to the tribune and shrugged

"I cannot answer that, Decimus. Perhaps she was going to kill you in the end. But I and my men arrived just in time to thwart her plans. As it is, after she leapt out of the window and made her escape, she killed several more legionnaires before she disappeared into the darkness."

Decimus closed his eyes and sank deeper into the pillow. He felt better. But tired. Incredibly tired. Yet pressing matters convinced him he would not rest. Caesar's spy was in his house. He knew the man was not here in concern for his health. The man was filled with news.

"What else, Caius? Why do you hover near me like some summer's fog unwilling to drift away?"

"Uh," the spy began, pausing and clearing his throat. "We, uh, we think we have found the body of the priestess. Her face badly deformed. Quite dead. Mummified. The doctor identified her. Apparently, she has been dead for several weeks."

Decimus, eyes still closed, nodded silently.

"And we found another body as well. A man's body. Stuffed in a wooden sarcophagus in the building's basement. Died from an arrow wound inflicted on him a few days ago."

Decimus frowned and opened his eyes.

"Have you identified him?"

"I suspect it is the assassin who attacked you a few days ago. But I can't be sure. None of the building's inhabitants would say a word about this man. Too afraid to talk. It didn't matter how much we tortured them. No one would say a word. All they would say was something about *the dead shall rise and the wicked will suffer eternal damnation.* Whatever the Hades that means."

Caius Lucius frowned, shaking his head in frustration. He walked across the room to pour himself a goblet of wine. He did not see the doctor's reaction when he chanted the classic curse the followers of Menket believed as gospel. But Decimus observed the doctor's reaction. Saw the color drain from the man's face. Saw the doctor's eyes widen in fear and surprise as he stared in disbelief at Caesar's spy before glancing at Decimus.

"Doctor," Decimus began, almost smiling. "You have something to say?"

The doctor was as white as a Roman senator's freshly cleaned toga. Fear clearly resided in the man's eyes. He tried to speak, found it difficult, cleared his throat and hurriedly glanced at the spy from Rome before turning back toward the tribune.

"While serving with the general in Egypt I saw many strange things. Witnessed many odd incidents. Inexplicable incidents. Impossible incidents. One of them was examining the body of a prisoner who had, unfortunately, been beaten to death by a centurion. Relatives came to collect the body. One mentioned to me the body was going to be mummified. Curious about the procedure, from a clinical standpoint, I asked if I could observe the procedure. To my surprise the Egyptian agreed to my request. A priest from the cult of Menket."

Caius Lucius, a sarcastic grin on his face and a glass of wine in his hand, faced the doctor. Although remaining silent, it was clear he was amused by the doctor's rambling tale.

"Well, to make a long story short, in the middle of the ceremony, after many magical chants purifying the body and introducing it to their spirit world, one of the priests uttered that very phrase. *The dead shall rise and the wicked shall suffer eternal damnation."*

"And you believed that believe this wild tale," the Roman spy retorted dryly.

"I thought it amusing at first," Aulus Nervanus answered, his face filled with fear. "But a week later the centurion who beat the prisoner to death in his cell was found murdered in his barracks room. His tongue had been cut out. His eyeballs removed. A sword protruding from his chest."

"Bah!" the spy spit out, shaking his head disgustedly. "One of the man's relatives killed the centurion. That's all."

Aulus Nervanus shook his head in disagreement.

"I was there, sir. I was called to identify the culprit. They caught the killer as he was about to leave the legion's fort. It was the same man. The one the centurion killed. The one whom I watched being mummified the week earlier. But sir, it ... it becomes even more strange."

"Bah! Impossible, dammit. Simply impossible!" Caius Lucius hissed angrily, lifting the glass of wine to his lips and showing his back to the doctor.

"Continue with your story, Aulus," Decimus put in quietly.

"I examined the prisoner. I saw the bruises all over the man's body where the centurion had beat him. They were dark and deep in the flesh. But healing. I tried to ask him questions. Tried to get him to talk to me. He didn't say a word. Just remained as silent as a stone.

"Later that night, asleep in my quarters, I was dragged out of my bed by soldiers and told to report to the prison immediately. The prisoner was gone, tribune. He had, somehow, disappeared."

"What do you mean, disappeared?" the spy shot back, turning to glare at the doctor.

"Just disappeared! In the middle of the cell floor were his

clothes. The clothes he wore when he entered the fort and murdered the centurion. And before you ask, either of you, let me say it. He could not have escaped. Two guards were assigned to watch the prisoner twenty-four hours of the day. They chained the prisoner to the cell wall and both soldiers stood in the cell with him and observed the prisoner."

"What did they say occurred in the cell?" Decimus asked.

"Both were dead. From unnatural causes," Aulus Nervanus answered. "From the expressions on their faces, I'd say they died from sheer fright. Whatever happened in that cell literally scared them to death."

Both the spy and the tribune eyed the doctor for some seconds in silence. Caius was filled with anger mixed with doubt. Decimus' face was an unreadable mask. He neither believed nor disbelieved. Belief or disbelief was held in suspension until all available facts had been gathered and reviewed.

In the end, it was Decimus who broke the silence.

"What you are suggesting, Aulus, is that I should expect a future confrontation with our dead friend. Fear not. I have anticipated such an event to occur."

"Wonderful," growled Caius Lucius, shaking his head in disbelief. "Just wonderful. The old hag for a priestess is dead. Her assassin servant may, or may not, be dead. Depending on which story you believe. Sulla is still missing, along with his wife. And oh, I forgot to tell you, Decimus. The Senate is in an uproar over the attack and abduction of one of their most illustrious members. They are demanding to know what in Hades are we doing in finding the general and returning him back to Rome.

"As if I don't have enough troubles on my plate, Caesar Augustus is still enroute to Gaul and will not return to Rome relatively soon. Tiberius Caesar is off in Dalmatia chasing rebels, and the Senate is breathing fire and brimstone down my neck demanding answers. But the *biggest* question I have to answer is the obvious one. If the priestess is dead, and if her assassin is dead, and have been dead for several days now, who in Hades is the person disguising themselves as a goddess of war and is the mastermind behind this catastrophe?"

The tribune smiled with a wiry smirk on his lips and nodded. The entire case summed up succinctly. Who was the mastermind behind all this chaos? For indeed, it was chaos wherever one looked. A magnificently manipulated but *planned* chaos designed to obfuscate and demoralize all of Rome in its dark machinations. A well thought out series of disasters thrust upon the mighty reputation of Roman invincibility only a sick mind of genius rating could devise.

In the beginning he assumed Shebet, the mother of Hatshepsut, was the master plotter—her hatred for Rome well known. Her devious assassinations and terrorist acts in Egypt equally well known. Undoubtedly intelligent enough to conceive and plan in detail such a devilish scheme while exiled in the deep desert years ago, she had the time and possibly the money, to recruit the dozens, if not hundreds of followers who would submit themselves to her every whim.

Perhaps she was the creator of the chaos. The visionary who believed a revolt against Roman rule in Egypt would be successful if enough chaos and terror was created elsewhere. And what greater havoc could there be but to threaten Rome? The beating heart of the empire itself. Perhaps a rebel invasion? Perhaps capturing the fears and terrors of the Roman people by destroying an entire Roman legion so near to the Roman capitol?

Interesting, Decimus thought to himself, the wiry smirk for a smile flashing across his thin lips again. *The lucky break of a provincial revolt happening just as Shebet's plan to destroy a Roman legion, kill Gaius Cornelius Sulla, and possibly abduct her daughter and return her to Egypt, all happening at the same time.* Was there some connection, perhaps a link, where Shebet secretly fanned the simmering hot coals of revolt always glowing in the hearts of the various Dalmatian tribes, and converted the simmering hatred into a full-fledged raging inferno?

If so, and if it could be proven, it would make this old Egyptian woman one of the greatest enemies Rome ever faced.

But it appeared as if Shebet was dead. She came to Rome and confronted her daughter and grandson knowing she had but a few days left of life in her. With her death, *if* she was the mastermind behind this grand plot, and *if* the second phase of her plot was about to commence with the destruction of the Ninth, her premature death should have, like a house of cards, collapsed into nothingness immediately. It had not.

Decimus grunted, pulling on the lobe of an ear thoughtfully. There was only one obvious conclusion. She had an accomplice. She knew she was dying and planned for just such an eventuality. But more importantly, *her accomplice was every bit as devoted, and as ruthless, and as intelligent, as the master planner herself.*

"Decimus," the spy's harsh voice growled menacingly. "I see that look on your face. What evil little thoughts are running through your head? Don't be coy with us now. Far too late, with our circumstances too grim, for you to be reticent now. Speak up and tell us what you are thinking."

"I am thinking," Decimus began, wincing in pain as he struggled to pull himself off the sleeping couch he was laying on. "That I must return to Asa as fast as possible. Our adversary is about to spring their next big move on us. I suspect it will involve Asa somehow."

"But what about our search for Sulla and his wife?" Caius Lucius grunted, coming over and assisting the doctor in pulling the tribune off the couch. "We've just started the manhunt. It will take days to complete it. You need to be here. We need to be here, in Rome, keeping the Senate from melting away into rabble and turning the city into a madhouse."

"No, no, no. You won't find Sulla and Hatshepsut in or around Rome," Decimus said, leaning on both men weakly and shaking his head. "Nor will they be found anywhere in Italy. They're gone. The attack, the destruction of the general's villa, the abduction of both, even their escape, were planned to the last detail long ago. Sulla and Hatshepsut are nowhere near by. With luck, and if we hurry, we might find them close to Asa with the rebels. Our adversary is moving fast. We must intercept them before they go too far."

"You are in no condition to travel," Aulus Nervanus blurted out moving the tribune, with the spy's help, over to the nearest chair and setting him down. "We have no idea who this adversary is. How can you intercept them if you do not know who they are?"

"Ah, but I have my suspicions, good doctor," Decimus said, smiling and shaking his head slightly. "And if they are correct, we must be in Asa to capture them."

"We?" Nervanus echoed, lifting an eyebrow. "Surely you do not mean I am going with you? I have patients here in Rome I must attend to!"

"You have a very large practice, with numerous skilled physicians on your staff," Caius Lucius said, dismissing the doctor's words with a wave of his hand. "And the tribune here will need an expert physician by his side for the next few days. So yes, Aulus Nervanus. You're going to Asa."

The physician saw it in the eyes of both men. There would be no room for argument with either. He was going to travel with the tribune to the small Dalmatian port city of Asa. A sigh of resignation escaped his lips. He asked for permission to return to his house and do some packing and to inform his staff of this sudden development. Both tribune and spy nodded in agreement. When the little doctor left them alone in the room, Caius Lucius poured a glass of wine and handed it to Decimus, then sat down in a chair beside the weak tribune.

"Caius, I have a few questions, and a couple of favors, to ask from you. But this is only between us. Only us. If I am wrong in my theories, better to keep it between two professionals like us rather than involving a large number of people."

"Ah. Limiting the damage, in other words." Caius Lucius smiled wickedly. "If you are wrong, that is."

Decimus Julius Virilis nodded, smiled, and lifted the glass of wine to his lips.

Yes indeed, old friend. If I am wrong.

XXIII

7 AD
Dalmatia
A dark, wet night

Angry, dark gray clouds hung low over the huddled rooftops of Asa as the sharp prow of the Roman trireme slid into the confining waters of the harbor. Here and there in the half-moon shaped protected waters, riding the rough waves on strong anchor chains, were a half dozen large transports. But no traffic between the ships and wharves moved across the gray water. In fact, standing on the stern of the deadly warrior of the seas, wrapped in the heavy bright red wool cloak, trimmed in patrician purple of an infantry officer, Decimus saw nothing moving on land or sea of the city's populace. It was as if sailor and landlubber all could feel the approaching storm. A brisk, cold wind was churning the harbor's surface into a rolling washboard of mini-white caps. Sharp, ice-cold rain squalls, off and on, kept rolling in from the sea, making life miserable for man and beast.

Asa looked almost deserted. Its glistening cobblestone streets were empty. The sturdy but small stone buildings and homes clinging desperately on the rocks surrounding the harbor looked despondent and abandoned. Cold and wet to the bone, nevertheless, Decimus stood on the trireme's stern and surveyed the harbor and town. As the *Mars Supreme* slid past the first of the large transports, his eyes saw at last, signs of human occupation. On the long military wharf, a large puddle of torch light glowed in the gathering dusk. Illuminated in this puddle of light were Roman soldiers. Soldiers of the Ninth waiting in the biting cold and wind for him.

Forty minutes later, stout hands reached down and pulled first Decimus, and then Gnaeus, out of the bobbing captain's longboat and hauled them onto the heavy wooden planks of the wharf. In the eyes of the men surrounding him, the tribune saw expressions of genuine relief and deep concern, looking back at him.

"Welcome back, sir!" both centurions chimed in at the same time. Behind the two, the eight-man squad of Roman legionnaires looked as relieved as their officers were with the tribune back among them.

His centurions looked haggard. Too many nights with little or no sleep. It could mean only one thing. A crisis was looming. An imminent and dangerous crisis.

"Report, Cletus. Any news of our inquiries?"

"Much to talk about, praefectus. But let us get you out of this foul weather and off these miserable streets."

In silence the group of Roman soldiers made their way up the rain-slick cobblestone streets. No one spoke. But the centurions and their eight-man escort seemed on edge. Heads kept swiveling around to closely inspect side streets and alleys as they moved up the steep hill toward the legion's headquarters. Another rain squall, fierce and cold, began slanting down from the dark skies with a vengeance. They marched in step past a dozen or more homes and businesses without seeing one light gleaming from within. Again, the impression of a deserted town crossed the tribune's mind. A city under siege.

The group passed through a heavily guarded outer perimeter, the rain soaked legionnaires on duty saluting smartly as they saw their tribune back amongst them. Entering the large warehouse the legion was using as its headquarters, everyone shed wet capes and grabbed towels to wipe faces, arms, and hands dry, before the two centurions led Decimus and Gnaeus into a different room.

"Report."

Simon, the silent one, turned and said the obvious.

"We're cut off from contact with the legions up north. The enemy has severed the road, isolating Asa from the rest of the country."

"They have also cut off most of our food supply as well," Cletus followed up, walking over to a large table which had a map of the surrounding countryside opened and illuminated with burning candles. "Farmers have refused to enter the port and sell their goods. Only a few fishermen go out to sea now. We're almost to the point of going to half rations."

Decimus stepped up to the map table and gazed down at the detailed rendering of the surrounding country. The coastline was rugged and dangerous. The hills surrounding the port up close and quite steep. Two roads led to Asa. One, the one he was familiar with, turned in a sharp curve toward the northeast and led off into the interior. Only two weeks earlier the Ninth had almost been annihilated on the road. He frowned. Just two weeks had passed since that fateful day. It seemed as if an eternity had passed.

The second road drifted out of the single gate in the city's outer wall and cut through a pass in the steep hills and meandered down a valley toward the southeast. And a river. The river was the Narenta. The town was Narona. Known enemy territory. The rebel's southern forces were somewhere off to the southeast. How large, no one knew.

He bent over the table and, with one long pointing finger, tapped the map three times and looked at his centurions.

"How far is this village from here?"

The two centurions looked at the map at the same time, with Cletus answering the tribune's question.

"Approximately fourteen kilometers, sir. Eight kilometers behind enemy territory. I'm told it's a small village in the hills noted for its apple orchards and iron mines."

"It is the only village on this road for a number of kilometers," Decimus grunted thoughtfully, rubbing his jaw. "If you had a force surrounding an enemy, where would you build a supply depot to feed and clothe your men?"

Both centurions glanced at each other and then back at Decimus. Gnaeus, the silent one, to one side and just behind the tribune, pulled his lips back in a knowing grin. The tribune was contemplating some audacious move. He knew the tribune better than any man in this room. In a tight situation, faced by superior numbers, Decimus Julius Virilis was not one to stand and wait for the inevitable. Not if he had time to study the situation and formulate a counterplan.

"What forces remain in here in the port?"

"We have the second, third, and fourth cohorts from the Ninth," Cletus answered. "Tiberius has decided to break up the Ninth and use most of the men as replacements for his legions up north."

"We do have two centuries of auxiliary units. Syrian bowmen. They arrived three days ago," Simon put in quietly. "And sometime this week transports are supposed to arrive with a contingent of Spanish cavalry."

About twenty-five hundred men, if the gods smiled upon them, would be available in the next few days. If the weather cleared up to allow the transports to enter the port. If the Spanish were truly coming and had not been diverted elsewhere. Looking up at his two centurions, Decimus smiled. A smile all too familiar to the two. A smile that made them instantly nervous.

"We will wait for the cavalry to arrive before we do anything," he said, standing up from the table and folding arms across his chest. "Now tell me what you have learned about our other matter?"

"We found a survivor of the first cohort who had been assigned to the main gate the night the explosion happened. A Gaul by the name of Renaud. Badly burned, but coherent. He has an interesting story to tell you, sir. We thought you would want to hear his story personally. He's upstairs in the infirmary resting. As soon as we can we're shipping him back to Brundisium, along with about two hundred of the other wounded, to better facilities."

"And we have a prisoner," Simon piped up. He lowered his voice. "A rebel who claims he was one of the men who were forced to prepare the hole and set the canisters of Greek Fire in place. He says he saw the Greek who supervised the project. He awaits in chains in the holding cells downstairs for further questioning."

"You believe this prisoner? Was he actually one of the diggers?" the tribune queried.

Cletus and Simon eyed each other, both silently asking the other if they believed the rebel's story. Both nodded at the same time and looked back at the tribune.

"His name was given to us by a reliable informer, sir," Simon chirped, with Cletus nodding silently. "We found him in an old farmhouse up in the hills a few miles from here. He resisted. But a couple of hours of Marcellus' handiwork convinced him perhaps there might be a less painful way to die."

Marcellus was a legionnaire belonging to the third cohort, fourth century. *The Hounds,* as they liked to call themselves. Marcellus was an average soldier at best. But he did have a talent. He could extract information from a prisoner. And somehow tell the difference between a truth and a lie in the process.

"Very well," Decimus said, frowning. "Tonight, I want the sentries doubled along the walls. And I want a guard on our prisoner. Much has happened since Gnaeus, and I left for Rome. Suffice to say the threats we face here in the city have increased considerably. I'll brief the two of you tomorrow at sunrise and then we'll interview the prisoner. Rotate the duty roster often. Keep them fresh and vigilant. I suspect military action is imminent. We must be ready."

Cletus and Simon saluted and left the tribune and Gnaeus standing beside the map table. The smaller, older Gnaeus looked into Decimus' face. His hands moved quickly.

You think this assassin will attempt to kill you tonight?

"Yes," Decimus answered, not looking at the older legionnaire. "Either me or our prisoner downstairs. This game we play is rapidly coming to an end. It cannot go on much longer."

Should we take more precautions? Assign a protective detail to guard your bedroom for tonight?

Decimus shook his head *no.*

"We will try to draw them out into the open. If we can capture our apparently risen from the dead assassin alive, perhaps we can extract from him some valuable information."

Offering yourself as bait? Tribune, I don't like this. It reminds me too much of Alexandria.

Alexandria.

Decimus peered speculatively at his old comrade. He remembered the incident quite well. Ten years earlier, as a centurion in route from Spain to Jerusalem, he and Gnaeus stopped over in Alexandria. While there, someone tried to assassinate a powerful provincial official. The assassination failed, but the intended victim, an old friend of the tribune's, asked him to find the assassin and bring him to justice.

A two-day layover in Alexandria turned into a week's worth of intense field work in tracking down the assassin. They were successful. Almost. The killer, a follower of the Egyptian god Amon, the God of the Underworld, attempted to kill the tribune. He failed, dying in the process, not realizing the tribune had set a trap for him. The remaining gang of assassins were tracked down and killed. Those who assisted the assassins were rounded up and imprisoned. Egyptian and Roman officials congratulated Decimus and Gnaeus on a job well done. A few parties, an official banquet in their honor, and bright and early one Egyptian morning the two of them boarded a ship and slipped out of the Alexandrian harbor. The harbor was heavy with traffic, both large and small, from all over the Mediterranean. But as they passed one large Egyptian dhow, standing on the port side up against the ship's railing, was a man, a hand over his head, waving farewell.

An Egyptian. Looking directly at the tribune with a cunning, foxlike smile on his face.

Without a doubt the same Egyptian who died a few days earlier.

Decimus smiled and shook his head.

"I don't believe the dead rise from the grave and return to the living, Gnaeus. The person we saw on that ship as we left Alexandria was not the assassin we tracked down."

Are you sure? It was apparent he knew you. I don't mind admitting it. That smile on his face as he waved at us, gave me the willies. But now we face another assassin risen from the dead. A coincidence, you think? Or perhaps something more sinister.

Decimus shrugged but made no answer.

A junior staff officer entered the room, saluted, and offered to escort the tribune to his personal quarters. Outside the rain squall evolved into a full-fledged thunderstorm with crashing thunder and howling winds.

A good night for a murder, Decimus thought to himself, as he followed the young staff officer to his quarters.

XXIV

7 AD
Dalmatia
The dead come calling

The storm continued building its fury long after retiring. Rolling thunder, deep enough to rattle the rafters of the old warehouse being used as a headquarters, continuously shook the night. Rain, driven by gale-force winds, ripped across the roof and splattered against the building's brick walls with a fierce insanity.

Shifting his position in the chair slightly, one eye half open, the tribune tried to find a comfortable spot. But the hours of sitting motionlessly in the chair, awake and aware, were taking its toll on him. Wrapped in deep shadow in one far corner of the room, unseen and motionless, he sat and waited for the assassin to strike. He was sure the Egyptian would. Twice the Goddess Menket sent agents out to kill him in one fashion or another. Twice he somehow parried the death blow. Twice Decimus subtly altered the meticulously detailed plans of this long-cherished conspiracy. Not necessarily changing the end results yet. But posing a very real possibility that the whole affair could begin unraveling like a threadbare Persian carpet if he was allowed to live much longer.

So, in the darkness, sitting in a chair in the corner facing his bed and the dimly lit image of what seemed to be a sleeping form underneath the bed's sheets, he was confident Menket would send her assassin out a third time to complete his mission. This time he was determined to capture this apparently immortal creature alive and tear from his lips what he wanted to know.

Who now led this conspiracy? Was the new leader of this conspiracy the same person who wore the mask of Menket? Where did such a creature learn to fight like a true goddess with amazing agility and blinding speed? What, ultimately, did this creature expect to accomplish after her plans were fully put in place? Was Gaius Cornelius Sulla and his wife Hatshepsut dead or alive? But the most intriguing question of all the tribune was asking himself was a bit more arcane.

Assuming Shebet was the one who originally came up with this decades-long plan for revenge, and assuming this entire conspiracy was aimed at destroying the House of Sulla, what insult or mortal blow did the general inflict upon the Egyptian priestess to warrant such hatred?

A revolt in Upper Egypt, a revolt led by Shebet against the Romans, never impressed Decimus. In that part of the world there were always revolts and rumors of revolts circulating among the desert tribes. A reason why Rome grasped tightly the reins of Egyptian politics and daily life with its military presence. Egypt was considered the wealthiest of all of Rome's conquests. So wealthy the province did not belong to Rome but to Caesar personally. It was Julius Caesar who originally took Egypt from the last Queen of Egypt, Cleopatra. It was

Octavius Caesar, the current ruler of the empire, who ripped it from the dead hands of a rebellious Markus Antonius and his scheming seductress, Cleopatra. The same Cleopatra who originally seduced the first Caesar.

No.

An audacious plan by a minor priestess who devoted herself to a minor Egyptian goddess to ferment rebellion and challenge Roman suzerainty over Egypt did not sound in the least bit compelling to Decimus. But what did seem more palatable in comprehending all this death and destruction was the belief that it had to be something personal. Deeply personal. Shebet had been personally mortified. Insulted. Possibly ridiculed in public by an arrogant Roman general. Perhaps rejected by a lover. Or tortured by a Roman while proclaiming her innocence. There were any number of possibilities. But in his mind, there were no doubts. No reservations. Whatever the cause for this undying hatred, it had to have involved, so many years earlier, both Sulla and the dead priestess.

The old saying was true, *Hades hath no wrath like that of a jilted lover.*

He almost smiled as that thought drifted across his consciousness. But he froze, moving not one muscle, even his breathing, before his lips moved. A sound, *droplets of water crashing onto the stone floor of the bedroom,* falling from out of the dark rafters above, sounded to him like a thousand men screaming their battle hymns just before lunging at the enemy. One, two, three droplets hit the stone floor with an audible clarity impossible to dismiss. Screaming in their death plunge as they dropped from out of the unknown.

He held his breath. Dared not move. Not even moving his eyes to peer upward for fear of alerting the hidden figure above. The assassin had arrived. The ghost-like creature found a way into the warehouse from above. Unseen and in complete silence. Only three droplets of rain water sliding off his clothing and disappearing into the gloom suggested his deadly presence.

Situated in a corner of the bedroom, facing the made-up form of a figure covered in the sheets of his bed, the tribune paused even his breathing, thinking it would be enough to alert the assassin something was amiss. Seconds ticked by. No other sound, other than the violent storm outside, came to him. The seconds turned into a full minute. Clenching his teeth, his body forced him to finally to exhale silently through his nose before inhaling a breath of air. As he did, a massive bolt of lightning hit something near the warehouse sending a shaft of white light searing across the bedroom floor. A narrow shaft of light, vivid in its brightness, solely illuminated his bed. That brief flash was enough to see the dark form of the assassin approaching the bed, dagger in hand. He lifted the curved blade in preparation to kill his intended victim.

"Now!" Decimus yelled, leaping out of the shadows, gladius in hand. He still stood some distance away from the hooded Egyptian.

Two Roman soldiers, plus Gnaeus, emerged out of the darkness. But instead of gripping sharp-edged weapons, each held the heavy net, the *reta*, used by the *retiarii*, the trident and net warriors of Rome's gladiatorial games. As if moved by one hand, each man stepped forward and expertly threw their nets toward the cloaked form in front of them. The assassin, unable to escape quickly because of the sword bearing Decimus, sidestepped one of the nets easily enough and tried to block the second net descending out of the darkness. Unfamiliar with this form of fighting, he did not know he had made a grave mistake. The heavy net, weighted down by lead weights, entangled itself around the assassin's hand gripping his dagger. As it did, the third reta, now fully open like the many arms of an octopus, enveloped him completely from head to toe.

The two legionnaires plus Gnaeus leapt onto the struggling figure and drove him hard onto the stone floor of the warehouse. In moments the assassin was stripped of his weapons and bound, hands and feet, tightly by short ropes. Stepping close to the now motionless creature, Decimus, still gripping the traditional short sword of a legionnaire, stared down at the man who had tried to kill him weeks before.

"Remove the hood hiding his face."

Gnaeus reached up and jerked the heavy cloth hood down. Staring back at the four Romans were the dark eyes of a desert tribesman. The creature, neither angry nor resigned on his capture, had on his visage an unreadable mask. With a steady gaze he looked up at the tribune and remained silent. As Decimus had anticipated.

"Awake the doctor," he said, turning and sheathing his sword at the same time. "Have him examine the man thoroughly. Body cavities and all. I want to make sure there is nothing hidden on, or in, the man's body which might offer him an escape. He must be alive and healthy so Marcellus can work on him unhindered in the morning."

He watched the men lift the motionless assassin off the floor and carry him out of his bedroom. For several seconds Decimus stared at the door the men closed behind them leaving the room. Thoughts, hundreds of them—jumbled and mostly too hazy to call true thoughts—raced through his mind like a sudden gust of wind. Emotions, strong ones, swept through him as well. He felt an uneasy hesitation rolling around in his consciousness. Mixed with heavy doses of anger and regret. But no fear. No doubts. His gut, his *emotions*, were telling him this nightmare was rapidly coming to a close. But there were questions, so many questions, yet to be answered.

Grunting to himself, he turned and tossed the sheathed gladius onto the bed. Pulling the hastily constructed dummy from out of the bed sheets he tossed it to one side. And then, fully clothed, dressed in the light armor of a tribune, he laid down, rolled onto his right side, and fell asleep.

Tomorrow would be another day. Another opportunity to find the answers plaguing his tired mind.

XXV

7 AD
Dalmatia
An uneasy feeling

Sunrise.
Not a cloud in the sky. The sun, just a glowing pink promise in the east, filled the air with enough light to see clearly.

A soft warm breeze greeted him as he stepped out onto the roof of the warehouse and walked to the edge of the building. Facing west, looking in the direction his men were pointing to, he nodded. Far away, just on the horizon, he saw the unmistakable dots of a line of ships. He counted ten black dots strung out along the horizon and knew immediately what they represented.

The arrival of an entire wing of Spanish cavalry. One thousand men and horses. Combat veterans arriving to put down the rebellious Dalmatians. Glancing at the view again, his eyes drifted down and looked at the huddle of buildings which made up the small port city of Asa.

He knew the port's history. Six hundred years earlier a small clan of Latins immigrated from Etruscan domination on the mainland and settled onto these rocky cliffs overlooking a very small harbor. Escaping from the constant strife over the harsh Etruscan effort to dominate and rule over an ever-growing combative Roman desire to expand, their intentions of starting a new life free from constant bloodshed. Before Rome became Rome, before the might of Roman armies finally defeated her enemies on the mainland, the Etruscans ruled that part of central and northern Italia which included the very small village of Rome.

The Etruscans were a strange but wondrous civilization who had, somehow, immigrated to central and northern Italia from afar. Related to none of the Latin clans around them, they were nevertheless very sophisticated and knowledgeable. They were the first to build cities. The first to have a written language. The first to work with iron. For generations they dominated the land, building cities and sharing their knowledge. One of the many semi-barbaric villages they held control over was one situated on seven hills overlooking a river called the Tiber.

These villagers called themselves Romans. From the very beginning they were a belligerent, combative group of people who were inordinately proud of themselves and their accomplishments. It came as a surprise to no one when this small village called Rome began to grow and expand. Warfare, it seemed, was an integral part of their soul. As was envy. Envious for anything and anyone who claimed to have more, or be superior, to a Roman.

It was very clear to anyone who opened their eyes and peered into the future that these Romans were eventually going to destroy the Etruscan empire and dominate all the Latin clans which surrounded them. Best to leave their homes and find someplace new. Someplace where life might be more peaceful. Someplace far away from Rome.

But that was six hundred years ago. Fate had been cruel to the small group of Latin refugees who settled onto these rugged cliffs and named the small village Asa.

Asa. Meaning *home*. Or *sanctuary*. Or s*helter*. Or *refuge*.

It was a place of refuge the small group of Latin immigrants looked for and were hoping they found here. They settled. They built their small town. They intermarried with the local indigents who, like them, had fled from some other endless war in some homeland far away. And faded from the pages of history as time marched endlessly onward.

Now, in the current timeframe, Asa was a small port who neither hated nor loved Roman occupation. Being a fishing port and a commercial trading post combined, they were familiar with Romans and tolerated them. With the latest scuffle Rome found themselves in with the inland Dalmatian tribes, they knew what their fate would be. Rome would come and occupy them. They would claim the port and use it as a launching site to feed its armies into the hinterland and toward the war. They did not resist. Nor actively assist in Rome's efforts to reconquer a rebellious province.

Decimus grunted quietly, feeling a small flicker of regret for those Latin ancestors now forgotten, and faced one of the soldiers standing behind him.

"Give the centurions Simon and Cletus my compliments and ask them to join me here on the rooftop."

The soldier hurried past the darkly tanned, balding Gnaeus who had stepped onto the roof and was approaching the tribune. His old friend Decimus waited for the silent one to speak.

Our wounded soldier is awake and ready to give his testimony. But I am afraid he is not of this world for much longer. His burns are quite extensive and he's unable to keep food down.

"And the Dalmatian prisoner?"

Alive, and also waiting for your arrival. He's very willing to tell you anything he knows about what he did and saw weeks ago. He has no desire to come under Marcellus' care anymore.

Decimus waited. He saw it in Gnaeus' clear eyes. Something else had to be said.

I worry about our assassin, tribune. He sits on his haunches, leaning against the back wall of his cell. He does not eat. He does not drink. He does not move. Aulus Nervanus examined him very thoroughly last night, per our orders. I observed the examination. Quite thorough, I might add. The man was stripped of his clothing and chained to a table. Nervanus used probes to examine all of his cavities. The man had nothing on him. I was impressed. The doctor's examination was not gentle.

"What concerns you about our assassin guest? Something does. Tell me."

Gnaeus turned his eyes away and shrugged.

I don't know. This Egyptian is young. But he is no raw recruit. His body is littered with old scars. Apparently, he had been wounded with an arrow a few weeks ago when we first met him. He's healed remarkably fast. And he exhibits no fear. He knows he is going to be tortured today. But it seems he has no concern about it. He just sits, motionlessly, in his cell and waits. Maybe that's what bothers me. His frozen immobility. It's like he not only knows what is going to happen to him. But he is not resigned to his fate. He has no fear. No concerns. He is like a rock waiting to be thrown into the abyss. That, tribune, is what worries me the most. It is unnatural for any human to be this calm before his death.

A true believer, this assassin, Decimus thought to himself.

Trained to kill. Trained to die. The most dangerous of all creatures. Egyptian civilization was as ancient as man. Stretching centuries back into the dim past. What the Egyptians learned of death and dying were unknown. Secrets kept closed from the outer world. He asked himself, did he believe in magic? Did he believe the dead could rise again? Could flesh and blood slip through walls of stone and never be seen again? The answer to all the questions was short and concise. No. No, he believed none of the legends. None of the myths.

On the other hand, in his twenty-plus years soldiering all over the empire, he witnessed strange things with his own eyes. The incident in Alexandria being, for instance, the most recent. But there were others. Others as inexplicable. Best to be prepared. To be suspicious.

"When Marcellus comes to collect the Egyptian, make sure he is accompanied by a squad of men in full combat array. Tell Marcellus to be careful while he works in his specialty. Very careful."

Gnaeus nodded and walked away. As he did, the centurions Simon and Cletus stepped onto the roof and approached. Decimus peered out at the distant approach of the Roman transports.

"Gentlemen," he said quietly as the two came to stand beside him. "We have a quick, and I'm afraid quite bloody, journey in front of us. It is time we take the fight to the enemy."

XXVI

7 AD
Dalmatia
A Gaul named Renaud

He laid in the makeshift bed, one of dozens lined up side by side along a brick wall, his body from the chest down covered in blood-soaked bandages. He stared at the ceiling, his face contorted in pain. Half of his body had been burned the night the explosion devastated the Ninth. The rest of the hospital's patients were victims of that night as well. Or the wounded from the short but fierce fighting repelling the rebels soon after. Stepping onto the floor of the hospital ward, Decimus took in the wounded and the dying and then turned his attention toward the legion's approaching doctor.

"Doctor, my apologies for disturbing your work. But I've come to talk to a certain patient of yours. A talk I am afraid cannot be delayed any further."

"Yes, I was told you were coming, sir. It is just as well," the man said, turning to look deep into the long hall of the upper warehouse that was now his hospital. "The Gaul is not going to last much longer. His body suffered major trauma. The burns too extensive. There is nothing I can do. I have nothing here to relieve him of the pain. Nothing to heal the burns. A quick death would be far more merciful."

Decimus, with Gnaeus standing just behind him, eyed the distant bed which held the burnt man. Neither said anything for a moment or two. Finally, the tribune nodded to the doctor and began walking down the long aisle between beds toward the Gaul. As he walked, he felt the eyes of the others following him. A few even formally saluted while lying in bed. He acknowledged each soldier's salute. He stopped a couple of times to say a few words to a number of them before reaching the bed of the Gaul named Renaud.

The Gaul saw the tribune approaching. With the clear image of severe pain filling his face, the soldier tried to lift his right hand and salute his commanding officer. But Decimus gently pressed the one part of the man's body which was free from burns down gently as he pulled a small wooden stool up to sit down.

"Relax, soldier. We can dispense with formalities for the moment. Now is the time to heal yourself before you return to your century. The fourth century of the third cohort, isn't it? *The Northern Wolves,* aren't you?"

"Yes ... yes sir."

Pain. Immense pain seeping out of this man's body and soul with a palpable wave of suffering. Decimus forced himself to keep the smile on his face and the tone of his voice light and cheery.

"Colorful, soldier. I'll give you that. How long have you been a legionnaire?"

"Ten years, sir. Me and the boys joined up together back in

Massalia. We were part of Third Augusta until we were transferred down to the Ninth."

"The Third Augusta," the tribune repeated, smiling fondly. "Know it well. Got my promotion to optio while serving in the Third. My centurion's name, let me think, what was it? Ah. An old warhorse by the name of Bolgios. Had this thing about whacking people across their legs with his baton if they didn't move fast enough when he gave a command. Wonder if he's still alive."

The Gaul painted a smile on his lips for a second. It quickly disappeared in a spasm of pain. But the pain slipped away, and the man relaxed somewhat.

"Retired, sir. A year after me and the boys joined up. Found some German wench and went off to become a pig farmer."

"Ha!" Decimus laughed, shaking his head. "A pig farmer? Never thought that'd be Bolgios' fate."

The Gaul started to laugh but a wave of pain overcame him. Pain so intense he gripped the tribune's right hand in desperation with a vice-like grip of sheer agony. Decimus made no effort to remove his hand. He gripped the man's hand firmly and waited for the pain to subside. It took over a minute for the pain to lessen.

"Soldier, I'm here to ask a few questions. Important questions. Think you can answer them for me?"

"Yes sir. I'll certainly try."

"The night the hill exploded, you were on guard duty at the main gate, weren't you?"

"Yes sir. Me and eight others. Plus, our optio. We'd just come on duty."

"I need you to tell me about that night. What did you see? What did you hear? Did anything occur which seemed unusual that night? Anything at all."

"The hills, sir. The first thing we noticed when we came on duty were the hills. A thousand burning eyes looking down on us."

Decimus nodded. The enemy's campfires dotting the dark hills burned brightly and in large numbers. Hundreds of campfires glowed in the night. Almost surrounding the Roman camp. Bright, unblinking eyes staring down at the Romans below. He remembered the image all too clearly.

"Have to admit," the Gaul whispered, closing his eyes and holding the pain down to a dull throb. "Had me and the boys jittery. Really jittery. But then, about a half hour into our watch, we began to hear voices."

"Voices?" Decimus echoed as Gnaeus stepped closer to hear better.

"Ye ... yes, sir," the soldier said, his body stiffening. He closed his eyes. Muscles in his jaw extended. For a few seconds he barely breathed as he fought the pain. And then he relaxed, a wave of relief rolling across his sweating face.

"We heard horses approaching. Out in the darkness. The gate commander started to raise the alarm. But the noise subsided and then sounded as if they were riding away. That's when we heard the voices."

Decimus glanced at Gnaeus. Gnaeus' hands were moving.

The enemy probing the lines? Maybe these unknown Roman officers? Who?

Decimus shrugged, turning to look down at the dying man again.

"Could you hear what these voices were saying? Have any idea how many voices spoke?"

"I heard three voices. Others thought they heard four men. Angry voices. Angry voices but kept low so we could not hear them clearly. They went on for quite some time. But ... but about five minutes later we hear someone leaving. One horse.

Riding away very fast. And then, out of the darkness, five Roman officers approach the gate slowly."

Behind them, the other wounded men in their beds moaned softly or asked for something to quench their thirst. A few of the ambulatory men shuffled down the hospital aisle on crude crutches to relieve themselves in another room. The lone doctor and his three attendants moved with efficiency from one patient to the next changing bandages, holding heads up so the wounded could sip water from a cup, or carting off the dead who had silently slipped away into the forever without making a sound.

The tribune paid no attention to that which was happening behind him. His full attention was directed toward the bandaged patient in front of him. Gripping the man's hand again as another wave of pain rolled through the soldier's body, he waited for the man to regain enough strength again to speak.

"You let them through the gate," Decimus began. "Why?"

"They knew the day's password," the soldier whispered, his strength waning. "A short man. A centurion. Said he had been sent by Caesar with urgent dispatches for the legate. Had to speak to the general immediately. I looked at the gate commander and he said to pass them through. Five of them, sir. Five."

"Did you see any of their faces? Recognize any of them?"

"Two of them looked like officers. But the one in the middle, the one wearing his cape with the hood thrown over his head... I ... I ... dunno. There was something, something, something odd about him."

"Odd?" Decimus repeated, leaning close toward the man's weakening voice. "Odd in what way?"

A fine veil of sweat covered the soldier's face. He clenched his hands into fists as he fought the pain. And he was rapidly losing strength. Yet the soldier fought his weakness and approaching death in an effort to answer the tribune's questions.

"He seemed to be in pain. He was leaning forward in the saddle, one hand pressing firmly into his stomach. I saw him wavering. One of the officers reached out with a hand to steady him on his horse. But, but here's where it becomes strange, sir. When they leave the camp, the hooded man is taller. Sitting upright in the saddle. He's moving around on his horse as if there wasn't a thing wrong with him."

Decimus sat back on the stool and glanced at the silent Gnaeus. The look on the mute's face was telling. He too realized what had happened. Someone in the camp replaced the injured horseman and left with the others. Threw on the wounded man's cape and hood as a disguise and left the camp when the officers left moments later. Gnaeus curled his eyebrows up in thought. Who had been replaced? Why would the wounded man agree to stay behind, knowing he was about to die in a massive explosion?

Decimus observed the silent ruminations move across his friend's face. Gnaeus was like a Roman scroll written by a scribe's precise hand. Easy to read. Easy to decipher. His friend was questioning himself, trying to interpret the information they'd just acquired. But he had not fully comprehended the implications of this revelation yet. He would. Eventually.

He leaned toward the wounded man again, gripping the soldier's hand.

"Is there anything else you remember? Anything at all?"

"Smoke," the weak whisper replied.

"Smoke?"

"Ye ... yes. Smoke coming out of the legate's tent. I saw what I thought were flames inside the legate's tent, and then I saw the smoke. I yelled to the watch commander and began running toward the tent. The next thing I remember is waking up here in this bed. That's, that's it."

The Gaul's last few words were so weak the tribune barely made them out. Seeing that the man could no longer continue, he glanced at Gnaeus and stood up. Stepping away from the bed he saw the legion's physician at the far end of the line of beds. The physician looked up at Decimus approaching and stepped away from the patient he was attending to.

"Sir?"

"Renaud. Is he expected to live?"

The younger man glanced down the long row of beds and frowned. He shook his head and returned his gaze to the tribune.

"No. The burns are just too severe. Fever and infection are setting in. There is nothing I can do."

"There is," Decimus said quietly. "Give him something to relieve him of his pain. To permanently relieve him of his pain. Let him pass away peacefully in his sleep. If you need it in writing, I'll sign the order."

The doctor gazed into the tribune's face for a long time before he, quietly, nodded in agreement. No written orders were required. Men died on this ward every day. Another death would go unnoticed. Especially the Gaul's.

Decimus and Gnaeus left the doctor standing at the end of the long hospital aisle staring down at the floor. Taking a deep breath and exhaling slowly, he walked over to a long table filled with vials, instruments, and various bottles of medicine.

He wanted to save lives. If only he could save lives instead of snuffing them out much like one snuffed out the flame of a nearly consumed candle. But, maybe, in this case, it was better to relieve the pain and just fall asleep. Fall into a deep sleep and never awake.

XXVII

7 AD
Dalmatia
The dead prisoner

Dead. The Dalmatian prisoner. Dead in his cell. Lying on his bunk, lifeless eyes staring up at the cell's ceiling. His throat cut from earlobe to earlobe. Discovered the moment the prisoner's cell door was opened by the guards to allow Decimus and Gnaeus to enter.

Both men stared at the dead body for some time. Neither said a word as they took in the scene before them. Eventually the tribune turned, stared at the two stunned and legitimately terrified soldiers who were on duty and told them to bring to him their watch commander. When the fat little Tesserarius stepped into the cell and saluted, he almost fainted the moment he glanced at the dead man lying in the blood-soaked bunk.

With the bleached, colorless little officer following him

around like a leashed puppy, Decimus closely examined the body. At the same time, he interrogated the Tesserarius.

"When was this man last seen alive?"

"Last night, sir. The evening meal."

"You personally saw him?"

"Yes sir. I supervised the meal. It was the shift's first job of the night. Feeding the prisoners."

The tribune's questions ceased momentarily as he paused and stared at the dead man. Bending down somewhat, the tribune twisted the man's head slightly to the right. Grunting in interest, he bent down even further and examined the dead man's face carefully. Gnaeus, standing beside Decimus, folded arms across his chest and kept his eyes on the fat little man standing behind the tribune. Long used to the predilections of the tribune when it came to examining the dead, he thought it best to make sure the visibly shaking junior officer didn't faint, or panic and make a dash for freedom, until the tribune had another question for him.

There were bruises on the victim's chin. Fresh bruising. The victim's hand had cut marks on them. Especially deep in the man's open palms. His knuckles were bruised. Frowning, Decimus straightened himself up and continued to examine the dead.

"After the evening meal, did the deceased have any visitors?"

"N ... no, sir. Per your orders. Quarantined and placed off limits."

"You're sure no one came to see this man after the meal?"

"Po ...positive, sir."

The young officer's bladder was screaming at him. His knees were shaking so badly he could barely stand. The murder of a valued prisoner in his own jail, under his supervision, was a breach of protocol which meant one of two possibilities. Either twenty lashes across the back or execution for dereliction of duty. If the former was administered, and if he survived, his career in the army was over. He would be a junior officer, if he kept his rank, for the rest of his enlistment. Word of mouth from one legionnaire to another would spread. No matter where he went, or what legion he served in, he would always be looked upon with a disapproving eye. No one would trust him.

Best, he thought, if he was executed. His shame would end with him. A few seconds suffering as the garrote slipped around his throat and the executioner applying pressure, and then it would be over.

"Soldier..." a voice. Faint. Far away.

The open palm of a hand came across his chubby cheeks. Hard. Cruel. Snapping his head to one side so violently he staggered back in pain and surprise. In front of him was the balding, darkly tanned silent Gnaeus, eyes blazing in fury. The tribune's gnome-like servant tilted his head toward the tribune, a silent gesture saying, *pay attention, fool! The tribune is talking.*

Decimus grunted, eyed the little officer, and frowned.

"Between the evening meal and discovering the body, I need to know what happened outside this cell. Every moment."

The chubby officer, as pale as a freshly washed cotton sheet, said he would collect the guards who were on duty and return with them immediately. Decimus nodded curtly and watched the man fly out of the jail cell. Gnaeus waited for the officer to leave before he turned and began speaking with his hands.

How did this happen? Did our assassin bleed through the walls again and kill the Dalmatian?

Decimus shook his head and told Gnaeus to check and see if the assassin was still in his cell. It only took a few seconds.

Walking back into the dead man's cell the silent old soldier nodded. The assassin was alive and unmoving.

"I don't believe in ghosts, old friend. But I do believe in conspiracies. Someone of flesh and blood entered this cell last night, had a struggle with the Dalmatian, and finally stabbed him in the back before cutting his throat to make sure he remained silent. The evidence is quite obvious."

But who? Soldiers assigned to guard the two prisoners were not Egyptian. Gauls and Italians only. As per your orders.

"I think I know, my friend. There can only be one possibility."

Gnaeus' eyes registered surprise. The tribune knew? How? Frowning, he glared at the three legionnaires who stumbled into the prison cell at the same time. The Tesserarius had two soldiers with him. Both looked as if they were two steps away from death. White complexioned, bent over in pain, each holding their stomachs, they barely had enough strength to stand.

"Let me guess. Sometime last night the two of you, assigned to guard this prisoner's cell, came down violently sick. Vomiting. Diarrhea. The works. Correct?"

Both men nodded, too weak to speak. The Tesserarius, surprised, looked at his men and then at Decimus. He knew nothing about this.

"Late last night you ate or drank something. Someone brought you something to eat or drink. What was it?"

"Wine, sir. A sweet tasting wine we were unfamiliar with," one of the guards whispered, the effort making him lose whatever color he had left in his face.

"How soon after that did it take you to become sick?"

"Maybe, maybe a half hour, sir," the second guard whispered. "Both of us threw up at the same time. We yelled for help. The officer on duty told us to hurry to the doc. He said he would watch the prisoner until men came down to replace us."

Decimus nodded, expecting the answer that was just confirmed. His eyes sought out the Tesserarius.

"The name of the officer on duty last night."

"Silas Festus. Optio of the sixth century, Forth Cohort."

"Find him. Bring him to me. And send these two back to their hospital beds."

The young officer nodded, pulling the two soldiers roughly as he vacated the cell. Decimus gazed at the dead man and spoke quietly to Gnaeus.

"Do not be surprised when the news comes. But I suspect they will find this Silas Festus dead, old friend. Very dead."

Gnaeus looked at Decimus, his face filled with curiosity.

Is this a guess on your part, tribune? Or have the gods been quietly talking to you in your sleep again?

A dry, almost cruel smile played across Decimus' lips. Gnaeus saw the evidence he saw. Always by his side in such adventures, nevertheless his loyal friend could not see the evidence as it was. Everything told a story. The dead. The pieces of evidence left behind. Markings on the body. Even how the blood spilled from a body. Everything. If you took the time to read the clues, you would see it. The story. The evidence. The possibilities.

But Gnaeus was a simple man. A common Roman soldier straight off the streets of Rome. What he saw was the obvious. The dead were dead. Blood was only blood. There was nothing to read from anything in the dirt. But if the tribune saw something, which he usually did, from this or that body, or on a wall, or in the dirt, and he guessed correctly on how it happened and who was the perpetrator, it could only mean one thing. The tribune talked to the gods.

There could be no other possible explanation.

Twenty minutes later the young officer returned. The look on his face told Decimus everything he needed to know. The optio, Silas Festus, was dead. Found in an alley in the city, his throat cut. His body lying half submerged in the waters of the harbor.

With one hand resting on his hip, Gnaeus looked up at the tribune, his face filled with a painting of smug satisfaction. The tribune did it again. Knew exactly what happened before actually *knowing* what happened. Shaking his head, grinning, he turned and stared at the young Tesserarius.

"Report to your centurion, officer. But before you go, double the guards down here and find another optio, a trustworthy one, to take over your duties. You're being reassigned."

The chubby officer gulped and paled just before he disappeared out of the jail cell. Gnaeus watched the young soldier leave. *Who is our killer? Should I send men out to bring him to you? What is our next move?*

"We do nothing, Gnaeus. Not now. But soon. Very soon. Right now, we wait for Marcellus to do his specialty on our other guest. After that, we'll see. We'll see."

XXVIII

7 AD
Dalmatia
The river Neretva

In the moonlight he watched as Spanish cavalrymen, one after the other, led their mounts off the wide beamed transports and down the long wooden ramps from the ship to the river's left bank. It would be an all-night disembarkation. Unloading a thousand horses and men took time. More time than normal since it was a nighttime operation. Standing on a high knoll close to the river, Decimus could, underneath the bright moonlight, watch both the unloading of the Spanish cavalry, and a few meters upstream, observe the unloading of the Ninth's third cohort off a second transport.

By dawn he hoped to have both the third and fourth cohorts of infantry unloaded and most of the cavalry. Already the one century of archers he brought along had disembarked and fanned out into the night to provide cover. Soon enough they would be reinforced with infantry. By noon he hoped to have the entire force of infantry, archers, and cavalry marching down the road to Narona.

The Neretva was a navigable river which came out of the back country of Dalmatia and dumped itself into the Adriatic. It cut its way through some truly rugged mountainous country before it found the sea. But it was, fortunately, deep enough for ships to navigate for some distance upriver. In fact, navigable all the way to a little river port city called Narona. Where, if his spies were accurate in their intelligence gathering, Dalmatian rebels were occupying and using it as their regional headquarters.

Fortunately, the countryside between their disembarkation and Narona was not all rugged mountainous country. A valley opened a few miles inland from the Adriatic and that is where they were now. On the left bank of the river the land was flat, filled with farmland and orchards. Once on the move the men would move fast. Fast enough, he hoped, to surprise the rebels and drive them out of Narona. And in so doing, perhaps breaking the ever-growing siege around Asa in the process.

But we should be hunting for General Sulla and his wife. For those who abducted him. Gnaeus signed in the moon light and frowning, watched the horses and men move off the ships. *The longer we deal with the situation here, the farther the general and his kidnappers flee.*

Decimus shook his head in disagreement. From the side of his eye Gnaeus caught the vision of the tribune's disagreement. Turning, he looked at the tribune skeptically.

"Consider Gnaeus, the situation the general's abductors find themselves in. They have kidnapped a famous Roman general and senator, along with his wife, from out of their home. Armed men, in a military precise attack, kidnapped the general, burning the general's villa to the ground, killing dozens of Roman citizens in the process. The Roman Senate is screaming its outrage that such an atrocity could happen so close to the very gates of Rome. They're demanding action. Insisting the culprits be brought to justice after the general and his wife are rescued. All of Italy is searching for the general. All of the ports and fishing villages, any inlet where a small boat might land, are being scoured and watched by the army. The Roman navy is tracking down and searching ships leaving the ports."

Horses neighed. Men lifted voices into the night to coax their skittish mounts down the gangplanks. The clutter and clanking of men in arms, along with the accompanying smells any army equally possesses, filled the night air. Both menwatched from their vantage point as the cavalry continued to disembark as rapidly as they could from the black mass of the waiting transport for a few moments. But only for a few moments. Peering at Gnaeus again, Decimus resumed where he left off.

"I am convinced Shebet's followers are not in Italy. In fact, I suspect they embarked on a ship and left within hours after conducting the raid. Again, I believe all of this, the attack on the Ninth, the abduction of the general and his wife, the destruction of Sulla's estate. All of it Gnaeus, was carefully planned and rehearsed and refined and set into place months earlier. Perhaps even years earlier.

"No. Our kidnappers fled the country. They had a fast ship waiting for them somewhere on the Adriatic side of the peninsula. A hard ride of two, maybe four hours, and they quickly boarded a ship and slipped away. But where could they go? How can they hide from the Roman navy? They dare not set sail for Egypt in the hopes of outrunning the entire fleet. I'm sure fast ships have already been dispatched to Alexandria, and other ports, with the news of the kidnapping of Sulla. The moment any ship from Italy enters a port it will be thoroughly searched.

"They dare not sail to any port which might feel some form of sympathy for their actions. No nation with ports open to Mediterranean traffic would allow such a bold group safe passage. Many powerful leaders might sympathize with Shebet and her followers. But none are foolish enough to face the fury and wrath of an aroused Roman empire. Except one, old friend. Just one."

Gnaeus lifted a questioning eyebrow and used a finger to point downward at the hill they were standing on.

Here? In rebel territory? You think the one who now leads these fanatics, and may have the general and Hatshepsut as captives, are here in Dalmatia? In Narona?

Decimus' thin lips stretched into a wiry half-grin.

"They are not in Italy. Too unsafe on the high seas. There are no ports on the African coastline open to them. The only place for them to run to and have any margin of anonymity is here."

Gnaeus, surprise written clearly across his weather-beaten face, whistled softly, half-turning to gaze into the interior of the rebel territory.

Will we find the general alive? Or are both of them dead, their bodies thrown overboard already?

"There is no way of knowing until we apprehend our fanatical friends. But we must hurry. I'm sure whoever leads this madness has made plans for their escape overland. They will not stay in Narona for long."

That's puzzling me as well, tribune. If Shebet is dead, truly dead, who then leads this motley group? If, as you have said, she was the mastermind behind all of this, who now is powerful enough to keep this conspiracy alive?

The wiry grin returned to Decimus' lips as he chuckled and laid a hand fondly on the older man's hard shoulder. The balding piece of old leather that was Gnaeus was a hard, pragmatic, but somewhat superstitious, old soldier. Shebet was dead. But *was she really dead?*

"Gnaeus, you know the facts about this whole affair as well as I. Examine each one in detail. Fit the facts together. You know my methods of deduction. You know none of us are in possession of all the facts until the very end. But we know enough. We can construct plausible possibilities which fill in the unknown gaps and connects that which is known to us. We can surmise certain possibilities. Can you not suspect a few who could be our current fanatical leader?"

I confess, tribune. I've tried over and over to think like you whenever we get into these situations. I really have. But the more I think about it, the worse my head begins to pound. So, I've made a bargain with myself. When it comes to obeying orders and fulfilling your commands, I am your man. But the thinking part I gladly leave to you. With my warmest regards.

Decimus laughed softly as the last horseman led his mount off the gangplank and stepped ashore. Already seamen were using long wooden poles to shove the heavy ship away from shore even as others on board began hauling up the long gangplank. Oars came out and the ship backed its way into the river's mainstream. In a masterful maneuver, the ship reversed its position. It Rotated one hundred eighty degrees around, using only the starboard banks of oars, turning the prow downriver. Once done both banks of oars came out and the moonlit ship moved gracefully past their position on the high knoll and disappeared around a river bend. In an hour another transport would arrive with more cavalry and the process would start all over again.

If luck held and the enemy did not discover what they were doing before noon the next morning, nor have a large enough force nearby to challenge their efforts, they would be ready. *If.* Always in the life of a soldier. That one indefinable word.

If.

XXIX

7 AD
Dalmatia hinterland
The puzzle begins to come together

He gave the last instructions to the two civilian-dressed individuals, speaking in a low voice only the two standing immediately in front of him could hear. With curt nods the two turned, mounted horses, and rode off toward the southeast and away from Narona. Behind the tribune were almost a thousand infantrymen and one hundred bowmen. On both flanks, in the rear of the formation, and sweeping forward slowly and cautiously in front of him, detachments of cavalry were probing the countryside in search for the enemy, while a block of six hundred cavalry waited patiently behind the standing infantry for the signal to begin marching.

Gnaeus, eyeing the two men riding off into the distance, handed Decimus the reins to his horse, lifting a brow questioningly.

"Two of the best army scouts we have," Decimus grunted,

DEATH BY GREEK FIRE

stepping close to the silent Gnaeus and taking the reins out of his hands. "They'll keep an eye on the road leading out of Narona. If our guests depart before we arrive, we'll know about it soon enough."

Lifting himself into his saddle, he gave the order to move. Underneath a very bright sun, armor glistening, and the thud of a thousand tough leather sandals of the legionnaires marching in step, the two thousand strong arm of Roman might began moving with uncommon swiftness. There were no slow-moving wagon trains. The legionnaires were not laden down with the usual extra gear a normal legion would pack along with them. Usually each infantryman would carry on his back not only his weapons and armor, but wooden tent poles and sharpened wood stakes, or an assortment of digging tools, to be used later in the afternoon to build their encampment. A Roman usually carried close to eighty pounds of armor, weapons, and equipment on a normal march. A typical march would be approximately eight or ten miles a day. A half day of marching. A half day of building their fortified campsite.

But not today.

Narona was a little over twelve miles away. Without the extra gear to carry, a twelve-mile forced march was feasible. By nightfall Decimus hoped to crash into whatever rebel forces surrounded Narona and defeat them in open combat. And maybe, if the gods smiled upon him, capture the new leader of the cult worshippers of Menket and end this conspiratorial nightmare threatening Rome.

The Dalmatian uprising was two uprisings at once. Pannonia to the north, land which would, in modern times, be known as Austria, Hungary, and Slovenia— who threw off their Roman rule and vowed to make war on Rome itself. Their initial successes against Roman rule thrilled the Dalmatians to the south and they too rebelled. The real fighting, the true threat to Rome, lay to the north. Augustus had to recall Tiberius Caesar, his adopted son and heir to the crown, from Germany and pull him and much of his troops back to northern Italy in defense. Slowly but surely Tiberius, a seasoned general of excellent qualities, began building forces to face the formidable Pannonian forces. Eventually a Roman army of one hundred thousand strong would confront the enemy. The struggle would be bloody and brutal. A typical Roman war. There would be much destruction and massive casualties. Whole groups of ethnic Slavs, Greeks, and others would be rounded up and sold into slavery. Rome would endure and eventually win the war.

To the south, a Dalmatian leader by the name of Bato of Desidiatia raised an army and began waging war up and down the Adriatic coastline. Macedon and Greece were threatened. Roman forces in Dalmatia were minuscule at best. Worse, no one knew exactly the size of forces arrayed against what few Roman outposts remained. Only the small port of Asa remained in Roman hands. The interior hinterlands of the mountainous country were now a mystery filled with potential mortal danger.

Decimus knew he was marching blindly into enemy territory. He had no idea what he and his men would find in and around Narona. But he was convinced of one thing. A swift, brutal clash with an enemy force of any size, would reverberate up and down the Adriatic coast. Dalmatian forces headed north to reinforce Pannonian forces would have to turn around and hurry back south to confront the new Roman threat. With luck, a swift battle and victory against the enemy would send the Dalmatians scurrying to safety deeper into the mountains, relieving the pressure of the siege around Asa for at least a month or two.

He had no intention of striking deeper inland. Nor did he

plan to remain in the rebel city for long. His two thousand strong band of men were not so much an invading army as it was a well-armed raiding party. A quick strike. A sharp fight. Perhaps successfully raiding the stores of food and supplies which the enemy stored in Narona, was all he could hope to accomplish. Once completed it would be a rapid force march back to the river where Roman ships would be waiting for them.

The day wore on. The flood plain and farmland on either side of the river moved past them swiftly. The infantry marched at a rapid pace. Cavalry swept away only marginal resistance. The forward units of cavalry were already standing on high ground surrounding the Dalmatian river port, observing it from the heights. Luck held for Decimus and his command. By late afternoon the infantry had only five kilometers to go before seizing Narona. Stopping the command to take a short rest before making the last push toward the river town, horsemen from three directions were observed riding hard to the marching men.

The enemy had arrived in strength. From the north, a Spanish scout reported perhaps as many as three thousand rebels were marching rapidly toward the river. A second horseman said a second rebel force, maybe as many as two thousand strong, were coming up from the south. The southern force would arrive in Narona first. Only the river, with one bridge crossing it, separated the southern force from the river town.

But it was the third horseman which drew Decimus' interest the most. A non-descript Roman courier, straight from Rome, dispatched on a fast ship with orders to find Decimus at all cost, handed the tribune a sealed envelope. He recognized the wax seal at once. Caius Lucius sent the courier. Accepting the heavy packet, he waited for the courier to move away before breaking the seal and digging out the envelope's contents. The news was both grim and provocative.

Tribune,

We found the general's body. It was pulled out of the sea a few kilometers off the coast of Italy night before last. He had been dead for several days before he was found. No other body was discovered.

The inquiries you asked me to pursue have had some interesting results. You asked me to look into the histories of two subjects of interest. I have. As you anticipated, suspect number one is not exactly who he says he is. The subject is a Roman citizen. As are his parents. But his parents are from Alexandria. As a child, they moved to Rome and became quite wealthy in the import of rare medicines and spices from the Orient. The subject in question received his formal training in Greece before returning to Rome. Apparently while in training in Greece he went on several long trips back to Alexandria. To be sure, the best physicians in the world are found in Alexandria. It is conceivable these long trips were addendums added to his formal training. I have made further inquiries.

Subject number two is far more interesting.

After completing our interrogations with the followers of this goddess we captured in Rome a few days ago, we ascertained subject number two is skilled, and quite deadly, in several different fighting skills. Apparently over the years the subject has brought in specialists from all over the world for training purposes. To describe them as being dangerous would be a vast understatement.

Apparently, this person of interest is quite unstable emotionally. Rumors have existed for years of homicidal tendencies. People close to the subject have mysteriously disappeared. But no bodies have ever been found. The prisoners we interrogated are convinced the subject is indeed our primary suspect. How this can be is a puzzle to me. But I have no doubts what we have gleaned from the prisoners are believable.

If this person still lives, I advise you to be extremely diligent in your endeavors to capture this person. Their skill far surpasses yours in the areas of individual combat. Do not attempt to take this creature into custody on your own. It will be an impossible task.

As a closing note, we have subject number one under constant surveillance.

Good hunting on your current expedition. Waiting for further instructions.

Serveus

Caesar's spy never signed his correspondence with his real name. If, indeed, Caius Lucius was his real name. It did not matter. Turning the correspondence over in his hand, Decimus turned and motioned for the Roman courier to approach. Using the man's back he quickly scribbled out a few short lines on the back side of the letter, folded it, slipped it into the envelope, and handed it to the courier. As the courier sped away, he sent Gnaeus out to collect his cohort and cavalry commanders. The moment for action had arrived.

XXX

7 AD
Dalmatia
Battle

Rebels, in two long columns of marching infantry snaked down a dusty road like some monstrous thousand-leg centipede. The moving columns of men threw up a thin cloud of dust into the late morning sky as they approached the river bridge directly in front of them. The rebels were a mixed assortment of traditional Greek-like hoplites, the heavily armored mainstays of any Greek army, and lighter clad peltasts. Peltasts were men with little armor but armed with helms and javelins designed to hurl at the enemy prior the heavier infantry's advance. There was only two or three decuria of cavalry. A decuria consisted of eight horsemen. What Decimus observed from his vantage point was no more than twenty-five or thirty horsemen, providing flanking cover.

The road wound its way through well-manicured farmland on either side of the river, coming around in a sweeping curve just before the river and the arching stone bridge crossing it. On the far side of the Neretva the farmland was flatter, wide open, with no building structures or walls to impede the rebel advance. On the side of the river where Decimus and Gnaeus stood, the riverbanks slanted deep in the depths of dark shade created by a copse of trees. The ground close to the riverbank was not so tilled and open. Here and there large stands of trees appeared as if they were green islands of foliage in a sea of untouched brown soil and grassland. The narrow, well-worn dirt road moved in a twisting path in and out of the green forest. It was here, just after the rebels crossed the high bridge, where he planned to spring his trap.

A large patch of forest, four hundred meters away from the bridge, provided the perfect screening cover for his two cohorts of infantry. From the rebels' point of view marching toward the river, they would see the steep banks of the Neretva, the bridge, and on the far side an open space before the road plunged into the trees. What they would not see were the two cohorts of Roman infantry, roughly nine hundred and sixty strong, standing on the far side of the tree line waiting for the enemy to advance.

Nor would they see, Decimus hoped, his Spanish cavalry two kilometers away on the far side of the bridge, the rebel's side of the bridge, hidden behind a natural slope of the terrain. Dismounted, motionless, they waited to hear the noise of the rebels' pipes and drums hurrying their men up into battle formation on the other side of the bridge before they mounted. When that time came, they would leap into their saddles and sweep down upon the rear of the enemy. With Roman infantry engaged frontally with the Dalmatians, the Spanish of almost a thousand strong would come flooding over the bridge and straight into their exposed backside.

In the deep shadows of the forest where he stood, the

tribune had with him most of the bowmen attached to his command. Their job was to harass the large contingent of peltasts who would come sweeping out in front of the heavy Greek infantry. The bowmen's assignment was to wait for the enemy to approach within range and then begin tickling them with a ragged barrage of arrows. The apparent undisciplined barrage coming from the woods would suggest to the Dalmatians only a small force of Romans stood between them and Narona. He stood in the trees with Gnaeus, the bowmen kneeling and waiting in the darkness of the woods on either side of him. He was there to make sure the bowmen remained there only long enough to bloody the enemy some and not get swept away with the lust for battle.

As he stood beside one large tree, noticing one eight-man detachment of horsemen rattling over the bridge and approaching the tree line, an older bowman, dressed in leather, a large quiver of arrows hanging on his back, stepped up beside the tribune and loudly cleared his throat with a barking cough before speaking.

"Tribune, thank you for willing to stand with me and my men. It is an honor to serve you, sir. But allow me to be blunt. Would the commanding tribune please step away and haul his ass back to his position behind our infantry, and let us get on with our job? It is not the first birthday party we've been invited to. Nor will it be our last. The boys and I will handle our part of the plan. No worries about that. Now, please. For our own peace of mind, get the Hades out of here. Sir!"

Decimus, holding his surprise in check at being addressed so frankly, stared at the commander of bowman and sized him up silently. He was a small man about the size of Gnaeus. Balding, but like Gnaeus, had that look of weather-beaten leather. Or steel which had been tested time and again and not found wanting. Smiling, Decimus nodded, stepping closer to the man.

"Your name, soldier."

"Themistocles of Sparta, sir."

"Well, Themistocles of Sparta, I will comply with your wishes. Good luck to you and your men. Bring them back safely to our lines the moment it appears you're about to be flanked."

Gnaeus grinned a wolfish sneer, nodded at the bowmen in respect, and followed the tribune as he hurried through the forest and trotted out of the tree line back to the infantry.

Slipping through the lines of legionnaires he took the reins of his horse from a soldier and mounted. And waited. Two cohorts of infantry deployed in two massive blocks of men, stood patiently spread out across the rise of a small hill and waited for the enemy to arrive. It did not take long for the action to begin. Ten minutes slowly ticked by before the waiting Romans heard the pipes and drums of the rebel army wailing toward the heavens. Decimus almost smiled. Themistocles' bowmen must have taken out the probing cavalry. Marching infantry swept over the arch of the high bridge, saw their comrades lying in the dirt riddled with arrows, and knew the enemy were either upon them— or very near. The rebels were now hurriedly deploying their men into battle formations. It took time for a large group of infantry, a group of any size, to break out of marching order and deploy in the precisely regimented lines of battle. There would be old soldiers, long used to command, among the men barking out orders as they strode up and down the lines to dress them down properly. Officers, on horses, would be doing the same. The enemy was near. No one among the Dalmatians knew how large the enemy's force may be. But everyone, Decimus knew, would assume the rebels would come to the realization Romans were present on the battlefield and a fight was at hand.

Another twenty minutes ticked by slowly for the standing Romans as they waited for the rebel infantry to show themselves. At the end of this block of time, in the distance, faintly, everyone heard the screams of men and neighing horses. Almost immediately exploding out of the tree line poured Themistocles' bowman, retreating in ones and twos, but in an orderly fashion. Each man moved in a brisk walk for some distance before stopping and turning, lifting a bow and notching arrows up to fire into the woods. The Spartan's position was in the middle of the retreating formation, the closest to the advancing peltasts, firing his bow and encouraging his men at the same time.

Dalmatian peltasts, hundreds of them, poured out of the forest, filling the air with javelins hurled toward the retreating bowmen. But the enemy came to a halt the moment they looked up the hill and saw Roman infantry occupying high ground. An order was given. Peltasts knelt to one knee, strung out in a long, thin line. But two men ran back into the woods. Now the rest of the rebel army would know. Romans were present in large numbers. And they were not retreating.

Themistocles and his bowmen came trotting up the hill and rejoined their bowmen comrades. They were sweaty from their exertions. But exuberant. Decimus silently nodded his compliments to the old Greek commander. The Greek, a wiry grin on his lips, threw a half hearted salute toward Decimus as he disappeared into the mass of his bowmen.

The waiting began anew. Battle, it seemed, was more on who could maintain their equilibrium the best while waiting for the real fighting to begin. Sliding out of the saddle of his horse, Decimus conferred with his centurions who soon began walking through the ranks of the men telling them to stand down but be ready at a moment's notice. With Gnaeus at his side he began walking among the ranks talking quietly with individuals, even creating bubbles of laughter among the men when relating to one group or another some obscene joke or two.

As the men relaxed, below them at the bottom of the hill, near the tree line, the ranks of the rebel peltasts began to grow in strength. From one long, thin, single line of javelin throwers, the enemy's lines were now three lines deep. All three lines of peltast were resting on one knee, well out of the range of Roman bowman, apparently waiting for their heavier armor-clad brethren to make their appearance.

The classical Greek hoplite was renowned for their slow maneuverability on a battlefield. Heavily armored, with breastplate, round shield, their near-legendary eight-foot-long spears, along with greaves to protect their shins, and with their traditional Corinthian styled Greek helms, Greek infantry were not known to move fast. They took time to deploy. Typically, hoplites would deploy in long battle lines, shield pressing against shield, the first three ranks of infantry with the sharp points of their spears lowered parallel to the ground. This formation would be four to eight ranks deep. The back three ranks would have their spears raised to the heavens, waiting their turn to fight, staying in close proximity with the three forward ranks in front of them. When deployed properly and led adequately, Greek heavy infantry was formidable on a battlefield. They could be a juggernaut. Literately sweeping through any enemy resistance very similarly to that of a hot knife slicing through warm butter.

But their strength was also their weakness. Being heavy infantry designed to hammer away at an enemy's front, their inability to move rapidly meant that, if their flanks were threatened, they could not adjust fast enough to face the new threat. In the past, when the Greek hoplite was the Queen of the battlefield, the flanks of the famous Greek phalanxes were protected by swarms of Greek cavalry. Or, if the army was large enough, by reserves of Greek infantry placed on the left and right flanks.

The enemy before him had no cavalry. Decimus estimated the enemy to have about eight hundred hoplites and about twelve hundred peltasts. A powerful force. More than a match for his two cohorts of infantry if the rebel commander knew how to deploy his peltasts properly. But what the enemy did not have was cavalry in any large number. He did. His Spanish cavalry would be arriving soon, if all went well, and strike at the rear of the enemy. But the enemy's heavy infantry had to be fully engaged with his infantry for his plan to work. If not, cavalry facing heavy infantry alone meant disaster for the Romans.

What was beginning to gnaw on the tribune's nerves was obvious. The enemy was taking his sweet time in deploying his hoplites. Were they aware of his cavalry coming up behind them? Had the enemy commander decided to deal with the Roman cavalry first and then attack the infantry? It would take only a small token force stationed at the bridge's exit leading onto this side of the river to keep the cavalry at bay. With the Roman cavalry out of the equation, Greek heavy infantry supported by twelve hundred Greek-styled peltasts would be a serious challenge to face by any Roman commander.

Decimus had a decision to make. Remain on the hill in the hopes the rebels knew nothing about his Spanish cavalry and were just taking their usual slow time in planning their attack. Or assume the rebels were aware of the threat in their rear and were laying a trap themselves for the unsuspecting Spanish. He made a decision. Finding Themistocles again he told the old Greek his plan. The Greek listened, nodded, and returned to his men. Decimus turned, located the centurions Simon and Cletus, and ordered them to prepare their cohorts to move out.

One hundred bowmen fanned out in front of the two

cohorts and began peppering the rebels in front of them with arrows. Behind the bowman the infantry began marching. Straight for the clump of trees the Roman force marched. The enemy, seeing Romans advancing, wisely split into two forces. One group went left. The other to the right. Javelins began flying through the clear afternoon air. But even though peltasts outnumbered bowman by ten to one, the uncanny accuracy and longer range of the bowmen made the javelin-throwing peltasts cautious.

Advancing one hundred yards, six bowmen, flaming arrows notched to their bows, let loose their oil-soaked arrows in high arching flights. The arrows, all six, rose almost simultaneously into the sky and flew heavenward. They fell arcing from their heights into the densely compacted center of the trees in front of them. Six more burning arrows were sent aloft. In moments, the large copse of trees was a burning conflagration sending up columns of thick white smoke high into the air.

Hoping the growing columns of smoke would provide a warning to his cavalry, he ordered both cohorts to swing to their right and begin circling the raging inferno burning on their left. His plan was simple. Marching both cohorts around the burning forest, he was going to use the raging fire on his left, and the steep banks of the Neretva on his right to keep the peltasts from attacking his flanks. Placing his bowmen in the rear of the formation he hoped to keep the javelins at bay long enough for his infantry to confront and engage the enemy's infantry. Fully engaged with the Romans, he hoped to threaten the rebel infantry enough to forget about the approaching cavalry. With luck, an opening at the mouth of the bridge leading onto this side of the river would be created, giving the Spanish an opportunity to smash into the rebel's infantry.

The rebel commander took the bait.

Walls of bronze shields and gleaming spear points came

marching in multiple ranks toward the advancing Romans. The crash of the two different fighting styles slamming into each other was a calamitous din of sheer noise. Whereas the rebels relied on the Greek way of warfare, that of relying on spear and shield and literately using sheer weight of the mass infantry to drive their enemy back, Roman warfare was different. Roman shields were rectangular in shape and curved to fit around a soldier's body. Instead of an eight-foot spear for their primary weapon, Romans preferred their three-foot long, double-edge short sword, a thrusting and slashing weapon, to do their bloody work on the enemy. And bloody work it was. It took time, and a few casualties, to hack through the mass of spear points in order to get at the enemy. Initially the leading cohort gave ground to the enemy as they began their bloody work. But an hour into the fighting and it was apparent the Greeks would have to fall back.

Confining spaces with the flaming forest on one flank and the river on the other narrowed the field of battle for the massed rebel infantry. The sheer size of the burning forest, the heat generated from the hot inferno, made the right flank of the rebels almost untenable. Men from the rear ranks of the phalanx began to press away from the hungry flames, thinning the lines up front. Decimus, seeing an opportunity, ordered the leading cohort to put pressure on the enemy's left. At the same time, he sent orders to his second cohort to slam into the gap between the flames that the forward cohort had created as hard as they could.

In the rear of the Roman forces the rebel peltasts were becoming more daring, thanks to his bowman running out of arrows to keep them at a respectful distance. Reluctantly he gave orders to the two rear centuries of men, one hundred sixty men in total, to peel away from their cohort and move toward the peltasts. Using their curved shield to protect them as best as they could, the two centuries of infantry moved far enough toward their rear to create a gap between the peltasts and his infantry.

Decimus knew it was a fill in the gap measure. One hundred sixty Roman infantry against eighteen hundred rebel peltasts was a temporary measure at best. Fortunately, the burning forest on one flank and the river on the other, limited the number of rebels who could attack his covering force. He knew one of two things had to happen if Roman arms were to take the day. Either the heavy infantry in front of his attack cohorts had to suddenly break and flee for their lives because of their untenable position due to the burning forest, or the Spanish had to arrive on the scene with stunning ferocity.

At the end of the day it was the Spanish who tilted the battle toward a Roman victory. On the far side of the river Decimus spied a growing column of dust approaching. The dust cloud grew in volume, filling the air and mixing in with the white smoke of the burning forest. Soon the first elements of the cavalry were observed, riding with a furious intent down the curving road leading toward the bridge. More horsemen appeared, filling the road and spilling off into the farmlands on either side, all heading toward the bridge.

That was when the enemy's desire to fight broke. The rebel's heavy infantry wavered, thinned, and then dissolved into a fleeing mob in a matter of moments. Behind the Roman infantry the thousand or so peltasts vanished completely. Cavalry came in two columns thundering over the high curve of the stone bridge and swung around and smashed into the enemy's fleeing heavy infantry. The slaughter began in earnest. Spanish swords flashed repeatedly in the afternoon sun and rebels were cut down in large numbers.

Decimus, sitting on his horse, watched the Spanish go

about their grim work with gusto. He made no attempt to stop them until the sun settled into twilight and night began to fall.

They made camp beside the river and the high bridge for the night, attending to their wounds and counting the dead. Fortuna, the Goddess of Fortune, smiled upon Decimus Julius Virilis this day. He only hoped she would continue to be so generous as he and his men approached Narona.

XXXI

7 AD
Dalmatia
The trap is set

A hand touched him gently on the shoulder. Decimus opened his eyes, fully awake, his right hand gripping the bare steel of his gladius' handle lying in the makeshift bed he threw together on the ground beside him. Standing over him was Gnaeus. Gnaeus with a very troubled look filling his eyes. Behind his mute servant was a Roman soldier. A very tired Roman soldier.

Throwing the heavy soldier's cape off him, the tribune rolled off the ground and stood up. Around him the infantry slept peacefully. The camp, a typical Roman marching camp, took half the night to build. By the time it was done everyone was exhausted. The men slept the deep sleep only the exhausted could know.

"Report," he said quietly.

Sir, a messenger from Asa. Bad news, I'm afraid.

Decimus eyed the dusty, sweat stained soldier with the look a commander gives to someone expecting a short, concise report. No frills. No embellishments. No introductions. Just the barest of essentials and nothing else.

"Sir, the assassin you captured in your quarters four days ago escaped. His cell was found empty. The guards on watch that night in the cell block all dead. Throats cut. Swords missing. A search of the city was organized the moment the discovery was made. With no results."

Frowning, Decimus said nothing and continued to eye the courier.

"I also am ordered to inform you the physician, Aulus Nervanus, is missing. He cannot be found. His quarters had been ransacked. There was blood on the floor. But no body was found. My superiors think the man was captured by the fleeing assassin and murdered."

Decimus nodded. He told the soldier to find some hot food and get some sleep. There was no urgency to send a message back to Asa. When the young man saluted and walked away, Gnaeus' hands flew with blinding speed.

You knew this was going to happen. You knew. But the doctor? You believe the doctor is dead? Or is he one of the conspirators?

Thin lips curled back into a half snarl as the tribune glanced at his old friend.

"Think about it, Gnaeus. The old priestess comes to Rome, after so many years playing the martyr in the Egyptian desert and knows exactly where to find her daughter and grandson. The goddess Menket and her men know precisely where Sulla's estates are and picks the exact time to attack knowing when chaos and panic would be the most extreme. But more than that, old friend. Aulus Nervanus is chosen personally by Sulla to be his private physician. In turn, our friend, Caesar's master spy, recruits the doctor to be one of his select operatives. He does not know the doctor is already spying for Shebet. Caius Lucius does not realize he has handed the old woman the perfect gift. Aulus Nervanus becomes the old woman's eyes and ears as he attends to Sulla, and he becomes the perfect conduit of information into the operations of Caesar's head spy. What better method could you devise to worm your way into the inner most working of Roman society?

"But there is more, old friend. Caius Lucius is charged with finding those here in Rome who are in contact with the grumbling malcontents who follow Menket in Egypt. He suspects someone in the general's household. Does he suspect Hatshepsut? Possibly. Someone else? Perhaps. Perhaps the old general himself. We know Sulla was a proud man. Someone who firmly believed he should be Rome's natural ruler. There is bad blood between the gens Sulla and the gens Julii. Perhaps he was the one who is the mastermind of the growing unrest in Egypt.

"But it was not Sulla. There is no evidence indicating direct contact with the rebels there with the household of Sulla. The only creature who can tie all three together into one neat bundle is Aulus Nervanus."

The doctor was a double agent? He has been working for the old priestess all this time. Gnaeus look incredulous at Decimus, his eyes wide. *He has been spying on the general, and spying on the master spy, for decades now. But, but ... how do you explain the blood on the floor of his rooms back in Asa? How did he assist, if he assisted, in the escape of the assassin?*

"How else can you explain the impossible?" Decimus whispered, making sure only he and Gnaeus could hear the conversation. "The courier said the guards in the cell block had their throats cut. How could a prisoner, chained to the wall with shackles around his ankles, unlock the shackles, and then unlock the cell door, without making a sound? And where did he get the weapon to slit our men's throats? He had to have assistance. Who was the only person, other than you and me, who could see the prisoner?"

Marcellus the Extractor of Truth, Gnaeus began, and realizing the obvious, lifted his brows in surprise. *Aulus Nervanus.*

"We know our Exactor of Truth, as you call Marcellus. A good soldier. A loyal soldier. But the man is about as subtle as a boulder rolling down a steep cliff. He is not someone capable of deception. No, no. The blood on the floor is a ruse, old friend. Put there by the good doctor in case he's ordered to return to the fold and spy on us a little longer. He'll claim he was abducted by the assassin, wounded in the process, and taken away as a hostage. But he will not return. This complex theater of revenge has entered its last climatic act. The next time we see Aulus Nervanus, we will be forced to kill him. Along with the rest of the writers of this macabre production."

But he and the assassin have escaped. No doubt your life is in immediate danger again. Surely the assassin will come to complete his original mission. But the doctor? He will not accompany this killer. He's gone. Disappeared into the hills never to be seen again.

Decimus smiled. The half-sneer growing into the full grin of a man filled with secrets. A grin Gnaeus was all too familiar. A grin which exasperated him and filled his mind with intense curiosity at the same time. Shaking his head in frustration he remained quiet. His benefactor was a man who constantly surprised him. Even after all these years serving with him. Better to remain silent and watch the events unfold before his eyes than to ask questions the tribune would answer by shrugging his shoulders in silence or answer in vague terms.

Better to wait and see rather than to speculate and be egregiously wrong. A motto he had developed long ago. One that still served him well today.

DEATH BY GREEK FIRE

Late in the afternoon of the next day Decimus ordered the men up and moving. Breaking down the camp, cavalry groups galloped off into the distance to sweep the countryside for any waiting surprises. Moving out of the camp, the men marched past the bodies of the enemy lying in the dust. Most had been stripped of their armor and weapons. Anything of value was taken. The dead's belongings would be sold later, making tidy little profits for the soldiers' retirement funds. Bodies, hundreds of them, lay semi-naked in the sun, the sky now filled with circling carrion birds waiting for the feast to come.

Four hours later Spanish scouts reported the enemy no longer occupied Narona. Only the old and the very young, and a few women, remained in the town. Men of military age were gone. A number of ships had been scuttled and now sat on the bottom of the river. Only masts jutting out of the calm waters of the Neretva like the tongs of Neptune's trident were visible. Entering the city at the head of the infantry, Decimus saw very few of the inhabitants coming out to watch the procession. The city seemed deserted. Abandoned. But he knew better.

The two cohorts of infantry swept through the city hunting for any pockets of resistance. None were found. The few city residents remaining in the city were cooperative. Rebels fled from the city early last night after news arrived of the massacre the Romans inflicted upon the rebel forces marching up from the south. The rebel commander within the city received orders to withdraw. They were to pull out, rendezvous with the other relief force marching toward the city from the north and slip away into the hills. How many rebels were in the hills no one knew. But, given time, Decimus knew large numbers would soon come. Far more numbers than he had under his command. Another battle, this time facing a far larger force, was out of the question. There was only one option left open for him. His entire force would withdraw from the river port late tonight. As he planned to do from the beginning. Roman transports would slip down the Neretva under the light of a full moon. The infantry would board ships and depart. The cavalry, still a formidable force, would ride for Asa through the night. Asa was not more than fourteen kilometers away. The ride to Asa in the dead of night through enemy territory would be filled with danger. It was a calculated risk he was willing to take. The enemy, he was sure, would be completely surprised when the morning came. Narona would be empty of Roman troops.

Empty of Roman troops. But not necessarily empty of Romans.

XXXII

7 AD
Dalmatia
Confronting a goddess

On the river the moonlight played across the calm surface of the slow-moving water in a sheet of sparkling diamonds. Narona was bathed in the same ghostly white luminescence. The town was almost dark. One or two dull yellow lights glowed from an open window or two. But the rest of the town was shrouded in moonlight and nothing else. No one moved in the streets. No guards stood watch on the river docks. It was as if the town had died and seemed to be waiting for someone to come along and quietly tear it down.

Hours earlier the last of the Roman transports, riding deep in the dark water, rowed on powerful oars and slowly began their labored journey down river with the final two centuries of Roman infantry. An hour before the last infantry boarded, the Spanish departed on horseback for Asa with a loud clatter of noise and typical Spanish bravado. But now the countryside glowed in the moonlight. Silent as a freshly sealed tomb.

Decimus, kneeling on one knee beside a large tree, eyed the eerily quiet river town patiently. Beside him the smaller framed Gnaeus knelt as well. Both men were dressed in armor. The blades of their sharp steel unsheathed and draped across their bent knees in anticipation of possible action. Hidden from the moonlight, each noted how silent the countryside gleamed in the night. There were no sounds of insects buzzing. No hunters of the nocturnal kind moved in the trees. No owls darted through the night hunting for field mice. It was as if the animal kingdom knew some foul deed was about to take place. No creature of the night stirred in fear of falling victim to what was soon to come.

Yet two creatures did move through the darkness within the tree line. Noiselessly to human ears. But not so to the creatures of the night. On two legs each creature moved a short distance before taking a knee and resting. But each remained motionless for only a few seconds before rising to their feet, crouching low in the shadows, and moving a few hundred meters more before kneeling again. Moving and stopping, this leap-frog style of movement led the two figures straight to the tree the tribune and Gnaeus hid behind. Approaching through the trees the two Roman scouts knelt just in front of Decimus, close enough to whisper.

"The rebels are on the move. A large force is coming down from the hills and moves to cut the road to Asa. A second force of equal size is coming down the main road leading to the river from the interior. Both should be here in a couple of hours."

"The size of the combined forces?"

"Maybe ten thousand rebels," the second scout answered quickly. "Most infantry. But with perhaps seven or eight hundred cavalry flanking the main contingent of infantry."

"What of our quarry?"

"The goddess rides in the lead of the rebels coming down the road. But she's accompanied by a female companion. The rebels seem to be very differential to her. As if she is more in command than the goddess."

Decimus grunted in interest. Peering around the tree, he took a long look at the stillness of the river town, a frown on his lips. Slipping back into the darkness he viewed the black shadows of his two scouts again.

"Were you able to see the goddess unmasked?"

"No sir," the first scout answered, the black shadow of his head shaking back and forth. "But the woman, sir. The woman we recognized. It seems impossible. But we both agree. The woman we know."

"Sulla's wife, Hatshepsut," the tribune said softly. Confidently.

Gnaeus' head snapped around toward the kneeling tribune, his face a wondrous scroll of profound amazement. The army scouts glanced at each other, grinning in the night, surprised, but not too surprised hearing the tribune admit he already knew their revelation. They had served with the tribune before. They knew the officer's reputation. The gods spoke to the tribune in tongues. Tongues only the tribune could understand.

"Gnaeus," Decimus grunted, almost laughing, as he glanced at the silent little man. "You act surprised. You shouldn't be. It is the only possible conclusion an astute observer of the problem could have arrived at. But no time to explain. We need to be in and out of Narona before anyone realizes something is amiss."

He glanced at the two scouts and then at the town one more time.

"You know what must be done next."

Both men nodded in the darkness.

"Any questions as to what you will do after the deed has been committed?"

Both men shook their head. They needed no further instructions.

"Good. Be off, then. Set yourself up in position and be ready. Have the horses ready at the rendezvous point. We'll have a hard ride ahead of us"

The scouts disappeared into the trees like ghosts. Decimus waited for a few moments for the scouts to distance themselves from his position and then, nodding to the little man beside him, came to his feet and stepped into the bright moonlight. Moving quickly, staying low to the ground, the two moved to the river and used the low ground for partial cover as they turned toward Narona.

Entering the eerie silence of the small city, hugging the deepest shadows of the street, the two swiftly moved to their destination. Decimus believed the goddess and her immediate entourage would occupy the small temple of Mars and use it as their primary residence. The Egyptian Goddess of War, Menket, apparently dominated the Roman's most favored god in his own house. It was a symbolic gesture he knew the human conspirators behind this charade would not deny themselves.

In the heart of the city the temple lifted into the eerie light of the moon impressively with its marbled façade of six Dorian-styled columns and the bronze statue of Mars the Protector standing arrogantly in front of the marble steps leading up to the temple's portico. Kneeling again in the deepest shadows directly across the plaza from the temple, both Decimus and Gnaeus observed the brightly lit plaza for some moments looking for any suspicious activity.

Silently, Gnaeus used an elbow and lightly touched the tribune's arm and nodded toward the temple. Decimus saw the image almost immediately. At the top of the temple's steps, half visible in the moonlight, the lower portion of a woman dressed in white linen. The cloth moved gently in the breeze, flashing the golden sandals adorning her feet. The upper half of her body was bathed in deep shadows. But there was no mistaking the image. No mistake knowing who stood on the temple's portico waiting for him.

Hatshepsut.

"Decimus Virilis!" her voice rang out into the night clear and strong, filled with confidence. "I know you are out there. I know you are close enough to hear my voice. You hide in the darkness like the typical flea infested Roman mongrel your kind are. Step out into the light. There is no place to run. There is no place you can hide. Your fate has been sealed. Face the goddess like the Roman soldier you think you claim to be with some measure of honor. If, that is, any Roman knows what honor truly means."

The tribune glanced at his comrade, smiled wickedly, then turned back to stare at the woman across the way. The sounds of hob-nailed feet, dozens of them, filled the night air as twenty heavily armed rebel hoplites, round bronze shields in one hand, the long Greek spear in the other, stepped out of the darkness and rimmed both sides of the open plaza in long single files.

The tribune came to his feet, still hidden in the deep shadows of a tall building and stepped out. In his right hand was the wicked looking straight blade of his gladius. In his left was a small round object. An object small enough to be completely hidden with his hand curled into an apparent fist. At his side was the defiant Gnaeus. Sword in one hand. The leather coils of a wagon master's bullwhip in another. In perfect cadence, both Romans marched in step straight toward the waiting goddess, the lines of rebel infantry remaining motionless on their left and right.

It was a surreal image. The light of the moon radiating off

the white marble façade of the temple. The two lines of heavy Greek infantry lining the opposite flanks of the plaza. Hatshepsut, now fully visible, standing on the edge of the temple's portico, bare arms hanging at her sides. One hand gripping the cold blade of Roman steel.

"There you are tribune. I knew you would come. Others said a man of your stature and reputation wouldn't be so foolish as to step into such an obvious trap. But I knew you would come."

He came to a halt beside the statue of Mars and half turned to his right. Behind him Gnaeus came to a halt, the hand holding the coiled whip becoming a light grip as he glanced to the right as well. From around the edge of the temple's portico the image of a white-robed assassin moved into the moonlight. In his right hand the steel of a curved Egyptian sword. Decimus nodded as if anticipating such a move. Silently he turned his head to the left. Dressed in black stood the masked figure of the Goddess of Menket.

"You see. You cannot escape your fate. The gods have decreed it. Your sins must be atoned. And I am the instrument they've chosen to fulfil their wishes."

He studied Hatshepsut. She was remarkably beautiful in the soft white light that filled the still of the night. Facing him, her body draped in exquisite white linen. The whiteness of the gown almost glowing. On her face was the look of triumph. The satisfaction of, at last, seeing a very complex plan finally coming to fruition. A cruel sneer momentarily creased his lips, partially hidden underneath his helm.

"My compliments to you, Hatshepsut. My admiration for you and your mother for a game well played is boundless. I will openly admit, for a long time I was truly mystified in trying to understand this complex game of intrigue and murder. But, in the end, as it always does, the clouds of confusion were swept away, and I comprehended the game's entirety quite clearly. Too bad your accomplishments, and that of your mother's, will be forgotten in history. But rest assured I will remember you and your deeds for as long as I live."

She lifted her chin slightly, descending two steps, and laughed. An easy, song-like laugh of a confident woman. A sound which was, for him, quite pleasant to hear. Even from a mortal enemy.

"Unfortunately for you, your life expectancy is quite short, I'm afraid. As to the idea of my name being remembered down through the pages of history, such a frivolity means nothing to me. But knowing my mother and I have taken on the arrogant and mighty Roman Empire and humiliated them, rendered them hapless in their efforts to resist us, fills me with a sense of pride and accomplishment no one will ever take away from me."

Decimus's sneer widened underneath his helm as he gripped his sword firmly. Behind him he knew his old comrade was ready. Every good plan relied on precise timing. *His plan* was coming to its natural conclusion. He hoped everyone was in position and ready to act the moment the fighting started. He looked up at the beautiful woman and grunted in amusement. Grunted loud enough for Hatshepsut to hear.

"But you have failed, my dear. All your mother's plans so intricate and detailed spread out across decades of quiet implementation. All those years of you masquerading your true intentions and playing the role of a loving wife to Gaius Sulla. All of it, Hatshepsut. All of it comes crashing down tonight. You have fooled no one, princess. You are the one who is the fool."

She slid down two more steps, the confidence and amusement in her face turning into a dark mask of rage.

"You think I don't know? You think I am unaware of your

childish attempts to trap me and my subjects in this deserted city? My spies have watched you from the beginning, Decimus Julius Virilis. We ran off your hidden bowmen and your cavalry you hid in the city hours ago. Such a pathetic attempt to hide them in the city. I am surprised at such a clumsy attempt, tribune. Especially surprised coming from you. But then again, you are a Roman. A proud, arrogant, self-centered, typical Roman.

"I have followed your every move since you joined the ill-fated Ninth legion months ago. I knew, my mother knew, if there was any Roman intelligent enough to thwart our plans, it would be you. Your dark history is well known. I am aware of your secret missions the Caesars have given you over the years. I know the names of the victims of those you have secretly murdered in the name of Caesar. Don't insult my intelligence, tribune!"

Decimus laughed. A loud, arrogant, rude male laughter which lifted toward the heavens and unmistakably heard by all. The laughter created the effect he wanted. From his left came a scream of furious rage. The scream of a man's furious rage. The black-robed, golden masked figure of the war goddess came charging toward the tribune, sword over the man's right shoulder in preparation of a vicious downward slash. He met the robed creature's attack with his own sharp blade. Steel ringing against steel filled the night air. The robed creature was amazingly fast. Amazingly gifted as a swordsman. But the true surprise was the swift work of the tribune. Effortlessly, Decimus matched speed for speed, lunge for lunge with the blade facing his foe. Lunge, parry, sweeping slashes of the blade, all countered as the two men fought while Hatshepsut looked down from her position on the steps.

The fight ended as dramatically as it started. Suddenly and

catastrophically. Decimus lunged at the black-robed figure with the point of his blade. The golden masked figure blocked the tribune's steel with a powerful blow, forcing the Roman's blade down and to his left. At the same time, he brought his blade up for a sweeping slash through the tribune's neck. Decimus anticipated the blow. Waiting for the last possible moment, he slid his head underneath the robed figure's powerful blow. At the same time his right foot came up and kicked out viciously. The foot landed squarely on the side of the figure's left knee so powerfully it buckled unnaturally.

The masked figured screamed in agony and lost his balance. Decimus straightened himself, bringing his sword around in a backhand slash. The blade caught the hobbled creature in the back of the neck just above the shoulders. The sharp edge of the tribune's Gladius sliced through the creature's neck, sending the severed head flying into the night with a spray of black blood.

The moment the creature's head slammed into the stones of the plaza and rolled to one side, pandemonium broke out in three different variations.

From above, the screams of rage and horror emitting from Hatshepsut's lungs were loud enough to be heard throughout the deserted city. She leapt from the steps straight at the tribune, the sword in her hand flashing menacingly in the moonlight. At the same time the two lines of rebel heavy infantry snapped their shields up and lowered their spears, beginning their march toward the tribune. Equally, the white-robed assassin ran toward the tribune, sword at the ready, eager to finally complete his mission.

Chaos beget chaos.

While the tribune fought off the killing rage of an Egyptian priestess, the silent Gnaeus turned and faced the on-coming assassin. A flick of his wrist uncoiled the bullwhip, its long tentacle of leather spreading out across the plaza's stones. Stepping forward, the leathery strip of muscle and sinew that was Gnaeus brought his arm up and around violently. The leather tentacle sped through the air with a crack of snapping leather.

Weeks earlier in a small room above a country inn the assassin assaulted and almost killed Gnaeus as he and the tribune tried to capture the man alive. As Gnaeus stepped back and pulled his arm back viciously, this time the parameters of the confrontation were different. This time the outcome would be far different.

The far end of the whip wrapped around the assassin's ankles. Jerking back his arm, Gnaeus' unexpected attack took the legs out from underneath the white-robed killer, sending the flailing, out of control assassin through the air. With a bone-wrenching *thud* the Egyptian landed violently on his back. Momentarily stunned, the assassin collected his wits and sat up. Seeing the leather coil encircling his legs he swept his blade around to sever the black leather. But Gnaeus had other plans. A flick of his wrist somehow uncoiled the whip from the assassin's ankles just before the edge of his blade cut through leather. The long black coil of leather sailed away from the flashing blade, unbelievably, seeming to float in the night air expectantly.

Screaming in rage, the assassin leapt to his feet and turned to face Gnaeus. The silent man's wrist flicked again. There was a second sharp crack of the leather as the snake-like coil flew through the night. The assassin tried to duck underneath the floating snake. But too late. Coils of leather wrapped around the assassin's neck with a vise-like grip. The assassin staggered, his free hand grabbing the leather coil firmly, his sword hand coming up to cut the foul thing from him.

His steel never touched Gnaeus' whip. Using both hands this time, Gnaeus violently yanked back and downward at the same time. The motion, at the far end of the whip wrapped around the assassin's neck, was startling to observe. The killer in white seemed to have been yanked off the plaza by some invisible hand and violently tossed into the air. He flipped, head over heels in midair, and slammed hard on the stone pavement again. This time taking longer to rise, with the leather whip still wrapped around his neck, the assassin staggered back one step and died instantly.

From out of the night sky, clouds of Roman arrows rained down upon the rebels. Six heavy arrows slammed into the assassin. Three in the chest. Three in the back. In the night air the killer's white robe turned a dark black from his own blood as his lifeless body violently slammed into the hard stones of the plaza.

The approaching rebel infantry fell clattering to the stones as well from the unexpected onslaught. Arrows flew toward them in opposing directions. The twenty hoplite infantry took longer to kill thanks to their heavy armor. But die they did in a matter of seconds as clouds of arrows continued to rain down upon them from above.

Hatshepsut saw none of the carnage raining down from the heavens as she attacked Decimus with her sword. Insane with a lust to kill, she fell upon the larger, stronger tribune with maniacal fury. So swift, so intent on killing him, Decimus was forced to give ground immediately, barely able to ward off her blows in the process. She was inhumanly fast. Incredibly skilled. Three times the edge of her blade slid across exposed Roman flesh, drawing blood which ran from his arms and stained the plaza stones with large pools of dark liquid.

This was the creature who attacked them in the tenement

building in Rome days earlier and killed eight good soldiers so easily. This was the creature Caius Lucius warned him about in his last communication. She moved like the lion-goddess she worshipped. Powerful. Swift. Amazing. He knew it was only a matter of seconds before her blade slipped past his defenses and found a vital organ. The realization that a woman challenged him with steel and surpassed him so easily in skill, did not surprise him. Part of him admired her. But the cold realization was, unless he had some way to even the odds more in his favor, he was going to die. And he had no desire to die this day.

Her blade found his left thigh, the edge of her sword biting deep into his flesh. Hot blood streamed down his leg as he brought his elbow around and smashed into Hatshepsut's jaw. She staggered forward. Disregarding the pain from the various wounds which were, due to blood loss, making his sight blurry from tears, he raised his free hand and paused just underneath her chin. All this time he had in his hand a small, round leather pouch. A pouch small enough to conceal as if it was nothing more than a fist. He didn't hesitate. In his weakening condition with only seconds left to him, he squeezed the leather pouch in two swift clutches.

A fine white powder filled the air in front of the dazed Hatshepsut's face. Holding his breath, barely strong enough to continue gripping his sword, Decimus stepped back and waited.

The goddess and her Egyptian followers were not the only ones familiar with the use of poisons delivered through the air.

Hatshepsut's sword clattered to the stones. A stunned look of disbelief filled her eyes as she stared at Decimus just before she wavered and sank to her knees. She continued to stay upright on her knees. But her muscles were frozen. She could breathe. But barely. Her eye lids wouldn't work. She could not swallow. Her vision was failing. But she was aware of Decimus' close proximity. Aware of him speaking to her.

The bleeding tribune, barely strong enough to grip his sword and unsteady on his feet, gazed upon the immobile priestess with an expression one would have described more as regret than of victory. Limping to one side to stand directly in front of her, he wanted her to hear him one last time.

"Priestess, what I said about my admiration for you and your late mother, I meant sincerely. Truly I have nothing but genuine respect for you. To endure what you have endured all these years. To suffer the outrages and insults I'm sure your husband hurled upon you. I am familiar with Sulla's arrogance. I'm sure he humiliated you time and time again. But you accepted your fate and continued to train and become the master killer that you are now. All of this, I stand before you in open admiration.

"I want you to know what is to come next is a choice not of my making. My suggestion was to bring you back to Rome alive. There, in some dark prison, you would live out the rest of your life. But I was overruled. Overruled and, frankly, convinced with their reasoning why it would be such a dangerous decision to keep you alive. No one knows how deep your reach into Roman society extends. Without doubt you have silent allies in high positions within the government who would, eventually, rescue you from your bondage. Better to kill you than to risk another uprising. Your death will haunt me for years to come. You have suffered so much from the hands of your husband and from Rome. For that, I apologize to you. Rest in peace, Hatshepsut. Perhaps in Hades some day we will sit down at a table with a bottle of wine and talk of our shared past. There is so much I wish to ask you. So much I wish to know. But time is not on our side. Goodbye, Hatshepsut. May your soul find the peace it so desperately seeks."

Somehow her eyes moved. She gazed into his face. Saw the tears streaming from his eyes. Saw the pain. The anguish. She tried to smile. She tried to speak. But her muscles would not move. She saw him summon the strength to do the deed. The blade in his hand lifted.

Oddly, when the blow fell, she did not feel any pain. No pain whatsoever. And she was thankful.

XXXIII

7 AD
Rome
Caius Lucius

Hobbling along on one crutch tucked underneath his left arm, dressed in the pull over cotton smock of a Greek peasant, Decimus stepped out into the small garden in the back of his house. He smiled at the innocuous figure of Caesar's spy standing with his back turned to him, admiring a colorful display of Irises. To one side of Caius Lucius were two scribes standing politely some distance away talking to each other in soft whispers. All three men were standing and waiting for his arrival, casually enjoying the sun and the small, colorful garden so prized and lovingly cared for by the silent Gnaeus.

His home was no longer encircled with a squad of Praetorian Guards. Equally, the sense of impending disaster which hung over the house and all of Rome for the last several weeks, seemed to have dissipated into thin air. News from Pannonia was encouraging. Tiberius Caesar was pushing the northern rebels deeper into the hinterland, relieving the terror of a possible rebel invasion for the average Roman living on the streets. There were rumors another Roman army was being assembled with the goal in mind of attacking the southern band of rebels in lower Dalmatia and Moesia.

Stepping out onto the stones of the patio, the clacking sound of his wooden crutch made Caius Lucius face the tribune, a smile on his lips. A smile filled with obvious concern. The image of Decimus Virilis would make any person who knew the tribune feel concern. The man's right thigh was heavily bandaged from the hip all the way down to the knee. Both of the tribune's forearms were lightly bandaged. Yet it was the tribune's complexion which bothered Caesar's spy the most. The color in the man's cheeks was a pasty white. Around the eyes were a crow's nest of lines indicating the tribune was finding it difficult to sleep. And the way he hobbled on his crutch over to the wide table and struggled to sit himself down suggested the soldier, noted for his incredible endurance, was very weak.

Decimus, seeing the worry in the spy's eyes, smiled weakly and waved to the man to come and join him. Leaning the crutch up against his bench he looked into Caius Lucius' face and smiled.

"Tell Caesar all is well. I am mending and regaining my strength. There is nothing seriously wrong with me. All I have done is added a few more scars to an already impressive collection I've earned over the years. Now tell me, Caius, while we wait for the wine to arrive, what brings you to my humble home?"

"Decimus, I know in the past we have been rivals. Heated rivals one would say," the spy said softly, seating himself down opposite of the tribune and sitting back in his chair. "But I must be frank with you. The night your man Gnaeus, the scouts, and the bowman you somehow hid so effectively in Narona pulled you out of the town moments before the whole countryside was flooded with swarming rebels, I thought you were dead. You certainly were more dead than alive when I saw you in Asa a few days ago."

A light of bright mischief flared up in the tribune's eyes as he smiled.

"What were your thoughts, old friend, when you saw me lying on my possible deathbed? Regret? Or silent joy that another rival had been quietly disposed?"

A sly, cruel grin spread across Caius Lucius' lips, followed by a soft chuckle. Rufus came out of the house bearing a large platter which held stone goblets and a large jug of wine. Behind him Gnaeus appeared, in his hands a second platter filled with freshly baked bread, cheese, butter, grapes, and knives. Both men sat their platters onto the table and silently disappeared back into the house.

"I'll get back with you on that a little later, tribune. Let's just say that I was concerned and leave it at that."

Decimus smiled, started to reach for the jug of wine, but winced in pain and sat back in his chair. Caius turned and motioned one of the scribes to step forward and fill goblets for the two. When the scribe stepped back, the spy lifted his goblet in salute.

"To your health, Decimus Julius Virilis. I say this with no animosity or jealousy hidden within me. Rome and Caesar owe you a great deal for your recent amazing services. Caesar asked me to inform you he plans to personally reward you as soon as you can endure the journey to the palace. And let me add my thanks as well. Your initial reports indicating my limited participation in your investigation honored me greatly. For that I am in your debt."

"There are no debts to be collected, old friend. We did our

jobs. We worked side by side stopping Hatshepsut and her followers. As we were ordered to do. But tell me, what brings you to my house on this fine day with two scribes waiting patiently in the wings. Is this the official after-engagement debriefing I've been expecting? Or is this something more formal?"

The spy reached for a batch of grapes, popped one in his mouth, then turned and motioned for both scribes to approach before turning back toward the tribune.

"The Senate, and Augustus, both find themselves filled with questions concerning this encounter. The death of Sulla, the near destruction of the Ninth, everything apparently. Both have been waiting impatiently to hear a more full, detailed report, from the one man who figured it all out. Yesterday I was handed a series of questions the two interested parties want to ask you, and supplied, as you can see, with two scribes to write down every word said precisely. So ordered, here I am, with the scribes, to complete this mission. Are you recovered enough to begin? Or should we come back another day?"

Decimus shrugged and leaned forward, cautiously using a knife to cut himself a slice of bread and a slice of cheese. Sitting back, taking a bite of the combined food, he gestured silently toward the spy to begin.

"Very well," Caius Lucius nodded, opening a large papyrus scroll and looking at the first question. "Explain how an entire hilltop can explode. You mentioned in your initial report Greek Fire. But Greek Fire is not an explosive. It burns on contact with whatever it touches. How can it explode with such force powerful enough to rip apart a hill?"

"The hill the Ninth selected as their campsite was riddled with caves and crevices. Seeping from out of these cavities were various vapors. Vapors which burned and or exploded if they accumulated enough gas just before an ignition source was applied to it. Days before the legion pitched camp, rebels came in, dug large chambers underneath the hill which soon filled with gas, and planted dozens of pots of this deadly concoction in these chambers, knowing their addition would enhance the destruction a hundred fold. A brilliant idea designed to fatally cripple a new legion filled mostly with raw recruits. But not just cripple it, Caius. To destroy the entire legion in two swift blows."

"First the explosion. And then the attack by the rebel army," Caius grunted, rubbing his chin thoughtfully. "But I see a problem. For this plan to work, someone had to light a fuse to set the explosion off. Light the fuse and stay in the camp, in the legate's tent, to make sure no one extinguished it. Light a fuse and wait, knowing death was about to claim them. How could this have happened? The legate's tent had to have had officers sitting in the tent on duty. Surely they would have seen, and stopped, this outrage from happening."

"Indeed," the tribune nodded, smiling as he cut another slice of cheese and bread. "If they were alive. But what if they were already dead? We all know how duty officers live and work in the legate's tent late at night. They are constantly munching on food and drinking watered down wine. What if the wine and food were spiked with a deadly poison? They drink. They eat. And they die without a whimper, or a realization, they are dying."

Caius stared at the tribune for a long moment without saying a word. Behind him, the two sitting scribes sat with masks for faces waiting for someone to speak. If whatever had been revealed surprised or startled either of them, they revealed nothing. But the master spy, rubbing his chin with a single finger, narrowed his eyes and spoke.

"You suspected Gaius Cornelius Sulla the Younger, the

Ninth's legate, from the very beginning, didn't you? Even before you took his head in that fight the other night. Why?"

Decimus started to answer but winced in pain from his wounded leg twitching unexpectedly. Gritting his teeth together he fought to maintain his composure, eventually relaxing and looking up at the spy.

"It could be no one else, Caius. It was his decision to march straight away to that hill. It was his command to the engineers to set up the stakes indicating where the legion's cohorts would throw up their tents. He was the only one left alive in the tent after everyone else was poisoned. The only person who could make sure this plan could take place falls on the shoulders of the young Sulla."

Shaking his head in amazement, Caius glanced at the scroll lying on the table and then back up at Decimus.

"How did the young Sulla survive the explosion? That is a question a number of Senators have asked for clarification. Followed, of course, with the question of why he did this treasonous act in the first place."

"Shebet," Decimus said casually, reaching for some grapes.

"What? Shebet?" Caesar's spy echoed, confused. "Shebet is involved in the destruction of the Ninth?"

Decimus picked a grape, paused, tossed his eyes toward the truly confused nondescript little man and smiled.

"To answer your first question. Shebet was the one who lit the fuse and remained behind to make sure her plan would be followed all the way to the bitter end."

Caius Lucius' mouth dropped open. He stared at the tribune filled with incomprehension as an entire hand came up and moved across his mouth indicating his disbelief. Eventually he closed his mouth. The look of confusion left his eyes as he dropped the hand covering his face and crinkled his eyebrows together angrily.

"How in Hades did you come up with that hair-brained idea, Decimus? The entire hilltop was destroyed. The legate's staff, the entire first cohort, and several centurions were killed at the same time. We haven't a shred of evidence which tells us who was in Sulla's tent. But you are telling me Hatshepsut's mother, this ancient priestess, Shebet, lit the fuse and died as a willing martyr?"

"I have compelling indirect evidence, from two different sources, which convinces me Shebet was the one who volunteered to stay behind. One of the sources being our physician friend, Aulus Nervanus. No, before you protest, just sit back and let me explain it to you slowly and clearly."

Caius Lucius was about to erupt in an outpouring of questions, but the tribune stopped the man in mid-stride by lifting a palm and motioning him to sit back in his chair. Reluctantly, the master spy complied with Decimus' wishes.

"A few days past, Gnaeus and I interviewed the good doctor at his place of work. The interview was short but very interesting. Instead of talking in the crowded hall of the Basilica, he led us across the Forum of Julius, and we sat down on a bench on the portico of the Temple of Julius and talked. In our conversations, he told us of the time he saw the hooded figure of an old woman approach Hatshepsut and the young Sulla as they made their way across the forum."

"The hag being Shebet," the spy growled skeptically. "Here. In Rome. Underneath my very nose and I knew nothing about it?"

Decimus grinned and wagged a finger back and forth in a mildly chastising gesture.

"Never underestimate your enemies, my friend. Especially an enemy who bore so much hatred for all things Roman she was willing to devote her entire life in a scheme for revenge which is breathtaking in its complexity."

"But a woman, Decimus. A woman! How could she have done all this by herself? How could she be so cunning. So cruel. So ... so ..."

"Daring?"

"Exactly!" Caius Lucius shouted, throwing up a pointing finger at the tribune in confirmation. "How could a woman do all this? And over such a long period of time!"

"Have you talked with Caesar's wife lately," the tribune asked pleasantly, smiling as he watched the master spy's face.

"Livia? Last week. She's remained in Rome to watch over things while Caesar journeyed north. Of course, I've been keeping her fully informed of our moves ..."

Color drained from Caius Lucius' face. His eyes widened. He walked right into it. Had no inkling Decimus Virilis had so expertly, with a casual off-hand question, laid a little trap for he and his chauvinism.

Livia Drusilla.

Augustus Caesar's wife.

Caesar the man was all powerful. He was brilliant. Daring. A visionary. Ruthless. Generous to his allies and friends. Merciless to his enemies. A natural leader of men who flocked to his side any time he made a public appearance. Where he was weak in accomplishing, which he realized quite early in his rise to power was his lack of military acumen, he quietly acknowledged. The difference between him and other men, the difference which alone consigned him to be one of the most brilliant men of his era, was he was astute enough to admit the weakness and seek out and employ the best military minds he could find. Even admitting he had a weakness somehow endeared him to his followers.

But the greatest gift the gods showered upon Caesar was the gift of his wife. She was an equal to Caesar in all things. She was just as brilliant. Highly educated. Just as daring.

Perhaps, as the rumors often hinted, even more ruthless. She charmed everyone. Accepted everyone as they were. She rarely played favorites. She presented an outward picture of a classical Roman wife. Always faithful. Always subservient to her husband. But she was far, far more than just a Roman wife.

She, along with Caesar, co-ruled the empire. And no one disputed her authority.

"Aha," the spy muttered sheepishly, reaching for his wine and knocking back a deep drought before continuing. "Point taken. You were making a point about Hatshepsut's mother."

"Indeed," Decimus said quietly. "Aulus Nervanus told Gnaeus and I the story about a hooded figure limping badly and using a heavy staff to lean on approach Hatshepsut and her son in the Julian Forum. That hooded figure was Shebet. He described Hatshepsut as both surprised and distraught as she conversed with her mother. Hatshepsut was surprised seeing her mother here in Rome. Surprised her mother was still alive. Fearful of the ramifications her presence might create with her being here. Or that is what the doctor implied. But he lied to us. His story, the implied concerns for Hatshepsut and the young Sulla, all a fabrication to hide the truth."

"What was this truth?" Caesar's spy asked, a captive now of the tribune's narrative.

"All good lies are based on half-truths, Caius. You are aware of that as much as I am. We use lies in our profession to protect ourselves. Protect our missions. Protect those who are innocent. Or we use them to gain an advantage over someone. Precisely what Aulus Nervanus did. Protecting his goddess and trying to gain our confidence at the same time.

"He told the truth when he said he observed Shebet's meeting with her daughter in the Julian Forum. Equally he told the truth when he described the emotions playing across

Hatshepsut's face. The lie comes into play in *the reasons* which brought Shebet out of hiding so brazenly."

"Yes, yes. Go on."

Decimus smiled and continued with his narrative.

"Shebet was dying. In fact, so near death it could happen at any moment."

"What!" Caius Lucius' reaction was so startling in his voice's volume even the scribes looked up from the wax tablets in surprise. Decimus chuckled in amusement and reached for more grapes. Caius glared angrily at him for a few seconds before taking a long, slow breath and exhaling even more slowly.

"Decimus Julius Virilis, I have never believed the whispered rumors about you talking to the gods in your tent using odd voices and strange tongues. But by all that is holy, I'm beginning to believe there might be a seed of truth in them! How in Hades did you come to the conclusion Shebet was dying?"

This time the tribune laughed. But winced in pain the moment he started. Clamping down on his teeth, he paused and then reached for his goblet of wine. A few moments rolled by before he could return to the conversation.

"There are no gods intervening on my behalf. There's no magic involved. All that is required is for one to observe and to listen. You know my feelings about this, Caius. We have talked before about it. The job we do, these dirty little deeds Caesar and the Julii need done in order to keep the empire stable, require each of us to sharpen our skills far more intently than the average man. People see things. Everyday happenings, the little oddities which fill our lives visually. But they don't *observe*. Something in front of their eyes takes place. But they do not see the series of events unfold which caused that event to happen in the first place.

DEATH BY GREEK FIRE

"A soldier on the battlefield looks down into the dirt and sees a footprint. But he doesn't bend down and observe it. How old is it? What kind of footwear did the person before him wear? What direction was he coming from? Is there a drop of blood mixed in the dirt which might suggest a wound? Is there a piece of turf, perhaps a partial leave or twig which might suggest where he has been?

It is the small things most people do not observe. As they do not listen. We hear everything around us. Birds singing. Water running in a brook. People talking. But we do not take the time to truly *listen* to our surroundings. What kind of bird is singing? Is it near or far? Or take the water running in the brook. Is the running water a soft, gentle song? Or is it the prelude to a deluge? Is the running brook shallow? Or is it deep water. Are animals lurking close by waiting for an unfortunate victim to fall into their trap? It's the small things, Caius. The small details most people do not pay attention to but are so critical for us to be aware in order for us to survive."

"Yes, yes. In principle I agree with you, Decimus," Caius Lucius countered, waving a hand angrily. "But what does that long treaties have to do in you ascertaining this old hag's approaching death?"

"Returning to Asa a few days ago we were told there was a survivor from the hilltop badly wounded but strong enough to speak. A young Gaul who was not expected to live much longer. He told us an interesting story. On the night of the explosion, he was assigned to the camp's main gate on guard duty. During the night the entire gate personnel heard voices, speaking in Latin, arguing out in the dark somewhere. Too far to understand what was being said. But close enough to know it was Latin being used. A few moments later officers approach the gate. The riders were challenged. They responded with the correct password being used for the night.

That is clue number two. The password. Riders from afar would not know what the nightly password would be unless someone told them. A word is chosen, by me in this case as the Camp Prefect, on a daily basis. Used only by legion personnel. Yet these officers already knew it."

"Clue number two?" the spy asked, lifting an eyebrow.

"The officers arguing in the night in Latin. Apparently, a heated argument. It suggests the officers could only communicate with each other using Latin. But here is the main point I'm trying to make. Clue number three."

One of the scribes fidgeted in his chair, glancing up quickly and then back down to his tablet. Decimus' narration had captured his complete attention. He was eager to hear, and record, every word he said.

"Clue number three," the master spy piped up.

"Yes. Well. The Gaul said the officers approached the gate. One of them had their head covered in a hood. But the person sat on his horse gripping the pommel of his saddle with both hands. Leaning to one side as if he and been wounded or was in serious pain. But, and this is critical, when the three officers left only a few minutes later and galloped off into the night, the hooded creature moved with the sprite and vigor of a much younger man in the full of his life. No outward appearance of pain. No clutching the pommel of his saddle to maintain his balance. The image of someone completely different to the person who arrived only moments earlier."

"The hooded person entering the camp was Shebet. The hooded creature leaving the camp is ... is ... Gaius Cornelius Sulla the Younger?"

"It is elementary, my dear Caius. The only possible scenario which fits the facts. Shebet, the long-suffering martyr of Roman injustice, broods and plots and plans a very elaborate act of revenge while suffering in exile in an Egyptian desert.

She implements her plan. But before the final chapter of the plan is about to play out, she is told she is dying. So, what does she do? She modifies her plan. Replaces her grandson, who in all probability was not going to die in his tent anyway, and gladly dies in the explosion. She kills hundreds of Romans in one blinking of the eye. The ripple effect of her deed is felt all the way to Rome. I'm quite sure she died a happy woman. A very happy woman."

The master spy sat back in his chair and stared at the tribune. He had no words to utter. Listening to the tribune's logic and reasoning, fitting all the facts into one neat working theory, was absolutely convincing. There was not a shred of doubt in his mind. The officer in front of him painted a full and complete account no one would ever doubt. He certainly didn't.

Sitting up in his chair, glancing back at the two scribes, he cleared his throat as he stood up.

"We will take a short break, I think. Our scribes are hot and sweating from their work and sitting underneath the sun. I'm sure there are refreshments in the house waiting for the both of you. Shall we say ten minutes?"

There was a murmur of agreement. The scribes took their wax tablets with them as they marched off toward the house, each one massaging their cramped writing hands in the process. Caius Lucius watched the men disappear inside before turning to gaze down upon the tribune.

"While they're out of listening range, let us talk about Aulus Nervanus. How did you know he was a double agent?"

Decimus smiled, poured himself another goblet of wine, and sat back in his chair.

XXXIV

7 AD
Rome
The double-agent

"For the last fifteen years I have used this physician as my primary agent in keeping track of Sulla and his household. Spying on the general. Keeping track of Hatshepsut. Sulla and his family have been a pain in the side of the Julii for more than a hundred years. Sulla's grandfather tried to kill Julius Caesar at one point. So, it made sense to be aware of the general's intentions. Always."

The tribune nodded in agreement. It was the wise move, politically speaking, to make in these troubled times. He sipped his wine and waited for the spy to continue.

"We knew who Hatshepsut's mother was. That alone would make her a person of interest for the palace. For years we knew nothing of Shebet's whereabouts in Egypt. Many in the government thought she had died. In those years Hatshepsut's demeanor toward Rome and toward her husband were unblemished. No suspicion of any kind ever roused our interest. But we had to watch her anyway. Aulus Nervanus, for us, seemed the perfect answer. Loyal, observant, highly intelligent. A perfect spy. It never crossed my mind he was, in fact, working for Shebet and her daughter all these years. But you knew soon after you met him. How?"

Decimus glanced toward the house, saw his servants Gnaeus and Rufus drinking wine and talking to the scribes, clearly too far away to overhear their conversation, and turned to look at his friend and rival.

"Conjecture and a slip of the tongue," Decimus said, closing his eyes and replying weakly. "Let me explain. I became convinced this affair was a well thought out, long running marathon of epic proportions. A powerful woman early in her life had been wronged. Wronged in such a fashion that she thirsted for revenge. She began gathering her resources. Gathering recruits. Acquiring gold enough to carry through the plan. She sent people to Rome. People she knew who would wait patiently for her eventual arrival. And she made sure she had trusted people close to the one who had so terribly wounded her. Close to him, and at the same time, situated in such a position in life he could monitor the enemy state as comfortable as he could with the general."

"That being a successful doctor in the heart of Rome. A man with many patients in high positions working within the Roman government. And the personal physician to the general. Giving him, of course, even more access within the inner sanctum."

"Precisely," Decimus agreed. "Our good doctor. For Shebet's plans to work, there had to be such a man buried deep into her enemy's politics. He heard all the gossip. All the rumors. Knew of plans even before Augustus knew of them.

For fifteen years he fed this information back to Shebet. To her and to Hatshepsut."

"Very well," the spy began, frowning, but accepting the tribune's thoughts. "I see what you mean about the necessity of having someone like him here. But the slip of the tongue. What did he say that convinced you he was a double agent?"

"Remember the fight in the tenement house near the Temple of Sekhmet? The fight where the robed goddess and her sword wreaked havoc on several Roman soldiers in the upper floor hallway? Yes? Very good. She used a powdered poison, delivered through the air, to slow everyone's reaction down. Most of us walked through this powdery cloud and became affected by it. Aulus Nervanus knew what happened to us. Knew the ingredients of the poison. Knew the antidote. He even claimed he was quite familiar with it. He knew, Caius. He *knew*."

"But he's a doctor. He would know of these things."

"No. He would not," the tribune said, shaking his head. "This poison's formula is very ancient. Very Egyptian. Used only by fanatically trained assassin cults. The only way for him to know is to be part of the cult."

"Conjecture and a slip of a tongue," the spy grunted, shaking his head in disbelief. He glanced at the house, saw the scribes putting their wine goblets down and reaching for the wax tablets. The break was over. "Decimus, no one knows Aulus Nervanus worked for me. Not even Augustus. If word got out I had been duped by a double agent, well, suffice to say my life's work would be over. I ask you. I plead with you. Let this portion of the conspiracy not be part of the official record. I would be deeply in your debt if you agreed."

"It will be a debt I might someday demand repayment. Repayment in a time which might be dangerous to comply to on your part. Agreed?"

"Agreed," the master spy nodded, looking pale, turning to nod toward the scribes. "Shall we begin? Only two questions remain. Only two and then we can draw to a close this sordid affair once and for all."

The scribes reclaimed their seats; Caius Lucius sat down again and reached for his notes while Decimus sipped his wine and ate a piece of buttered bread.

"Hatshepsut," the spy began, glancing at his notes first and then up to the tribune. "She was involved with this conspiracy all the way back to its infancy?"

Decimus grinned. A cruel, one-sided curl of the lips which, somehow, chilled the air around the four men, even though they sat underneath a blazing sun.

"From the beginning. In fact, you could say she is the reason for this murderous affair."

"In what way?"

"What I am about to tell you, Caius Lucius, cannot be transmitted to the Senate in any fashion. Only me, you, these two scribes, and Caesar should know what I'm about to reveal. If anyone in the Senate discovered this information, there would be a leak. You know how notoriously porous the politicians are in keeping secrets. There would be a scandal. And the scandal would be the greatest in the already scandalous history of Rome. I am not exaggerating in the least. The fallout stemming from this revelation would decimate entire families and financially ruin many more."

Caesar's spy ran a hand over his lips, a gesture of obvious concern filling the man's soul, and eyed the tribune thoughtfully. There was an intellectual firestorm roaring in the man's brain. Two masters, that of the Senate on one hand and Caesar on the other, tore at his loyalties. In the end he made a decision.

"Very well. I can promise nothing. Other than give you the promise I will take this up with Caesar personally. The full account will be sent directly to him and to no one else. It will be a decision he will make on who reads the full report and who doesn't. But I will strongly urge him to consider your warnings, Decimus. He holds you in high regards. I have no doubts he will seriously consider them before making his decision."

He knew it was the only possible answer the spy could give him. He would have to trust Caesar's decision. The two scribes sitting behind the spy patiently waited to record the next sentence. Could these people be trusted? Would one of them see an opportunity to perhaps make a small fortune for himself by selling a copy of the original report to someone who would be willing to pay? Names of potential buyers instantly popped up in his mind.

Nevertheless, exhaling quietly, he knew he had no choice. Caesar would be insistent. The old man would demand from him the reasons why this bloody debacle blew up into the mainstream of Roman politics. Like a sudden, violent and unexpected summer storm. Sound and fury which, if left unattended, would threaten the very fabric of Roman society.

"Thirty-five years ago, Gaius Cornelius Sulla was a young tribune in command of a maniple of auxiliary cavalry. One night, while making their regular rounds through the desert near the Numidian border, they came across a small village. A village they were familiar with. A village which, in the past, was loyal to Rome. But on this night strangers were in the village and the minute they saw the auxiliary cavalry, they took up arms and began fighting.

The fighting continued well into the night. Many died. Included a large portion of Sulla's command. He himself was wounded. Enraged over his losses, and over his false conclusion the *villagers* participated in the fighting against his cavalry, he ordered his men to burn the village to the ground and leave no survivors. His men gleefully complied. Blood soaked into the sand. The cries of women and children rose into the desert night. Almost everyone is slaughtered."

"Almost everyone?" Caius Lucius repeated, leaning toward the tribune to hear better. "What do you mean almost everyone?"

"In the middle of the slaughter Sulla discovered a young native girl hiding in a hut. Very young. Just coming into her womanhood. He discovered her hiding in the dark. She had in one hand a long knife to defend herself. They struggled. Apparently, this girl was well versed in the art of combat. Sulla slapped the knife out of the girl's hand and threw her onto the floor of the hut. He rapes her. Repeatedly through the night as the massacre continues unabated."

"Oh no," Caesar's spy grunted, a look of horror in his eyes as he sat back and stared at the tribune. "Oh no, no, no. Sulla rapes a girl thirty-five years ago. Thirty-five years! The girl was, was ..."

"Shebet," Decimus answered quietly.

"Shebet. Later on, she has a daughter ..."

"Hatshepsut."

"That means, that means ..."

"Twenty years later Sulla returns to Egypt in command of a legion and discovers both Shebet and her beautiful daughter. He falls inexplicably madly in love with Hatshepsut and marries her without once realizing he has married his own daughter.

"But we are getting ahead of ourselves, my friend. Let me go back thirty-five years to that dark hut deep in the Egyptian desert. Eventually Sulla grows weary from his evening's entertainment and falls asleep. Shebet, although bound up like a sheep about to be slaughtered, somehow finds the knife Sulla slapped out of her hands and cuts herself free. She attacks the sleeping rapist. Plunges the knife deep into his chest. Thinking she has killed him, she flees into the desert.

"Sulla, on the other hand, survives the blow. But he is so badly wounded he cannot ride a horse. A wagon is found to carry him across the desert. They eventually find a Roman outpost. Questions began to be asked on what form of engagement this cavalry unit fought. Several of the auxiliary troopers told the truth. Gave the name of the village they pillaged and burned. Reports were written and sent up the chain of command."

"And forgotten, no doubt. Just another unfortunate event with the natives. Regrettable. But it happens."

"Not this time," the tribune replied, shaking his head grimly. "This time the Seventh level of Hades exploded all over Egypt, embroiling everyone who was involved in this incident. Sulla found himself in serious trouble. Apparently Shebet's mother was a well-known high priestess of Menket as well. But she was *an ally* to Rome's growing power in her country. She wanted to be friends with Rome. Convinced her followers Rome's law and justice would benefit them all. All that changed overnight after Shebet's escape. From potential and loyal allies, to committed enemies became Menket's followers. All thanks to Sulla's inability to control himself."

"Sulla is in trouble. Serious trouble," Caius Lucius echoed, frowning. "How serious and how does he deal with it?"

"An astute question, old friend. The reports of the massacre go all the way up to the legate in charge of Egyptian Affairs. Shebet's mother demands justice. Sulla must be punished for killing and raping so many innocent Egyptians. All of Egypt rallies behind Shebet and her mother. The political maelstrom rises to the loud cacophony of a near revolt. There is talk of clapping irons onto Sulla's wrists and shipping him back to Rome to stand trial in the Senate.

"And then, curiously, seemingly overnight, the outrage blows away into nothingness like a spring shower moving in off the sea and sweeping across a city gaily before blowing away."

Caius Lucius folded hands together in front of him, elbows propping arms up in the air in front of his face, and smiles like the scheming fox he was.

"Money bought Sulla his freedom. Lots of money."

"Precisely," Decimus nodded in agreement. "Sulla bribes everyone. The men of his command. All the officers who received the initial reports. The judges. The magistrates. The important native leaders. Money flows into the coffers of anyone and everyone who might know the truth. Even Shebet and her mother find themselves wallowing in bags of gold. All of the charges are dropped. An agreement is signed, in writing, between Sulla and Shebet's mother. All charges against Sulla are to be dropped in exchange for due compensation and the banishment of Sulla from Egypt for an indeterminate amount of time."

"Ha! I think I understand where this is going. Where you see scandal pillaging through Roman society if all of this is revealed to the public. You're thinking of the Romans who accepted the bribes. Of covering up a crime and keeping quiet after all these years accepting, only the gods know, gold from Sulla. Many of these men who were young officers in Egypt are now old men and in positions of power in the government. Even in the Senate. The ripple effect of the scandal would surge up and down all of Roman society. Causing irreparable harm.

"But Shebet, did she not break the agreement as well? She waged war on Rome. Even after she accepted the terms signed by Sulla and her mother."

"She had no choice in the matter, Caius. A young girl, loyal to her mother, she was told to accept her fate and raise her child. But Shebet never forgave, nor forgot, her night of terror. Hatshepsut is born. When old enough, Shebet begins training her as a weapon of war. The tool she will use to destroy the Sulla name and Rome itself. She plans her revenge in minute detail. We have seen, and experienced, the brilliance of her plans."

"Evidence?" the spy queried.

"The last words of a dying Aulus Nervanus. Duly recorded by a military scribe. And this."

Reaching inside his thin cotton tunic Decimus pulled out a heavy envelope. The envelope sealed in red wax. Red wax with the family seal of the Sulla Clan engraved deep into the wax.

"Sulla's copy of the original agreement. Found in Hatshepsut's belongings soon after her death. Evidence enough to convince Caesar my tall tale of intrigue and murder rings true."

"More than enough," agreed the spy, coming to his feet and taking the heavy sealed envelope from Decimus' hands. "We will leave you now. You are exhausted, and I have many hours of time consuming reports to write ahead of me. But know this. You have served Rome well. Few will ever know of your deeds and accomplishments. But the powerful who do know, hold you in high honor. Quickly recover, my friend. I eagerly await our next meeting."

Caius Lucius and scribes vacated the small garden in silence, leaving Decimus sitting in his chair underneath a warm sun. His stomach was full. The pain was tolerable. And he felt incredibly sleepy. A short nap seemed so inviting.

Yes. Just a short cat nap. Nothing more. Just a few moments in the sun asleep...

ABOUT THE AUTHOR

My name is B.R. Stateham. I am a 72 year-old male with a mind still filled with the wonders and excitement one might find in a fourteen year old boy. I write genre fiction. You name the genre, I've probably got a short-story, a novella, or a novel which would fit the description. I've been writing for over 50 years. Which, frankly, means very little in reality. Most writers can say the same thing. For a writer, storytelling is something built into one's psyche. From birth on, a writer was probably telling some kind of story to himself, or anyone close to him. Whether they listened or not.

For the last 37 years I've been married to the same patient woman. A school teacher, now retired, who has this thing of sitting down with me and discussing, or verbally outlining, concepts for stories knocking around in my head. We have three grown adults for children and six (if I got the current number correct) grandchildren. None of the children or grandchildren think that me being a writer is of any particular significance. As it should be.

I like writing dark-noir. Or hardboiled detective/police-procedural novels which border the demarcation line between dark-noir and hard-boiled fiction. In fact, I like mixing up sub-genres in my fiction. Don't be surprised if you read something of mine traditionally found in the dark-noir niche with tinges of Science-Fiction or the Supernatural thrown in to spice up the tale.

That's it. There's nothing else to say. I'm just as writer. But I hope you'll find something of mine to read and find it enjoyable.

———

To learn more about B.R. Stateham and discover more Next Chapter authors, visit our website at www.nextchapter.pub.

Printed in Great Britain
by Amazon